A MURDER IN DEHRADUN

A MURDER IN DEHRADUN

SIDDHARTH MAHESHWARI

PAPER TOWNS
PUBLISHERS

First Published in 2024 By
Papertowns Publishers
72, Vishwanath Dham Colony,
Niwaru Road, Jhotwara,
Jaipur, 302012

A Murder In Dehradun

10 9 8 7 6 5 4

Paperback ISBN - 978-93-6185-133-9

Printed and bound in India by Thomson Press India Private Limited

A Murder in Dehradun: The Book Bloggers' Favorite Whodunnit

When over 100 top book bloggers from India rave about a book, you know it's something special. From classic Agatha Christie vibes to its intricate details—like maps, floor plans, and character sketches—this gripping thriller has charmed the book bloggers' community. Here's what some of India's most influential book bloggers had to say!

Every twist and turn pulls you deeper into an electrifying mystery, where tension crackles, and each reveal brings new surprises. The suspense is masterfully woven, making it impossible to predict the plot twists or uncover the murderer's identity. Rich character sketches, captivating chapter titles, and clever word puzzles at the end add layers of intrigue, making this thrilling read an unforgettable journey.

Shruti Kantawala (reader_sm)

A masterfully crafted whodunnit that kept me on edge—13 suspects, countless secrets, and a jaw-dropping twist that I never saw coming. Every plot twist had me guessing and failing. Siddharth's writing is weirdly gripping and definitely had me in a chokehold.

Kriti Sachan (kritiisachan)

An absolute page-turner! Suspense, drama, and those twists? I didn't see them coming. Set in the serene hills hiding dark secrets, this book is perfect if you love fast-paced mysteries that keep you guessing till the end!

Smriti Nautiyal (bibliophile_halfblood)

Siddharth's book makes you forget you have other responsibilities. You just want to read and read and read just to know what happens next. And that's something remarkable.

Om Kini (nightowl_om)

It's like sitting in on the most dramatic family gathering ever, except it's snowing outside, and someone is probably plotting your murder. Intrigued? Same! OMG, the vibe of this secluded mansion during a snowstorm? Perfect. Maheshwari nailed the atmosphere—it's like Agatha Christie vibes but set in the hills of India, which is so cool. The little details—maps of the estate chapter titles inspired by nursery rhymes—make it super immersive. And trust me, those nursery rhymes? Kind of creepy, but in the best way.

If you're into closed-room mysteries with a deliciously dramatic family, snowy vibes, and twists galore, A Murder in Dehradun is your cup of chai. Definitely give it a read—you'll want to discuss it with someone the moment you finish!

Raya Das - (Booknightouts)

This is more than just a mystery book; it's a chilling exploration of the darkness that can reside within the human heart. Maheshwari's talent for creating atmospheric tension and complex characters elevates this novel above the ordinary.

Atul Sharma - (bookwale_sharmaji)

A masterfully crafted whodunnit brought to life in the hills of Dehradun with unpredictable twists and unforgettable characters. This murder mystery delivers intrigue, deception, and a jaw-dropping conclusion!

Aayushi Anandprakash (bookishcoffeelover)

A gripping tale of secrets, greed, and suspense set against the haunting beauty of snow-clad Dehradun. With vivid storytelling and unpredictable twists, it kept me hooked till the final reveal. A must-read for mystery lovers!

Mugdha Mahajan (confuzzledreader)

A thrilling closed-room mystery where secrets unravel, motives clash, and a shocking murder keeps you guessing till the end.

Sarita Pahuja (Instabook._.marked)

I can easily say Siddharth Maheshwari is the Indian Agatha Christie. The setting of a snow-covered and chilling Dehradun makes this murder mystery a perfect fall read with a cosy cup of coffee and blanket in bed.

Avani Shah - (avanireads)

Meticulously detailed storyline and a thrilling experience, with an unanticipated twist at the end! Loved the characterisation, which made it unputdownable!

Aryasmita Dhir - (readwitharyaaa)

Engaging from start to finish—a masterclass in suspense that kept me hooked till the end!

Susheel Chaudhary (kitabeaurkirdar)

A chilling locked room mystery. If you love Indian murder mysteries that feel like a movie, you have to read this book.

Shreevanti (shreevanti)

A murder mystery book which is so good that you literally have to make notes. This is hands down the most intricately set whodunnit murder mysteries.

Ishaani Chaturvedi (ladylectiophile)

It starts with Karan Johar vibes and ends up giving you a Tolstoy.

Gaurika Gandhi (gaurikagandhi)

Very much twisty and addictive. For anyone who is a fan of Agatha Christie, this book is a must-read.

ishanika (ishnika_reads)

As an ardent lover of locked room murder mysteries I highly recommend this book.

Sulagna (diaryofsulagna)

I was amused by how an Indian murder mystery book can actually be so interesting. Can easily be compared with the works of Agatha Christie.

Ruthvi (livinginthebookshelf)

Trust when I say that Siddharth Maheshwari is slowly becoming one of the finest writers of the country.

simran (booktographer)

The book is dedicated to my mother,
Smt. Sunanda Maheshwari

ACKNOWLEDGEMENTS

Human behaviour and characteristics are unique. No two people are alike. Nor is behaviour predictable. Humans are grey.

Inspired by my mother, a die-hard Agatha Christie fan, I ventured from spy thrillers to craft a classic whodunnit. Using human behaviour as the essence and flavour of my story, I wove a tale in hopes of impressing her, for she will always be my first reader. I hope I have done at least a half-decent job.

I shall forever be grateful to my Nani ma, Late Smt. Leela Devi Somani, who initially inspired me to write. I hope she is looking over me from the heavens above and enjoying my journey. I am indebted to my parents, Anand & Sunanda Maheshwari, who taught me everything I know and have, through impeccable sacrifices, turned me into the human I am today. All my experiences in life and the practical knowledge towards approaching an issue stem from their knowledge and hard experiences. I cannot thank my father enough for everything he has done for me. A special shout out to my mother, who not only had a twinkle and belief in her eyes when I told her that I had started writing but has now managed to push me to change my genres. Her critique and support made it possible for me to write the story. She acted like a soundboard while I discussed my raw plot line with her.

I thank my elder brother, Aditya Vikram Somani, who painstakingly went through the first draft and suggested the required changes and formatting. He gave me insightful critiques at every step and thus encouraged me throughout the journey.

I also wish to thank my dear friend Abhijai Singh, who gave me insightful critiques and helped shape the raw outline into a meaningful story.

I thank my aunt, Nandini Patodia, for her on-point critiques and additions to the characters, especially those of Shirin Dinshaw and Shehnaz Contractor.

I thank my wife, Sakshi, for her on-point critical analysis of the story and patiently bearing with me while I typed away in solitude on countless nights. I also thank her for drawing the illustrations and bringing each character to life. I know it was not a very convenient time for her to do it, so the painstaking effort is all the more appreciated.

I thank my friends for being an immense pillar of support at all times.

I thank Paper Towns for giving me the opportunity to tell my story to the world.

A special shout out to Manik Jaiswal and Narendra Singh for executing the project in such a professional manner. I know we were working on some very tight and strict timelines, but they pulled it off with panache.

I thank Meenakshi Mulani for pinpointing character flaws and Aanchal Gupta for plugging the plot loopholes. You both have eyes for spotting the minutest of inconsistencies, and your efforts helped make the story so much crisper and better from a logical standpoint.

Lastly, I thank Simon and Schuster for ensuring the book reaches readers across the country.

I thank all my readers. I sincerely hope you enjoy the story.

One doesn't recognise the really important moments in one's life until it's too late. —Agatha Christie

A sprawling estate, frigid weather
A family assembled but moods wither,
Lurking murmurs, growing discord
Tempers flaring, failing accords

So pick your poison, be wary of treason,
Avarice has abandoned reason,
On a dreary night, under a crimson moon
There has been a Murder in Dehradun

By Abhijay Singh

Dinshaw Family Tree

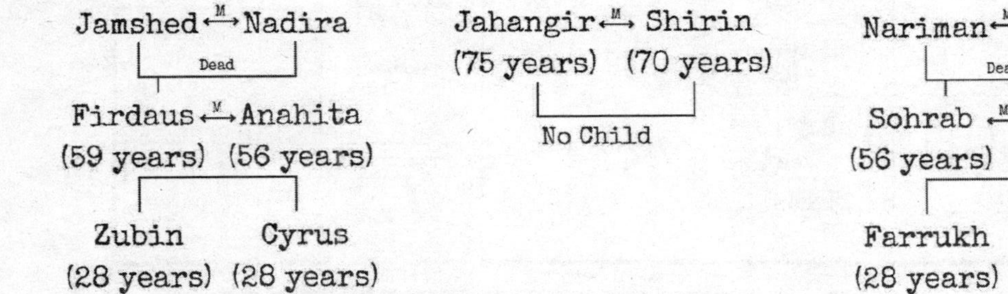

Other Characters

Butler – **Jawahar**

Lawyer – **Bejan Contractor** (75 years old & Jahangir's friend)

Crime Reporter – **Shehnaz Contractor** (56 years old & Bejan's daughter)

Cousin – **Jim**

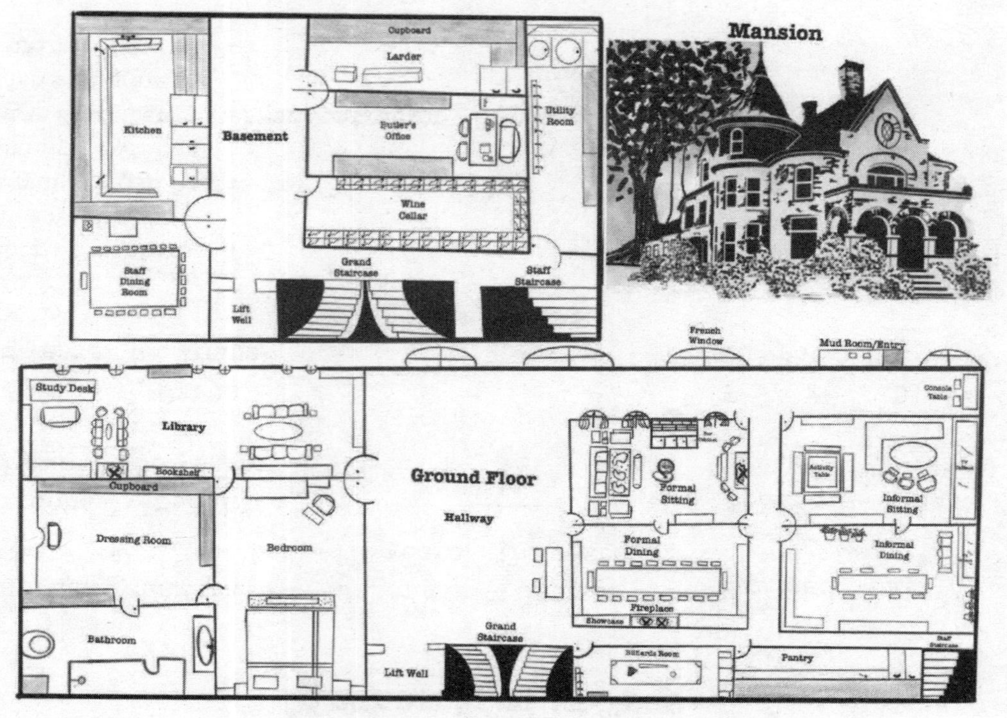

Floor Plan – basement, ground floor and the mansion

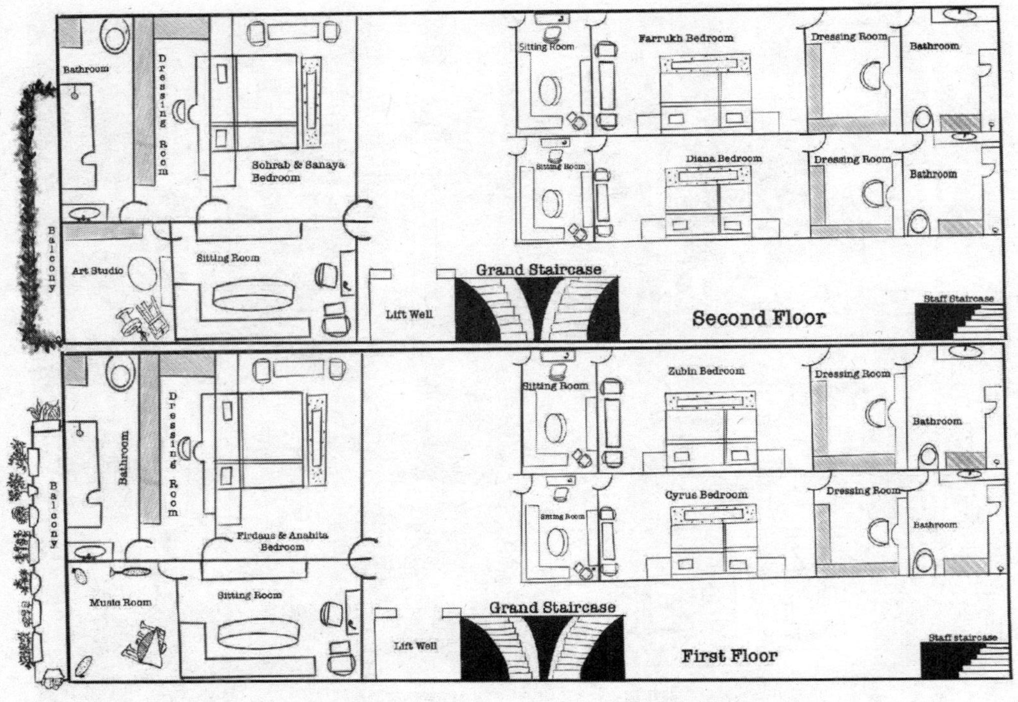

Floor Plan – First and Second Floor

Dinshaw Estate
Fruit Orchard
Farukh's Workshop
Garden Shed
Greenhouse
Vegetable Patch
Entry to the Estate
Silo
Main Lawn
Big Pond
Cow Shed
Small Pond
Stable
Green Field
Mansion
Koi Pond
Swimming Pool
Guesthouse/outhouse
Lawn Tennis Court
Staff Quarters
Kennel
Apiary
Silo
Archery Ranch

CONTENTS

Acknowledgements *xiii*
Prologue 1
1. Old MacDonald had a Farm 4
2. This little piggy 11
3. Little boy blue 18
4. This is the house that Jack built 24
5. How does your garden grow? 30
6. Here we go round the mulberry bush 40
7. Girls and boys, come out to play 48
8. Old king Cole 53
9. Baa baa black sheep 61
10. Little Jacky shall have but a penny a day 64
11. Wee Willie Winkie 76
12. The King was in his counting house 84
13. When the bough breaks 93
14. The Saints go marching 103
15. Scavenger hunt 112
16. Sing a song of six pence 122
17. Dame, what makes your ducks to die? 132
18. Can I get there by candle light? 149
19. Some like it hot 156
20. When she hollers 164
21. Stick, stock, stone dead! 171
22. Peter Piper picked a peck of pickled pepper 174
23. A hunting we will go 180
24. A Pig in a wig 195
Epilogue 208

PROLOGUE

Monday, 16th January 2023
5:00 AM – 7:00 AM

Just as a private Honda Jet skid while landing in Delhi's Indira Gandhi International Airport, at Palam, a prodigious black Rolls Royce entered the borders of Delhi. The single occupant of the Jet stepped out onto the tarmac and felt the winter chill on his face. The smog made his eyes itch and water. But the determined Gentleman dressed in a bespoke black suit, carrying a prim leather Swaine Adeney attaché, steadfastly moved forward and entered the BMW waiting for him. His company had notified the Indian Immigration Department of his arrival even before he departed from London. A copy of his credentials had already been sent ahead. The Gentleman had been cleared on the tarmac itself. It took the skilled chauffeur eighteen minutes to reach Man Singh Road, where the mighty Taj Mahal Hotel was situated. It was 5:30 AM, and the Brit could feel the warmth of the rising sun on his white cheeks, which flushed pink owing to the nip in the air, as he entered the grand hotel.

Briskly, he approached the reception desk, showed his ID, and said, "I am expected at the chambers. Could you please escort me there?"

As one of the receptionists waddled and moved out from behind the desk, the Brit asked, "Is my host here?"

The Brit knew that "The Chambers" was an elite club of the Taj, where membership was by invitation only. He silently wondered if The Chambers was the luxurious den where the rich bad boys found their offices away from their quotidian workplace. He also wondered whether the place allowed people to hold closed-door confidential meetings along with some very posh alcohol and gourmet food being served round the clock.

The Brit was registered as a guest by the person who had booked one of the conference rooms. The receptionist was about to answer when the black Rolls Royce halted just outside the Hotel foyer, and she saw the guards pave the way, give crisp salutes, and open the doors for the gargantuan personality of Jahangir Dinshaw. The petite man walked in casually, with his hands in his pockets, wearing a white polo neck t-shirt, jeans and a plain black Versace leather jacket. It was not his boots but his personality that reverberated through the grand foyer. It was almost as if the figures of the famous painting *Three Stanzas* by M.F. Husain would turn their heads to admire Jahangir Dinshaw as he nonchalantly strolled through the lobby.

When the opportunity presented itself, Jahangir organised this meeting. The appointment was important for him. Yet, Jahangir did not want anyone to know that, so he had dressed casually, almost as if he did not care about the outcome of this meeting. Generally, people dress according to the occasion, but Jahangir was shrewd enough to throw an observant mind off its tracks. Gesturing with his right hand, he silently indicated to the receptionist to lead the way.

The young receptionist was bowled over by Jahangir's personality. She quickly composed herself and said, "Good morning, sir. Welcome to the Taj." Then she turned around and led the way.

The elevator pinged and silently halted on the fourteenth floor. The doors opened, and the guests were greeted by a sling of caricatures of Winston Churchill, Satyajit Ray, Mother Teresa, and Pandit Ravi Shankar, among others, created by R.K. Laxman, the pioneer of cartoons in India. The wall opposite felt proud as another M.F. Husain hung from it.

Ignoring the opulence and the beautiful artwork as if these were some everyday phenomena, the two men silently followed the receptionist.

Upon settling down in the conference room, Jahangir waited patiently for the Brit to begin.

The foreigner began by clicking open the locks of his leather attaché and taking out a thick brown manila envelope. Without saying a word, he handed over the documents inside to Jahangir. The old, wise capitalist went through the documents meticulously, and as he turned the pages of the report, the paper rattled softly in the eerily silent room.

A while later, Jahangir looked up and with a piercing gaze asked, "How accurate are the figures and what is the possibility of a takeover?"

"Very high. The due diligence has been done by Morgan Stanley. Whether you choose to stay or en-cash your stake, you will be a very rich person soon. You would probably make more money than your entire existing wealth combined," replied the Brit firmly.

Jahangir smirked and replied, "Son, at this stage in my life, money and loyalty both are worthless. It is me against those who want what I have, and they are not outsiders. They breathe, dine and live with me. They are my kin. So, it gets down to whether I can manipulate them better than they can manipulate me. It is my vision of the future that I am now fighting for and striving to achieve. Therefore, I will make my exit now. Prepare the documents."

Saying thus, Jahangir got up and left.

CHAPTER 1

Old MacDonald had a Farm

Tuesday, 24th January 2023
5:00 AM – 10:00 AM.

A light, watery breeze ruffled through the nicely trimmed white hair of the Gentleman, wearing a pair of khakis and a soft cotton full-sleeves white polo-neck t-shirt, as he casually pedalled a limited edition Fendi cycle around his estate. It had been raining continuously for the past three days, and today, on the twenty-fourth day of January, the thunder had finally halted in the early hours of the morning. The Sun probably felt threatened by the deep cloud cover and had decided not to show its full prowess. The mild rays of the sun created a misty atmosphere, with heavy raindrops still lingering in the air, unable to decide whether to fall on Earth as droplets or still linger on and take in the warmth of the rising red sun which covered the Doon Valley and all of Dehradun like a shroud.

Nestled between the Song and the Asan rivers is the picturesque hill station of Dehradun. And within this quiet and simple retreat was the majestic estate of Jahangir

Dinshaw, which grandly sat overlooking the valley of flowers in Dehradun. Although the travel guides, brochures and the now rampant travel influencers would point to the road by the river as "The Song Road" and would list scurrying through the small quaint shops selling local artefacts, woollens and souvenirs as the main thing to do, Jahangir had unofficially named the obscure off-beaten road leading to his estate as the "Song Road". He had a small wooden gate constructed at the entry of the road to mark the beginning of his territory. Though even a mountain hare could have hopped over the feeble gate, the creaky structure had served its purpose and deterred most from venturing into the old Parsi's private lands. Anybody coming up to the Dinshaw estate was expected to first open the gate themselves, shut it back and then drive about three kilometres up the hill on the winding dirt road to the estate. Jahangir enjoyed such idiosyncrasies. He could have had the gate manned, but his nerves tickled, knowing that his guests probably suffered a tiny bit before reaching him.

The Dinshaw patriarch had a penchant for cycling around his estate, which allowed him to keep an eye on his ninety-three acres of property, all of which was registered under the family trust.

Such was his affinity for cycling that he had a bike path curated around his property dotted with bulkit lights and canopied stands to be able to ride leisurely at any time he so wished. Even while it was raining, during the past three days, he had coolly biked around. Jahangir had a grand collection of expensive bicycles, and although two days ago, the brakes of his bike had unexpectedly failed, which had caused him to fall head-on into a ditch, he had survived with just minor scratches on his face and had continued to bike around his estate.

Jahangir was fond of exquisite, materialistic things and regularly collected antiques, rare historical items, paintings, sculptures, first editions of books and anything else that, by virtue of time, would appreciate in value. He was a shrewd businessman, and for him, the increasing worth of his various investments held more value than the sentimental value of his collections. All of his treasured collectables and assets, including gold bonds, shares of various companies, mutual fund investments and properties, had been accumulated within the family trust.

Jahangir had celebrated his seventy-fifth birthday four days ago, surrounded by his immediate family. He was of the generation where people often had wrong birthdays printed on their official documents and were really born on a different date. Jahangir loved to celebrate on both days, especially as the difference between the dates was of a mere nine days. His real birthday fell on the twenty-ninth of January.

The slow retired life he had been leading for the past three decades, the controlled healthy diet, and the daily meditations that he practised showed on him. His cheeks flushed pink, his body was well-toned, and he did not have any major ailments. To an outsider, he could pass off as a man in his early sixties.

Switching to the fifth gear, Jahangir casually pedalled his bike as he crossed the cow pasture and the horse stables, which were surrounded by colourful, lush hydrangeas that had come to life after the rains. At 5:30 AM, the animals had still not stirred from their slumber. His khakis were dotted with specks of mud, which flew as the soft tyres splashed through the occasional puddles, and his t-shirt was drenched in sweat and stuck to his lean body. Finally crossing over the small wooden bridge that he had built over his Koi fish pond, he arrived at the apiary. Jahangir would stop at the apiary on his way back and observe his bees every day. He never wore any bee suit, as not in the slightest bit he ever felt threatened by the bees. He would meditate for thirty minutes, and the melodious hum of the bees would help him relax his nerves. After his meditation, Jahangir would ride back to the Mansion, have his morning espresso with a slice of William Curley's most divine dark chocolate and then head for a cold shower. Today was no different, and after his morning routine, Jahangir casually slipped on his lamb wool lined crocodile skin Gucci loafers under his silk suit and treaded softly as he crossed a bunch of Monet's that depicted a surreal European nature, for which Jahangir had no interest, and entered the baroque family library. Normally, he would read a bunch of newspapers before delving into the fictional novel that he would be reading. But not today. Today, he was going to make some much-required amendments.

Since his birthday party, for which all of his family had assembled, he had had a strange feeling. A feeling he was not able to shake off. His subconscious brain told him that he was in mortal danger, and so Jahangir wanted to make some changes before the big party on the thirty-first, for which most of the now departed guests would be visiting again. Although to the outside world, he depicted himself as a lion ruling in a jungle, he did at times have pangs of anxiety and felt like a scaredy-cat. The bane of sitting on a golden throne was that the iron nails would still pinch the bottoms.

Donning his smoking robe that was thrown over his chair to make himself comfortable and warm, with a firm resolve, Jahangir started making meticulous notes. After about two hours, he opened a safe that was concealed behind a group of visibly cheerful ballet dancers painted by Edgar Degas, who at the time may never have imagined that his creativity would be used as a front for hiding a numbered locker. Till 9 AM, Jahangir slowly re-read his last will and testament and made copious notes. This was no longer going to be his last will. He had given strict instructions to the house butler, Jawahar, that he was not to be disturbed and that he would have his breakfast in the library at the usual time. Jahangir was a stickler for rules and had always controlled his surroundings. In his world, meals were supposed to be eaten in the dining room, but he was allowed to break his own rules. In his eyes, these were the small perks of being the head of the family.

Sharp at 9:45 AM, after finishing his fruit bowl, which had consisted of a green apple, a banana, some strawberries, blackberries, grapes and cherries, he unapologetically burped, cursed his slowing metabolism and then making a groaning sound while getting up from his plush leather chair, gingerly walked towards the window. After letting out another burp and taking in the warmth of the sun, he took out his iPhone and dialled his long-time friend, confidante and family lawyer, Bejan Contractor.

On the fourth ring, Bejan picked up and said, "Morning Jeh, how are you?"

"Not quite well, my friend. I want to discuss an urgent matter with you. How soon can you come?" asked Jahangir with an urgency.

"I am coming for your birthday celebrations on the thirty-first. Should we discuss the matter then?" asked Bejan with a hint of equanimity in his voice.

"The question, how soon can you get here, was a rhetorical one, Bee. I would like you to come over now." Jahangir respected his friend for his wisdom and legal prowess, but that did not mean that Bejan could make him wait. Jahangir was not used to waiting for anyone. In fact, he had the habit of controlling everything and everyone around him. He felt secure in knowing the predictability of his surroundings.

"Very well. I'll arrive at your house tonight, so take out your rare whiskey bottles. I will need a stiff drink to help my brain cells work better," replied Bejan light-heartedly. He was wise enough to not provoke Jahangir, especially since he was paid generously for the retainership.

"Also, I remember you mentioning that your daughter is now the lead editor and co-owner of the leading news channel Secular 24/7."

"Yes. She was recently promoted to the post of lead editor and also given a share in the company after she received the Ramon Magsaysay Award for her unfaltering commitment to professional and ethical journalism of the highest standards and for her moral courage to stand up for the truth."

"She has grown to be a woman of high integrity and principles. Would it be possible for her to take a break and enjoy the hospitality and the serene calmness of my estate for a few days? I could use her experience in discerning the bent of criminal minds and her input could be vital for setting my future structuring of the family trusts. I would like to have her opinions and discuss matters at length with her. Besides, in her childhood days she did visit the estate with you and maintains a warm bond with my nephews Firdaus and Sohrab."

"Yes, I will appeal to her emotional side and make her accompany me as I do believe that she could do with a short holiday. Moreover, I agree that her recommendation might be valuable for our discussions as we set your plans that would control the future of the Dinshaw family in motion."

"Then, this is agreed. I will see you both soon, Bee," replied Jahangir and cut the phone.

On the other side, Bejan silently wondered that God really did craft his friend Jahangir's brain with leisure and precision, placing each neuron and cell carefully. The sly astuteness of his friend was not missed by him, and that was one of the things that he admired about Jahangir. As Bejan looked out of his New Delhi apartment at the congested interconnecting motorways with hundreds of cars moving through the capital city, he realized that it was Jahangir's similarly functioning complex brain network that was the reason for his grandiose and formidable personality.

The recent conversation had sparked an old memory in Bejan, and with warmth, he remembered his daughter having so many stories to share about Jahangir's nephews, Firdaus the Naughty and Sohrab the Quiet, fun secret names they had given to the boys. He wondered how the family members would behave now. Not just because of his friendship but also by virtue of the work that he did, Bejan's interaction had mostly been with Jahangir.

CHAPTER 2

THIS LITTLE PIGGY

Tuesday, 24th January 2023
10:00 AM – 11:30 AM

As Jahangir slid his phone back into his black velvet smoking robe with a green dragon embroidered on its back and lit a pipe, he saw his eldest nephew, Firdaus, go for a late morning jog.

Jahangir saw the time on his watch and muttered to himself, “It is 10 AM; even if the weather is so pleasant, it is too late for a morning jog. The man is fifty-eight years of age but still acts like a young, foolish boy.”

Muttering under his breath, he switched on the 75-inch OLED screen in front of him and settled on the sofa. As the screen came to light, it displayed the vivid blue jersey of the Chelsea players, who were shaking hands with their counterparts from Liverpool before the kick-off. Chelsea had a better line up of players and in this match, Liverpool was considered the underdog. Where most people would like to see the underdog win and put up a strong fight, Jahangir thought that being the better team, it was Chelsea's right to win and be arrogant about it. In his world, the weak were dominated and preyed upon.

Firdaus Dinshaw, wearing white boxer shorts and a loose black t-shirt with a pair of Bose headphones nicely placed on his oval head, stretched his long legs on the stone statue of a lion that had been royally placed at the entrance of the mansion. He then began his jog slowly, placing his legs gingerly yet surely on the damp mud. As the slow instrumental music rhythmically drummed in his ears, Firdaus thought about his early years in business, when he had cracked a deal with the Sri Lankan Defence Minister and ensured the island government's long-term dependency on his company.

Firdaus, much to the objection of the board, had started by dropping the prices of his products below the market rate and supplying a superior quality before time. This strategy ensured his entry into the Sri Lankan Defence market. Then, Firdaus had maintained a steady supply line for over a year. Once he was sure that the Defence Ministry was totally dependent on him, he had slowly started increasing his prices, which were still below the prevailing market rates. By the third year, Firdaus was charging them a little over the market rate, but by this time, the Lankans had severed their ties with the other suppliers and had become quite dependent and comfortable dealing with Firdaus. Firdaus was an astute businessman but, over the years, had become very lazy. Therefore, he invested his money in blue chip stocks and only backed companies that he calculated to be a sure-shot winner in the market. He did not have his uncle's inexorable risk appetite and thus always took planned risks. He never invested his money in start-ups. Three years ago, Firdaus had retired from active business after selling his company, Fira Pvt. Ltd. The company had been in the business of manufacturing bulletproof jackets for the Indian Army and had been started by his father Jamshed and his uncles, Jahangir and Nariman Dinshaw. Firdaus, at the age of five, had lost his parents in an air crash. Jamshed and Nadira had been returning from Indonesia after their yearly holiday on an airline out of Malaysia when the airline mysteriously crashed into the Indian Ocean. There had been no survivors.

Firdaus, after attaining his MBA from Judge Business School of the University of Cambridge, joined the company and grew the enterprise under his uncle Jahangir's tutelage. He had worked hard to make Fira one of the largest defence manufacturers in the country. He had brokered contracts with the defence ministries of various low-level countries like Egypt, Turkey, Sri Lanka, and Thailand and thus had expanded his enterprise.

Once he was at a considerable level, instead of taking his company public, he had chosen to sell it to his largest competitor, much to the anguish of his uncle, Jahangir. The consideration offered had been handsome, and Firdaus had used his share of the money to invest in a few Real Estate ventures to garner a steady rental income and parked the balance in bonds and shares. He now enjoyed a routine, quiet life in the hills within the family estate.

Unlike his uncle, Firdaus appreciated all forms of art and routinely produced plays for the theatre circuit in New Delhi and Mumbai. This was his one passion where he frequently lost money, merely due to the fact that he would insist on lavish sets and would get the best of the actors to perform for his production company. But his consistency had gained him popularity in the thespian circles of Delhi and Mumbai. Firdaus had a very giving nature and would regularly contribute to charities, especially those that would provide for the destitute and the homeless. He always gave his old clothes to the staff that worked at the estate or helped them out in any way that he could. Firdaus was not a spendthrift, and although he dressed in fine clothes, ate gourmet meals and owned a few sports cars, he was not married to this lifestyle and so, most of his clothes and possessions were a decade old, at least.

With sweat drenching his t-shirt, Firdaus continued his jog, with his thoughts drifting towards his investments and the recent loss that he had booked in his production company despite the success of his eighteenth play, "How to Kill Your Family?" It was a satirical dark comedy which explored the need for the human mind to right the wrongs that a family patriarch unknowingly passes on to his successors. Finally, after completing his circuit, he arrived back at the estate at 11:15 AM. Through the entrance on the right was the grand family library, where he saw his uncle smoking his pipe and sipping on a cup of freshly brewed coffee. He could smell the aroma of the Arabica beans, but without a second glance he went to the second floor to have his daily long shower. Just as he took off his sweaty t-shirt, he saw his wife, Anahita, come out of their private terrace with mud sticking to her fingers. Anahita loved botany and would maintain her collection of bonsais herself.

While still undressing in the dressing room, Firdaus said, "I believe I should ask uncle to increase my quarterly allowance. What do you think?"

"C'mon, Freddy! We have enough. Why would you ask him for more allowance? You have invested our share of the wealth well. We get money from the rentals, the dividends from the stocks and the interest on the investments, which provides us with more money than we need. The allowance that we get from the family trust is anyway an added bonus," replied Anahita with a slight concern in her voice. She got irked by her husband's insouciant nature of unhesitatingly asking favours from others to further his own goals.

"Yes, we have multiple sources of income, but I have recently lost some money in my latest theatrical production," explained Firdaus with a grim voice while casually stroking his pencil-thin moustache.

"So, pay the creditors in small instalments over a period of six months. That way, you will also be able to manage your cash flows," replied Anahita, wisely.

"Hmm…let me think about it. How is the old man's injury now? He gave us quite a shock after he fell off his cycle into that ditch," asked Firdaus as he now prepared to step into the hot shower.

"He is tough as an iron bar. A light fall won't put a dent in him," replied Anahita coldly. Then, with a slight sense of irritation, she quickly added, "Also, just the other day, Aunt Shirin was grumbling about me spending too much time with my Bonsais and not participating much in the house. I don't know why she gets these sudden pangs and starts lashing out. She is a complicated character."

Firdaus did not react or comment and simply walked into the bathroom.

Hearing the gush of water and looking at the light steam emerging from the bathroom, Anahita walked out to the terrace and bent down to tend her most prized possession, a bonsai of the desert rose, or as the botanists preferred to call it, the Sabi Star. Looking at the stunted thick grey trunk with multiple crooked branches which were enveloped by thick rigid leaves, Anahita wondered about how ugly this expensive plant actually was. The only saving grace, which she felt, were the blossoming delicate flowers with red petals and a white centre. What gave the plant value was not the fact that it was a desert plant and thus difficult to grow or that it required tremendous care but the fact that the very delicate-looking flowers of this dwarf plant were poisonous and could potentially kill a human.

Anahita was an interior designer by profession; at most, she would take up three projects a year. She only took assignments which interested her and charged a moderate fee for her designs. Most of her contemporaries would also manufacture the furniture for the clients, but Anahita never bothered with the hard part of dealing with labour. She just gave her clients the designs and left them to fend for the furniture as per their budgets.

After tending to the bonsais, she dumped her floral-printed gardening gloves and strolled out from the terrace into a smaller room, which was adjacent to her sitting room. This room had a lot of planters and seamlessly blended with the terrace. Right in the middle of it was a black Bösendorfer Piano, which she played every day for an hour before lunch. Just as she was flipping through the pages of the sheet music to identify which score she would play, the butler, Jawahar, softly entered and gingerly placed a flute of chilled mimosa on a side table by the grand piano.

Anahita observed the time was 11:30 AM and felt uncomfortable at the precise mechanical nature of the butler. After the butler left, Anahita softly murmured to herself, "My life has become monotonously dull, and nothing is going in my favour." She quickly gulped down the chilled orange drink without much care for the exotic cocktail or for the dry brut that was used to make the perfect blend. Today, she chose to play the haunting tune of "Ride of the Valkyries" composed by the controversial German maestro Richard Wagner.

Anahita Dinshaw

CHAPTER 3

LITTLE BOY BLUE

Tuesday, 24th January 2023
11:30 AM – 1:00 PM

As the tune played through the house, Sanaya Dinshaw grudgingly exclaimed, "Oh! I can't bear to hear her haunting tunes. Why can't she play nice melodies? Has the sound of music really escaped her?" But there was no one around her to partake in her cribbing. Dumping the charcoal and the artists' scalpel with which she was creating strokes of unequal haphazard lines across the canvas, which her patrons called modern art while sipping on champagne, Sanaya declared, "I will need some peace and tranquillity to be able to create art. I'll go for a walk to clear my mind." With the determination and stubbornness of a toddler, Sanaya wore her Gucci trainers and hurriedly stepped into the elevator and pressed the ground floor button. While the elevator slowly clambered down, she put on her air pods and put on a light instrumental song.

Sanaya was the late Nariman Dinshaw's son, Sohrab's wife. She had a very temperamental nature and was frequently irked by the smallest of occurrences, yet her brain's artistic streak was on point as her black and white modern art sketches were coveted and renowned the world over. Sanaya was born to wealthy Parsi parents and was their only daughter. She was brought up like a princess, and even without the enormous corpus of Dinshaw wealth and family trust of which she was now a part, she was rich in her own right. Yet, she never cared for money or for the exorbitant luxuries that came with it. Her art sales got her enough that she never bothered about the quarterly allowance that came from the trust into her account. Walking eastwards along the dirt road, she reached the tennis court. There, she sat in silence and saw the mustard ball covered in soft brown mud being rallied across the net by the two players, who occasionally grunted when the effort to slam the ball across the net became tough. Observing the duo play, she murmured, "Winning is not about not failing, but about never quitting. And so, I must persevere. Hitting a roadblock should not shake my quest. I am determined and will not quit until I have achieved my goal."

Of the two players, the leaner one with a salt and pepper goatee was her husband, Sohrab and the other, who was a bit heavier and was constantly finding it difficult to run the breadth of the clay court, was their guest, Jim. He had flown down from Mumbai for his Grand Uncle Jahangir's upcoming birthday celebrations. At 12:20 PM the players finished their match with the set being called 4-2 in Sohrab's favour. As the players stepped out of the court, wiping their sweat with their respective white towels, Sanaya joined them. As they began to walk back to the mansion, Sanaya asked Jim, "When did you arrive, and how was your flight to Dehradun?"

"Oh, I arrived this morning. I had booked my tickets via points and so I landed a seat near the rear toilet. And there was this rather skinny passenger with a round head, and he kept swaying his head and fidgeting to find a comfortable posture to sleep in, but very quickly, he decided to rest his round head on my shoulders, and I had to keep flicking it back." Continuing with his bickering, which was making him feel good, Jim exclaimed, "There was no overhead space for my hand luggage as everyone else had already placed theirs in the limited space present. I had to keep mine under the seat in front of me and thus couldn't even stretch my legs. There was also a group of about forty people travelling together. I gathered that they were coming to attend a wedding. But they were the most obnoxious group of travellers, for they refused to sit on their assigned seats and kept exchanging their seats with each other throughout the journey. All of them spoke so loudly that I can still hear their voices booming inside my head."

Then, throwing his arms up in the air, Jim relented to his harrowing experience and stated, "But other than that, the flight was okay, and it landed on time at 6:30 AM. I reached the mansion just in time to greet grand-uncle as he was stepping into the library. Then, after settling in the outhouse, I met uncle, and we decided to play a game of tennis."

"What brought you here? I thought you would be busy sketching," asked Sohrab.

"I just couldn't stand Anahita's haunting music and needed to get away to clear my head," replied Sanaya bluntly.

Sohrab gave a slight laugh and while shaking his head said, "The Dalai Lama rightly said, and I quote, 'In the practice of tolerance, one's enemy is the best teacher'."

"Well, I really don't need to torment myself for your acquiescence. Anyway, you both are stinking and should shower before the family sits down for lunch at 1 PM," retorted Sanaya with a sense of authority and marched ahead back to the Mansion.

With an intention of lightening the mood, Jim casually asked, "Is business good? I heard that uncle Firdaus sold the company that made bullet proof jackets."

"Yes. We got good money from the sale. The company's shares were split equally amongst Firdaus, the family trust and me. The operations of the company were being looked after by Firdaus. Though uncle was not very happy about it, I see merit in Firdaus's decision. The publishing company that I look after is under stress as the industry is going through a tough phase. We have more competitors than the demand in the market. I am trying to export our books and set up a brand name for the arm of the publishing house which publishes school curriculum to be able to sell the company," explained Sohrab with a hint of dejection in his voice.

"You seem to be in a tough spot," said Jim sympathetically.

"Well, since the company is in losses, I am not able to get any sweat equity, and all the labour and time that I put in is converting into a free-of-cost service. The situation has become quite frustrating for me."

The two had now reached the outhouse, and Jim left to take a shower.

Lost in his own thoughts and almost like an innocent lamb, Sohrab silently treaded back to the mansion. As he entered, he saw his uncle sitting upright at the dark rosewood library desk and scribbling in his diary while the smoke from his pipe created a light haze around his face and persona. Sohrab entered the library as the golden rays of the afternoon sun hit the heavy wooden furniture and basked the room in a golden hue.

Walking up to the table, Sohrab said, "Uncle, I wish to discuss something with you."

"You are sweaty and are stinking. Go take a shower and come down for lunch. We will talk later," replied Jahangir in a stern voice without looking up from his desk.

Dejected, Sohrab went for his shower.

As he undressed, he calmly told Sanaya, "My parents were the oldest in our family. They struggled and laid down the foundations of our various businesses and investments. They built everything from the ground up. Together, they collected the various art pieces that adorn the walls of this house. Over the years, Uncle Jahangir favoured Firdaus, and he sold most of the family businesses. But when I speak about selling the publishing business, the obstinate old fool pays no heed to my experience and perspective. He insists on running the business and is needlessly pouring more money into it. The situation is becoming tough for me."

"Oh, darling, why do you bother? I have enough funds myself. Even if your business shuts down and Uncle removes you from the family trust, I'll take care of you," replied Sanaya casually as she giggled and poured herself another glass of cold Champagne after quickly tying her hair in a messy bun.

Sohrab was a poised and mature gentleman and chose not to retort to his wife's comments. He stepped into the bathroom for his shower, hoping that the cold water would lower his mind and body heat.

Sanaya Dinshaw

CHAPTER 4

THIS IS THE HOUSE THAT JACK BUILT

Tuesday, 24th January 2023
1:00 PM – 2:15 PM

As the big hands of the magnificent timepiece inside the well-carved seven-foot-tall grandfather clock with cylindrical brass pendulums struck one, the Dinshaw family assembled in the large baroque dining room. The chair on the head of the long glass dining table was reserved for Jahangir, but he had retreated into the library and had informed the butler that he was not to be disturbed. Firdaus pulled out the intricately carved chair with white silk upholstered around its back and on the handles, which was on the right side of his uncle's seat and sat down. His wife, Anahita, sat next to him. Sohrab sat opposite Firdaus with his wife, Sanaya, beside him. Firdaus's twins Zubin and Cyrus, who were twenty-eight years old, sat next to their mother, per the hierarchy in the family. Sanaya's daughter Diana and son Farrukh, who were twenty-seven and twenty-eight years old, respectively, sat opposite Zubin and Cyrus. Jim was a guest and sat next to Cyrus.

Finally, Jahangir's wife, Shirin, softly treaded into the room placing each step with such delicacy as if she was afraid her feet would spoil the plush Kashmiri carpet underneath her. Putting her cane on one side, she allowed Jawahar, the butler, to pull the chair back for her and then nicely tuck her back once she had settled her soft bottoms on the silk upholstery.

Just as she settled on the opposite end of the dining table, Shirin looked at Jawahar and said, "Dim the lights a bit; the brightness makes me blind."

Silently, Jawahar adjusted the regulator to decrease the brightness of the lights emitting out of the LED bulbs placed inside the Murano chandelier, which hung over the middle of the room.

A few minutes later, three menservants brought ten white bowls which had a thin gold line around its rim, per the standard Dinshaw household gold line cutlery. Even cutlery becomes standardised after one accumulates a certain level of wealth. As the cloches were removed, Jim remarked, "There is a strong whiff of ginger and garlic. What are we having?"

Dipping her bouillon spoon into the broth and after moving around the chopped onions, carrots and green beans, Diana replied, "Did the sweet smell of chicken miss you? It's a chicken bone broth with vegetables."

Taking a sip of the flavourful yellow broth and while chewing on bits of the soft potato and zucchini pieces, Jim replied, "Ah. I could never have guessed by the smell." Then, throwing a barrage of questions, by making good on his right as a guest, Jim inquisitively asked, "How long has it been since you graduated? What did you study? What are you doing now?"

While struggling to chew the leafy coriander and parsley bits that would get stuck in her teeth with every spoonful that she would take, Diana replied, "I graduated six years ago. I studied psychology at Oxford and now work directly under Grand Uncle. We invest in start-ups." Hearing about the investments in the start-ups, Firdaus, who had been following their conversation, frowned but kept mum. Sohrab silently observed his cousin Firdaus's facial expressions, but he too decided to remain mum.

Diana continued her explanation while ignoring the whiff of the chicken and allowing the broth to cool a little, "After graduation, I worked for three years in the M&A departments of various companies. I believe that the field I had chosen in college was intriguing and hard, as psychology is largely based on perceptions, and every human has a unique way of looking at a situation. But the ability to study the human mind gives me an edge while assessing the people and their ideas when I invest in their newly founded businesses."

As the last of the soup broth was slurped and the bowls cleared, three small bowls were placed near everyone's plates, and a large basket of pav was kept in the centre along with two earthen jars.

Taking a few pieces of bread from the basket, Jim said, "I agree with you, Diana, but not everything is a matter of perception," and then, without specifically looking at anyone, he continued, "Statistics and numbers also reflect human and organisational nature." Then, dipping his pav into the first bowl, from which he got a strong whiff of turmeric and ginger, he wrapped a few pieces of the succulent mutton chunks in his pav, and as he chewed on to it, Jim could taste the flavours of tomato, onion and jaggery and the fact that the juicy meat had been thoroughly marinated in vinegar. Gnawing on the slivers of fried potato sticks that were generously sprinkled on the Salli Boti, Jim looked at Farrukh and asked him, "Are you planning to join Uncle Sohrab in his business?"

Farrukh, who preferred to eat in silence and was an introvert, had been concentrating on the second bowl, which had tender pieces of chicken wrapped in fiery chillies and spices and again sprinkled with fried potato sticks. It was the chilly and not Jim's prying question that made him sweat while softly smacking his lips with each bite. As Farrukh continued to dip his pav into the Salli Marghi and eat in silence, Jim, with suppressed eagerness and the meddling right which every guest is bestowed with by virtue of their short-lived elite status at the host's home again repeated the question in a louder voice.

Attacking the inquest, Zubin, Anahita's son, smirked and replied, "Uncle Sohrab's business no longer has room for dear old Farrukh. It hardly churns any monies, and Grand Uncle regularly injects funds into it from his investments. It would be better for him to start looking at jobs in the UK, that is if he is able to complete his doctorate from Cambridge."

Firdaus silently smirked at his son's comment but, with a straight face, asked Sohrab, "Should I speak to Uncle on your behalf?"

Sohrab was a refined gentleman and did not react to such childish condemnation. He understood his position and knew how to take a punch on the chin and, so he confidently replied, "No, Firdaus. I am discussing the matter with Uncle. There may be merit in his point of view, and maybe we can turn things around."

"Now, I really can't distinguish between you two twins. You look and sound so similar, and my eyes are not as sharp as before," said Shirin in a delicately soft yet commanding tone. Bending over, she gently peeled the green banana leaf which had been used to steam the pomfret. The light steam from the cooked meat was filled with the aroma of garlic and chilli. Shirin cut a piece, and as she chewed the supple meat and, her heart-shaped face bobbed in agreement while she tasted the mild coriander, mint and coconut chutney that was generously spread on the fish, she then sternly looked up and said, "Which of you were mean and must you pass such despicable comments about your own kin?"

Before Zubin could reply, Cyrus doused the rising tension by saying, "Oh! Grand Aunt Zubin did not mean to be rude. He was just having fun with Farrukh and Jim." Then Cyrus quickly reached for one of the earthen pots, removed its lid and served himself some rice.

After chewing her morsel of fish, Shirin, without particularly looking at anyone, exclaimed, "Rudeness is a weak person's imitation of strength."

Chewing on the berries and nuts and devouring the saffron-flavoured berry pulao, Zubin curtly stated, "No matter how good one's heart is, eventually one has to start treating people the way they treat you."

"Zubin! You are being unwantedly hot-headed. No one here has ever wronged you. You are making a mountain out of a molehill. Why don't you eat your food in silence and try not to be rude to Uncle Sohrab, even if it is inconvenient for you." stated Anahita sternly.

The family then continued to chew in silence, but after a while, Sanaya, on impulse, remarked with a sense of excitement, "I believe we should either shut or sell the publishing house. We still own rights to some novels and we can sell the rights to other publishing houses and to various production houses in tandem with the authors."

"Oh, darling, must you behave like the kids and discuss business and disparaging issues on the table?" questioned Shirin and then flicked her hands indicating to the butler to clear the plates and bring in the desserts.

The manservants quickly brought a platter of cheese sprinkled with candied walnuts and a portion of apple crumble with vanilla ice cream.

The family ate the sweets together and suppressed any bitterness they felt as the dopamine kicked in and calmed their nerves.

Shirin Dinshaw

CHAPTER 5

How does your garden grow?

Tuesday, 24th January 2023
2:15 PM – 4:30 PM

After the scrumptious lunch, Shirin softly ambled into the pantry where she found a young maid taking out some ingredients as per the list handed over to her by the chef. Looking at the matriarch, the maid hurriedly collected the last of the few items, scanned the list and withdrew from the room. Shirin prodded around the neatly arranged array of shelves, bumped her walking stick into a stack of grains without any adverse effect on herself or the grains and finally managed to reach one end of the room. There, she meticulously examined a few jars of pickles that she had prepared herself, opened a few and smelt them and then as her old shrivelled bony hands were closing the lid, she unconsciously grumbled, "Sanaya gets excited too quickly. A woman of fifty-six years of age should show some maturity and restraint. She is always so cold and calculating."

Just as she mumbled these words, a pang of jealousy towards Anahita and Sanaya hit Shirin as she felt sad about her inability to have children and being creatively inept as compared to them.

On most days, her brain would subdue any such feelings. But the occasional arguments with Sanaya or Anahita would revive the suppressed feelings and that kept her sad for the next couple of days.

After checking on her pickles, Shirin slowly prodded towards the library.

Jawahar, who was sitting across the library on a single armchair which sat beside an ornate console table, looked slightly up from the newspaper that he was reading. He knew better than to intrude on the decision of the matriarch to approach her husband. So, while Shirin slowly moved towards the library, he neatly folded his paper, put it beside a delicate white vase which depicted a blue dragon gliding amongst the blue clouds that had been ornately painted by a master under the Ming dynasty, and promptly stood up to open the heavy rosewood doors.

Shirin entered and found Jahangir slumped on his desk, with his hands moving fervently as he scribbled away his thoughts on a piece of paper. A light cloud of smoke formed around his oval head as he puffed on his pipe. Jahangir, even at this age, was perceptive and alert. Before his wife could announce herself, he, without looking up, asked, "Curiosity got the better of you, Shirin? I thought you would retire to your room after lunch."

"I walk ever so slowly, without much commotion. With your back turned towards me, how did you guess that it was me?" asked Shirin, still impressed and in love with the man whom she married almost fifty years ago.

"I did not guess. I heard the door open, and as you walked towards me, I could smell the light scent of your rose perfume," replied Jahangir casually.

"Well, to answer your earlier question, I came to check upon you. What has been bothering you?" asked Shirin.

Still continuing to scribble, Jahangir said with a slight chuckle, "It is nothing that I can't resolve. With a little firm hand, I'll entangle the unassuming souls together forever."

"You know, I sometimes wonder if we should have had children of our own or, at least, adopted one. You could have had someone to rely upon," said Shirin with a heavy voice.

"You know I couldn't have fathered children. And I don't need to rely upon anyone", exclaimed Jahangir sternly. Then, without waiting for a reply, he said dismissively, "Anyway, now is not the time to discuss this. Tonight, Bejan is coming over. I must discuss certain issues with him. Then, tomorrow morning, I will convene everyone together. On your way out, please send Jawahar."

Shirin got the cue and, guessing the importance of Jahangir's work, slowly ambled towards the door. Over the years, she had learnt to suppress her bitterness. With some effort, she opened the door and, with her bony thumb, indicated to Jawahar that his presence and services were required by Jahangir.

When Jawahar stepped inside and gave a slight cough as an indication of his presence, Jahangir continued with his scribbling and, without looking up, said, "Tell Diana to come and see me at once. Then inform everyone that I want them to gather in the library tomorrow morning, sharp at 11."

"Understood," replied Jawahar softly and silently left the room.

Diana had been riding her chestnut pony around the estate. It was her way of meditating and focusing on the task at hand. After graduating in psychology from the University of Oxford, UK and her brief stint in the Mergers and Acquisition sector, she had been under the direct tutelage of her Grand Uncle Jahangir. He had moulded her into a shrewd businesswoman who now invested in start-ups.

Over the past three years, she had built a team of twenty people with whom she undertook the due diligence of the various companies that came to her for investments. Only after minutely going through the details, doing numerous background checks, and running references on the promoters in the market would Diana present the case to Jahangir.

If the promoters were able to satisfy Jahangir's grilling questions and show him the marketability of their vision, Jahangir would invest his money in their company. Of the twenty-five start-ups in which Jahangir had so far invested, nine had gone bust, three had given his money back before they were finally shut down, one had turned a unicorn, and he was still invested in the remaining twelve of them. This was a high-risk-high return game and Jahangir was slowly mastering the art of it.

Through the GPS tracker put around the Pony's neck, Jawahar was able to locate Diana. A manservant was sent in a golf cart to bring back the young heiress from one end of the estate. Almost everyone, including Diana, believed that her Grand Uncle had been training her to take over the reins of the family.

A while later, Diana hopped off the golf cart, took out her riding boot in the mud room located near the entrance of the house, and strutted into the library. As she entered, she saw her bag, still kept on the sofa, which she had placed there the previous evening during her conversation with her Grand Uncle. They had been discussing the status of their existing investments in the various companies. Strolling towards the bag, she first took a handful of fennel seeds kept in a silver box on a small side table set beside the sofa and then took out her crochet set from her bag and began sewing. Diana was a creature of the daintiest habits and had a compulsive itch to keep herself preoccupied. Her sharp mind did not allow her to remain idle.

A few moments later, Jahangir got up from his table and settled on to the armchair next to the fireplace. He beckoned with his hand for his grandniece to join him. Although Diana was busy doing her crochet, she saw Jahangir's silent instruction from the corner of her eye and followed suit. She took her crochet set and sat opposite Jahangir. Over the years, while working under Jahangir, Diana realized the virtue of being patient and mastered the art of listening without reacting.

With a piercing gaze, Jahangir looked at her and exclaimed, "Diana, listen to me carefully. Over the years I have mentored you and have taught you everything I know. But there are still many lessons for you to learn, for which I must now set the stage. Our family trust holds most of our investments, the publishing company, this estate, and our jewellery. The interest the investments earn are used for giving allowances to the family members, the upkeep of the estate and to keep the publishing company running." Other than the light crackle of the faint fire combined with the silent movement of Diana's deft hands moving about the crochet needle and the thread, only the deep baritone of Jahangir could be heard through the library. "Put down your crochet and listen intently," said Jahangir in a stern voice and then, as Diana looked up while her hands automatically put the crochet aside, he continued, "Our company, Dinshaw Finance, has been investing in multiple start-ups. Now you know that nine of them went bust, while we recovered our investment from another three. What you don't know is that the previous week, one of our investments turned into a unicorn. The food delivery company, Fool's Food Limited, pivoted into delivering groceries and medicines. It is now also setting up its own fleet of delivery boys and trucks to have a greater control over its supply chain and to better manage their logistics. An American conglomerate is looking to get into the Indian market and is going to buy out Fool's Food Limited. The value of our investment has increased by over three times. We had a 1% stake in the company, and the company at the time was valued at three billion dollars, but last week, I made the exit at a valuation of nine billion dollars. This morning, I received the ninety million dollars." Diana, who had been carefully listening, realised how her uncle began the conversation with "we" but ended it with "I." She, however, ignored her gut feeling and calmly asked, "Why did I not hear about this on the news?"

"This has been a closed-door deal. Three of the four investors, including me, have decided to en-cash our investment. The founder and the remaining investor have agreed to continue working for the Americans in exchange for sweat equity and some bonus shares."

Then looking straight at Diana, Jahangir continued, "But this is not why I have asked you here. I wish to tell you that the company Dinshaw Finance is not a part of the family trust, and the entire seven hundred crores shall be mine to will. Now, I'll be pulling out our investments from all the other start-ups and closing Dinshaw Finance."

"But I have participated and worked diligently under you. I should get a larger piece of the pie. And I think we should continue to deploy our wealth in start-ups and multiply our investments," exclaimed Diana, hiding her irritation about the rude shock of the news and the turn of events.

"You are not yet ready to handle such wealth. Prodigious wealth is created by a stroke of luck and by the grace of God. I do not wish to play this gamble anymore. You must find some other work to do or make good with the allowance from the trust. In time, after Shirin and I pass away, this wealth will be used for the betterment of the family and its future generations. And in my lifetime, if anyone proves to be more capable, then I'll give a bigger piece of the pie to that person. Till then, work hard, prove yourself, and enjoy life," explained Jahangir in a stern voice.

"I am not some hamster in a wheel or a pig in a pen, which you can use or slaughter as per your convenience. You are being unfair, Grand Uncle," blurted out Diana in a fit of rage, with tears welling up her eyes. The situation had made her go against her very nature.

"Your thinking reflects your immaturity. You have a lot to learn. Money is not for you to toy around with. Creating and handling wealth is a game of patience." Then jutting out his bony index finger and pointing it towards Diana, Jahangir continued, "The English poet, William Shenstone rightly said, a miser grows rich by seeming poor. An extravagant man grows poor by seeming rich."

Then, flicking his hands as Diana wiped her tears, Jahangir, in a dismissive voice, exclaimed, "Now, you must leave me alone. I have work to do."

Congregating her poise, Diana left the room quietly. She left the mansion, walked across the garden, turned left and continued to walk in silence. Her mind was numb, and as it processed the recent revelation and its repercussions, it blocked all other thoughts. After walking for about fifteen minutes, her mind suddenly captured the image of rows of barren blackish-brown tree trunks with twisted branches in front of her.

Diana stopped in her tracks and looked around. After a few seconds she realized that she was in the orchards of the estate and was standing in front of the dried dormant apple trees. Realising where she was, Diana went down the dirt road, and as she suspected, she could hear the whirling sound of a drill forcing its way into a block of wood. As she neared the barn, she could also hear the repetitive sound of a hammer repeatedly beating on a wooden block. Diana peered in and saw her extremely creative and resourceful brother, Farrukh, working on his latest design.

Looking at his sister, Farrukh stopped and, removed his headphones and paused the serene Sanskrit shlokas that he was listening to.

Diana, as always, broke the silence and probed, "I cannot understand your ways of meditation. How can carpentry give you peace of mind?" Then, gesturing towards the various sheets which had neat drawings and mathematical equations depicted on them, Diana inquired, "What are you working on now?"

"Well, carpentry is my meditation. And by meditating, I ensure that my thoughts don't control me. Besides, I love making things because if an opportunity won't knock on my door, at the very least, I would know how to build a door."

As Diana rolled her eyes, Farrukh explained, "I have created a new wine bottle holder. It will look like the flames of fire, and the curves will hold three bottles, one over the other, on each side. It will also have a small secret compartment, which I have added just for fun. Maybe we can keep the used corks in there." Then, looking at his sister's bored expression, he asked, "What brings you here?"

Diana gave a detailed account of the news that their Grand Uncle, Jahangir, had broken to her.

Farrukh listened patiently as Diana ended her monologue by stating, "Why does the elder generation obsess about controlling our lives till they are alive. What happens when they are no longer present in our lives? They should understand that they have given us the right education and sufficient exposure. Now, they must believe in us as we walk on our own path."

Ignoring her rant Farrukh decided to hit the nail on the head when he inquired, "Who is he going to will the larger chunk of the newly acquired wealth to?"

"He has always favoured Uncle Firdaus and his family over us. I suspect he will transfer most of the wealth to them. If that happens, I will feel cheated of my hard work and the hours that I put in the Investing and Financing business," bleated Diana.

"Why don't you speak to father about it. Meanwhile, I will speak to our family's old firecracker this evening when I place the wine holder in the library. He will eventually realize the logic in our argument," explained Farrukh.

"Well, I hope he does, for everyone's sake," said Diana and walked out.

Diana Dinshaw

CHAPTER 6

HERE WE GO ROUND THE MULBERRY BUSH

Tuesday, 24th January 2023
4:30 PM – 7:00 PM

Across the library, on the ground floor of the Dinshaw mansion, was the formal drawing room, which opened into the formal dining room. And across these, on the other side of the hallway, was the informal sitting, which opened into the informal dining room. Unless a guest was present in the house, the family always used the informal dining and sitting areas. But owing to the presence of Jim, who, although in the pecking order of importance of guests, would probably be classified as phytoplankton, the standing rules of the family were followed, and the formal areas were put to use.

Down the hallway, behind the formal areas, was the billiards room. The guests, after a scrumptious meal, would at times retire to this room to smoke a cigarette and discuss the nastier portions of business.

In here the twins were playing a simple game of eight-ball pool. As Zubin set the balls in the rack, he declared, "It has been a while since we played last. Let us see how much of the game do you still have in you."

"When you have played these games enough, the strategies become muscle memory. Anyway, why are you against Uncle Sohrab, his publishing business and his family?" inquired Cyrus as he took the break shot and hit the cue ball with his cue stick. The white ball powered ahead and made contact with the other set fifteen balls resulting in a loud clacking sound and the balls dispersing in different directions. None of the balls pocketed.

Applying chalk on the tip of his worn-out cue stick, Zubin mildly replied, "I don't have any beef with Uncle Sohrab or his family. I just find them to be slow and stupid. They are all such characters. Uncle Sohrab keeps seeking sympathy. Aunt Sanaya is forever zoned out. Diana acts as if she knows everything, and Farrukh is the slowest of them all. Irritation and anger can be feigned. I was just trying to rile up Farrukh to actually see what is in his mind."

Zubin then took a shot and pocketed the solid blue ball and as the ball trickled down the net, he declared, "I have the solids. You now have to target the striped balls." Once again after rubbing chalk on his cue stick, Zubin took another shot, pushing the red ball and the yellow striped ball closer to the pit.

Cyrus hit the cue ball and targeted the green striped ball which pocketed easily, as it was anyway dangling very near to the pocket, almost like an old man ready to trip into his grave. "But what would you gain by harassing poor old Farrukh. He is an introvert and hardly makes his presence felt," inquired Cyrus as he prepared to take another shot.

Targeting the yellow striped ball, Cyrus hit the cue ball with quite a force, but instead, this had the opposite effect, and both the red solid ball and the yellow striped ball rebounded off the edge and settled back in the centre of the table.

Looking at the effect of Cyrus's force, Zubin replied, "When you apply force, you are not always sure of the outcome of how things and humans react. I am not too happy about the family wealth being depleted and thrown down the drain for the sake of keeping the publishing business active and to ensure that Uncle Sohrab remains busy."

Then as Zubin took the shot, Cyrus rebuked, "Uncle Sohrab himself wants to shut the business or sell it, but Grand Uncle won't let him do it."

Zubin pocketed the green and the maroon balls in quick succession before losing his turn to Cyrus.

As Cyrus prepared for his shot, Zubin replied, "Well, at least we know now that it is true and that Farrukh has no intention of trying to revive the business. I had once heard mummy expressing concern to Dad about Uncle's business. Now the rumour seems to be confirmed."

After Cyrus took his shot, he said, "I saw Diana enter the library earlier today, but a while later, when she came out, her eyes were watery, and her face looked like she had seen a ghost."

"I don't understand the science behind becoming a venture capitalist. It seems tough to be able to work for the eccentric old man. Jawahar told me that the family lawyer is due to arrive later this evening and also that Grand Uncle has called for a family gathering the following morning. I hope common sense prevails on the elders," answered Zubin while flicking his head in a bout of irritation

"Well, I am going to pursue a PhD in economics and become an economist. I don't want family politics to ruin my future. I also hope they are either able to revive, sell or shut the publishing business," explained Cyrus as he hit another powerful shot and pocketed the last of his striped balls.

"Will you be able to survive in a demanding job, as that of an economist?" inquired Zubin, now realising that he was losing the game with three of his solid-coloured balls still juggling around the table.

"Well, what other option do I have?"

"Isn't the allowance that we get from the trust enough? Besides, you always have the option to start something of your own?" inquired Zubin with a hint of irritation still lingering in his voice.

Cyrus grunted and smirked in agreement as he thought about the upcoming visit of their family lawyer, Bejan Contractor, and their irritatingly prying guest, Jim. As Cyrus pocketed the black ball, claimed victory and kept his cue stick on the pool table, he declared with a sly smile, "Looks like it is time for my diplomatic skills to be put to use."

"What are you planning to do in life? You have completed your architectural studies and have gained a healthy experience by working in a number of firms," inquired Cyrus further.

"I am thinking of joining mummy's company and taking her projects forward. I am close to her and together, we make a good team. Besides, I feel calm when I am with her," replied Zubin in a soft voice while staring at a portrait of his parents that hung on the brick wall in front of him. As his eyes diverted to a very old black-and-white photograph that had captured his uncle, Sohrab and his parents standing in front of the Taj Mahal, his irritation festered into apparent indignation.

A while later, Zubin and Cyrus retired to their respective rooms on the first floor of the house. Their lavish bedroom had their own sitting, bath and dressing rooms. The old English-style mansion allowed its members to have a deep sense of privacy.

At 6:25 PM, with the onset of dusk, the sky in the Doon Valley started showing strokes of red and orange. Around the Dinshaw estate, a variety of birds sang and chirped as a black Mercedes E class smoothly rolled into the Estate gates. The family lawyer, Bejan Contractor, had arrived. As the car lazily strolled ahead, his daughter Shehnaz who was sitting next to him, noticed a herd of braunvieh cows grazing on the green hilly pasture while the caretaker was preparing to move them inside the barn for the night. The pasture had patches of frost as the temperature had started dropping rapidly.

A few moments later, on the lower plateau, she noticed the stables and the race tracks. A lone chestnut Mustang was trotting around and soaking in the lingering warmth of the evening sun. The car moved ahead on the winding road that was now covered with the canopy of the mighty Himalayan Cedar trees that had been planted on both sides of the driveway.

Shehnaz loved the red hues of the sun rays that filtered through the canopy and illuminated their path ahead. Though she had been coming to the Dinshaw estate since her childhood days, this time, the grandiosity of the place sent a haunting chill down her spine.

At last, the car stopped between the Grand Lawn and the Mansion. Jawahar, the omnipresent butler, along with a junior manservant, was standing outside to greet the guests.

As Bejan stepped outside and stretched his legs, indicating that he was tired from the long, arduous journey from New Delhi, Jawahar stepped forward and said, "Welcome, Mr. Contractor. I hope your journey was pleasant." Then, looking at Shehnaz, the butler bowed a little too deeply and said, "Welcome, Madam. Master is eagerly awaiting your presence." Looking back at the lawyer, the butler explained, "Your belongings will be taken to your rooms situated in the guest house near the tennis court. You will get your regular rooms." As soon as Jawahar said these lines, the young manservant got his cue, and he hastily moved ahead to gather the luggage in his luggage cart.

Ignoring the commotion, Jawahar continued, "Master Jim, who is visiting us, is also staying there and occupying one of the rooms. Would you like to freshen up, or should I escort you straight to Mr. Jahangir?"

Bejan looked at the butler, who was at least seven inches shorter than him, cracked his fingers and neck, and softly replied, "I will freshen up first, then meet my old friend." A thick breath vapour escaped from his mouth and nostrils as he spoke.

Then, taking off the grey tweed jacket that he had worn over his thick white turtleneck T-shirt, he quickly strode over to the guest house. Shehnaz followed suit. It took the father-daughter duo about thirty minutes, during which time they each had a cup of tea, freshened up and applied their perfumes. As Bejan ran his hand through his white beard and squeezed it a bit to drain the water his facial hair held, his daughter was tying her long black hair in a bun.

Wearing the same outfits, the two stepped out and began walking towards the mansion. While enroute, Bejan, who, despite his tall height and commanding personality, had a very soft voice, said, "Listen intently to what Jahangir says. Do not give your opinions to him too easily. He has a tendency to not rely on opinions and options shared too quickly and too easily. Let him feel that you are pondering over his problems. Make him hungry for your advice."

"Well, I am not their family lawyer. You are. Why would he include me in the discussions or value my opinions?" inquired Shehnaz.

"You are a fifty-six-year-old mature lady who has travelled around the world, is independent and successful. Your ambition has driven you from starting as a crime reporter to becoming the co-owner and lead editor of one of the top news channels of the country," explained Bejan and then, looking at the disbelieving look on his daughter's face, he continued, "Darling, you are wise and perceptive. Everyone is hungry for wisdom, but be careful while you impart it."

When Bejan and Shehnaz entered the mansion, they found Jawahar sitting on a petite visitor's chair by the console table, which was neatly placed near the entrance. The uninvited visitors were expected to wait by this table while the butler would ask the master where the guests would be entertained.

In this situation, however, the guests were expected and eagerly awaited. So, Jawahar took them straight to the library. As he opened the heavy, ornate ten-foot-tall door and heaved his way in, the visitors too quickly squeezed behind him through the door, not wanting to handle the heavy door by themselves. Once inside the library, they saw Jahangir sprawled across the sofa with his chest discreetly puffing. Bejan crept up to him and tapped on his shoulders. Jahangir woke with a start. After looking at Bejan for a few seconds, his sluggish brain comprehended the fact that his guests had arrived. Rubbing his eyes, Jahangir said, "I decided to take a quick power nap for I have much to discuss with you and realised that we may be in for a long night."

Then, looking at Jawahar, he instructed, "The three of us shall have our dinner here. We are not to be disturbed."

"Understood," replied the butler as he closed the door and left.

Then, indicating his guests towards the fireplace, where the dimly lit fire still crackled, Jahangir settled himself comfortably in one of the armchairs. At that time the weather took an ominous turn as dark clouds slowly started shrouding the Doon valley.

Zubin and Cyrus Dinshaw

CHAPTER 7

GIRLS AND BOYS, COME OUT TO PLAY

Tuesday, 24th January 2023
7:00 PM – 8:00 PM

Jim, who was Shirin's late sister Nina's grandchild, was close to Shirin and would often visit the Dinshaws during his early years with his grandmother Nina. Nina had died of old age complications, and her daughter Mehr had married a modest doctor for love. Jim realised that in the pecking order of society, he sat comfortably in the middle.

Strolling about in the archery range beside the lawn tennis court, Jim occasionally did feel the pangs of jealousy, looking at the casual opulence of the Dinshaw family.

With a variety of thoughts going through his head, he picked up a bunch of arrows, and as he took aim at the target placed twenty yards away, an arrow flew from behind him and hit the bull's eye. With a start Jim turned and saw Diana standing there and laughing with her bow loosely held in her hand, almost as if she was a professional.

"You could have hit me," complained Jim with a sense of concern in his voice.

"Well, you are in my crosshairs," said Diana, trifling with Jim.

As his cheeks flushed, Jim determined to show off his skills too, carefully aimed and punctured the target right next to where Diana's arrow had landed.

Then, whistling casually, he ran his hand through his hair and looked at Diana and said, "You seem to be in a jovial mood today. Care to share the news?"

"Well, I have just been used like a hamster in a wheel and discarded off by Grand Uncle Jahangir. So, I have come to let off some steam and think what I am going to do in life now."

"Let us go for a walk, and you can tell me all about it," said Jim.

"Are we allowed to be romantic?" inquired Diana while sliding her arm in his.

"We are not related by blood, so that should not raise any eyebrows, and besides, love does not require any explanation," said Jim as they both decided to walk towards the Koi pond, which was situated on the other end of the estate.

With a cocktail of giddy and mushy feelings with little butterflies fluttering in their stomachs, the newfangled couple slowly walked out of the archery range as Jim thought to himself, "Cupid's arrow seems to have hit his mark," while Diana thought, "He is nosy, inquisitive and does not look conventionally attractive, but he is intelligent and charming."

The dark clouds that had spread over the estate now thundered, and with the last rays of the sun fading out, a light drizzle started.

The solar lights and lamps illuminated the vast property, making the area look like it had been swarmed by fireflies. Just outside the library was the secondary lawn which was where the swimming pool was located.

To work up her appetite for dinner, Anahita was rapidly completing one lap after another as the heated swimming pool started to lose its warmth owing to the drizzle and the drop in the climate temperature. The lights in and around the pool shimmered and made her dusky complexion appear golden.

Sanaya was observing her from the covered pergola of her second-floor balcony and briefly thought about creating a sketch of a woman drowning in water. Then, talking to herself, she said, "It would be a depiction of the struggles humans have to bear throughout their lives. How just to sustain themselves and to remain afloat they must keep kicking the water. Yet in the end, we all die, and the earth consumes us all."

But an instant later she changed her mind and decided to complete her existing work.

Sanaya kept changing the location as she progressed through the art. She would start in her studio, then would set her easel and tables in her veranda or at times in the lawns or wherever she desired to seek her inspiration from. Once, she had gone to the apiary, but her persona could not become one with the bees, who, for some reason, decided to sting her the moment she had set up her paraphernalia there.

The cow pasture and barn had an acute smell of cow dung, and after stepping on a fresh pool of warm cow dung and spoiling her Gucci loafers, Sanaya decided never to set up shop there again.

Although the smell of dung, urine and hay was not really present in the equine quarters due to excellent ventilation, regular cleaning and changing of the dried hay mattresses in the stables, the horses, too, had not taken fancy to Sanaya's presence. When a young, playful filly had decided to bite a canvas on which Sanaya had spent months, she had angrily flung her tools at the poor, ignorant animal. Her behaviour had not gone unnoticed by the joey's mother, who had decided to charge onto Sanaya despite the jockey's best efforts to calm the horse down.

After her misadventures, Sanaya had resolved to sketch in open areas, preferably not in the presence of other living beings.

A while later Sanaya observed her husband slowly walking back across the grand lawn, with his hands outstretched and holding what looked like a bunch of roots. As Sohrab approached the swimming pool, Anahita, who had by now completed her laps and was sitting by the poolside and sipping a glass of red wine while wrapped in a soft olive-green gown, saw him and gave a slight squeal. With his arms still outstretched, Sohrab showed his loot to Anahita, who he believed to be an excellent cook. She looked at his dirt-ridden hands, from which sac-like cups were protruding, and as one of her eyebrows raised, she said, "What have you collected?"

"These are meadow mushrooms. Fancy a fungi pizza for dinner?" replied Sohrab coquettishly.

Taking a few in her hands and inspecting the white gills on the underside and the white spore prints, Anahita quickly threw the mushrooms in the dirt and, with a tense voice, exclaimed, "These are not meadow mushrooms. They don't have the standard pinkish-brown gills found in meadow mushrooms. These are wild poisonous mushrooms known as Destroying Angel or the Angels of Death. They look very similar to the meadow mushrooms. Where did you find these?"

"They were growing alongside the fruits and vegetables in the greenhouse. I don't know who planted them. I thought you had planted them, they looked ripe so I collected them," clarified Sohrab.

"I will have these removed from the greenhouse. We must now wash our hands," replied Anahita, smiling at Sohrab's innocence and simple nature.

Sanaya, who had heard the conversation between her husband and Anahita, owing to the latter's booming voice, flicked her head and agitatedly muttered to herself, "He is an idiot and keeps making a fool of himself. If I wasn't his wife, his family would have cast him aside long ago. He doesn't even know how to stand up for himself."

Elsewhere in the estate, when Diana and Jim reached the apiary, they found Firdaus rapidly texting someone. Finding her uncle there made Diana feel uncomfortable, so she quickly let go of Jim's hand and announced, "Oh! It is already 7:45. I am hungry and do not want to be late for dinner."

"Why don't you go ahead. I want to have a quick word with Uncle Firdaus," said Jim.

"As Diana stepped out, she heard Jim saying, "I saw your play "How to kill your family." I was at the performance when the troupe performed in Delhi. Later, I also came to the green room to congratulate you…" By this time, Diana was out of earshot and could not exactly hear what Jim was saying, but a few moments later, she could hear the two of them arguing loudly, and it was apparent that Uncle Firdaus was very upset. As he yelled, "This is preposterous…" his angry voice could still be discerned by Diana, who was now walking back to the estate and wondered if Jim had probably said something to irk Firdaus. In her mind Jim had the capability of getting on someone's nerves. Thinking of exploring this subject and probing Jim later, Diana hurriedly reached the mansion.

CHAPTER 8

OLD KING COLE

Tuesday, 24th January 2023
7:15 PM – 9:00 PM

In the library, Jahangir was in the midst of a deep conversation, and while using his index finger to punch numbers on his scientific calculator, he explained, "As you are aware, the family trust that was set up by my late elder brother and his wife, Nariman and Alaya Dinshaw, was done so with the purpose of ensuring the financial stability of the future generations of the family. The trust now has three hundred crores invested in mutual funds, bonds, equity shares and debt structures.

Since our idea was to preserve the wealth and the principal, the investments are conservative with the aim of yielding enough returns to beat inflation and sustain our lifestyle. The instruments roughly yield a cumulative annual return of just twelve percent." Then, clacking away at the calculator again and presenting an Excel sheet to Bejan, Jahangir continued, "Therefore, on an average, we receive an annual amount of rupees thirty-six crores, which means three crores per month. The monthly break up of funds is that half of this money gets reinvested, while the other half is distributed as follows, about forty lakhs is spent on staff salaries, upkeep of the livestock, maintenance of the estate, general repairs and footing the medical bills of anyone, including the staff, who may have fallen ill. Ten lakhs are allocated to our charitable trust. Twenty lakhs are allocated for paying the premiums of the life insurance of the family members. Me and Shirin collectively receive fifty lakhs, while each of my nephews, along with their wives, receive thirteen lakhs. Lastly, each of my grandnephews receives a sum of one lakh every month."

"While everything seems to be covered by the trust, what do the family members spend their monthly allowance on?" inquired Shehnaz.

"Well, there are certain standing rules, which everyone must abide by like everyone pays for their own toiletries and dry cleanings. The holidays that they take and any shopping that they might do or an experience they might indulge in are borne by the members themselves. Any tuition or classes outside of their school or college is borne by the members," explained Jahangir, while his shaking bony hands filled the vanilla-flavoured tobacco in his pipe. After a few long drags, as the nicotine tingled his throat, he continued, "If more than three friends are visiting, the hosting member must pay two thousand rupees per guest. For a gathering of more than twenty people a flat fee of thirty thousand is charged to the grand nephews and a fee of fifty thousand to my nephews. Although the fee does not always cover the décor and liquor charges incurred during a formal party, the rules ensure that no one treats the resources of the estate frivolously. Now, the cost of any businesses or hobbies that the members do is borne by them. But they individually reap the benefit that arises out of any such venture or activity. Lastly, other than the investments, the trust holds the estate, some jewellery, gold and all the paintings in the house. Therefore, the collective value of the trust, including the non-liquid and the immovable investments, is roughly seven hundred crores."

Taking the pipe out of his mouth and slightly tamping the burnt tobacco, the old bull relit the pipe and slowly sipped on it while churning the smoke in his mouth before exhaling it. A few moments later, he continued, "Now, Firdaus has multiple sources of income. From the businesses he has sold, he has developed a commercial property from which he gets a rental income of seven lakh rupees a month. He has also invested some of his corpus individually in mutual funds and shares. His wife, Anahita, earns from her interior designing and architectural projects which she sometimes picks up. However, they run a separate office with a staff of fourteen people, including five highly paid accountants, two personal secretaries, a receptionist, two runners, a draftsman and three junior designers who manage their company, collect the rentals, ensure the upkeep of the building, track their investments, work on Anahita's projects and manage their theatre group. Besides their salaries, Firdaus spends a lot on the production of various plays, acquiring scripts and getting the most talented actors to perform. On the other hand, Anahita plants rare bonsais, which she occasionally sells through her online website. I do not exactly know how much the couple earns, but I have heard rumours that Firdaus's theatre troupe regularly incurs losses, and if that is true, I wonder how they manage their lifestyle, company and hobbies. Also, of late, I have noticed that Firdaus has mentally aged a lot and has decided to pursue a slower life. He may be under stress or maybe the high-octane life that he led for so many years has left a scar on him."

The weather had taken a turn for the worse, and it had now started raining heavily, with pellets of hailstones hitting the windows and creating a continuous racket. Wanting to stretch his muscles and with his active mind demanding some activity, Jahangir, got up and softly paced the room. He called Jawahar and, owing to the chilly weather instructed him to increase the wood chunks in the fire to increase its intensity.

Turning towards Bejan, who had been intently listening, almost like an obedient student, the mature patriarch continued "Sohrab too has invested some of his money in mutual funds, but he keeps changing his hobbies. For a long time after his marriage, he would regularly trade in his wife's art pieces. He even opened a music studio for some time. He installed the best recording equipment and facilities there. His staff at the studio were skilled at operating the equipment and were thus highly paid. But a venture that was supposed to give him rental income, the genius managed to run it into the ground owing to a high working capital requirement. He then switched to trading of Kashmiri carpets. Although he was making good money there, he grew tired of it and, one fine morning, just gave it up. Now, other than the publishing company, which he is struggling to keep afloat, his newfound interest seems to be planting organic crops in the greenhouse and betting on horses. He is naïve enough to think that nobody knows about his gambling habits, but his secret seems to be common knowledge amongst the family members. I suppose his mood swings can be attributed to his temperamental wife, Sanaya."

Flicking his hands in a quick stew of irritation and wanting to light his pipe again, Jahangir fiddled with his tobacco pouch. Pinching the tobacco, he continued, "Sanaya comes from money. Through her art works, she earns a lot. But she also spends a lot on herself. She regularly purchases antiques and jewels. But she is shrewd and intelligent, and from what I have observed and seen over the years, she handles her money astutely. I wish Sohrab was not so fickle-minded and rushed towards every new venture that opens in front of him. To keep him in check, I insist that he does not retire and keeps working at the publishing company, for unlike Firdaus, I don't think Sohrab can handle his retirement with grace. I fear his callousness may cost him his share of the wealth."

As Bejan took extensive notes about the facts surrounding the family and the personal thoughts of Jahangir, his daughter Shehnaz pressed on with her inquiry, "What about your grandnephews? Are they happy with their allowances, and how do they spend their money?"

"Well, until their graduation, their share of the money, though transferred to their individual bank accounts, was invested into the debt structures of the market and in gold bonds. The idea was to preserve the wealth but not yield a very high rate of return. The trust does not want to be blamed for any loss of wealth. Now, Zubin is a trained architect and interior designer. I suspect sooner or later he will join his mother. He is hot-headed, but I believe he has a sense of shrewdness buried within him. He is close to Anahita, so it seems only natural that he would continue under her tutelage. I am not sure where exactly he has been spending his time or money after his graduation. Young adults are difficult to predict these days. His brother Cyrus is wise and diplomatic and very perceptive of the situations around him. I know that while acquiring his master's degree in economics, his dissertation topic was "the impact of mergers and acquisitions on the productivity of firms in an economy," and his thoroughly researched paper backed with logical reasoning won him the gold medal from the London School of Economics. He is generally quiet unless he is sure that his speech can positively impact a conversation. I like the young boy. He has the capability to achieve his goals by any means once he puts his mind to it. I feel he will carve out his own path."

As Jahangir settled back in his seat and eagerly sipped on his pipe, an air of thick smoke filled the room with the essence of vanilla lingering around. As Bejan scribbled the last of his notes and looked up, Jahangir began his monologue again, "Farrukh,

Sohrab's son, is shy and reserved. He has a knack for carpentry and creates beautiful woodwork. I know he spends his money on getting tools, tackles and some high-quality wood. He seems to have inherited his mother's artistic skills, though not her temperament. I am not sure if he is selling his creations in the market yet or if he is serious about pursuing his carpentry. He is just a graduate and has a degree in business administration. I don't really know about his plans. It is difficult to extract information out of him. He is resourceful and readily shares his feelings with his sister, Diana. And Diana is very intelligent and a diligent hard worker. She studied human psychology and helped me invest in a lot of start-ups. Her ability to read human minds is commendable. Under my guidance, she learnt a lot about business, and I, too, learnt certain tricks about how to read human minds through their behaviour and gestures. She is sweet but needs to go out in the world and explore for what it truly is. I believe she has the potential to carry this estate and family fortune forward. Her head seems to be in the right place, though due to her age, her immature mind makes her react faster than it actually should."

"Well, you seem to have everything worked out. What do you need my help for?" inquired Bejan, feeling slightly confused.

"Of the various start-ups that I was investing in along with Diana, one of them turned into a unicorn, and I received seven hundred crores. I formed a company which was not a part of the family trust, and therefore I am currently sitting on crores of liquid money. This money and its possible distribution are the root cause of my worry."

"You surely haven't called me here for financial advice. Is something else the matter?"

After a long pause and looking directly into Bejan's eyes, Jahangir softly said, "I believe one of the family members is trying to kill me. I believe myself to be in mortal danger."

"Who in the family knows about your newfound wealth?"

"Well, I told Diana out of moral responsibility, for she was involved in the process from the very beginning. Firdaus and Sohrab get daily updates about our bank balances and investments from our chief accountant. Though I don't really know how diligently they go through the reports," explained Jahangir, spreading his hands on his lap and sounding a little helpless.

"How do you want to distribute the wealth? Your nephews and their children will anyway get the wealth after you pass away. You are seventy-five; why would anyone take the risk of killing you and going to jail. They could shrewdly wait in misery."

As his lips slightly curled up and his active Machiavellian brain cells kicked in, Jahangir replied in a soft whisper, "I know how I want to distribute my wealth, and I want you to draft documents to that effect. As far as your question about someone waiting shrewdly in misery for my death, I believe an agitated mind requires the constant hammering inside their head to desperately stop and to achieve that instant calmness; it would do absolutely anything. And my kin are an agitated lot."

As Jahangir, Bejan, and Shehnaz talked and deliberated further on the matter at hand, the family, who had just finished their dinner, was now dispersing to their respective rooms.

Bejan and Shehnaz Contractor

CHAPTER 9

Baa baa black sheep

Tuesday, 24th January 2023
9:00 PM – 11:00 PM

On the first floor, Anahita, wearing a long, lush golden silk nightgown with intricate lacework running along its borders, was sipping her hot black coffee and reading about the adverse effects of certain rare Orchids in a book titled "The Big Bad Book of Mayan Botany."

Looking at his wife, Firdaus, still irritated after his argument with Jim, grudgingly said, "You are always preoccupied with your plants and botany books. You don't take interest in anything else that is going on in this house or in the lives of those around you."

"I am quite aware of everything that is going around me. I know your uncle is sitting with his lawyer and, planning the distribution of his newfound wealth and drafting his final will. I also got to know that you had a row about something with Jim. Instead of quarrelling with young boys or willowing your time in the theatre, why don't you, for a change, take an interest in me or the lives of your boys?" snapped Anahita with a flare in her voice, yet not lifting her head from her book. Her face was so close to her book that she could have probably smelt the book if not for the strong aroma exuded by her coffee, whose vapours slightly fogged her glasses. Yet, her ego prevented her from looking at her husband and made her continue to rant from the depths of her book, almost like a ghost wailing from the attic of a house.

"I am not in the mood to fight. Why can't we ever have a conversation like a civilized couple? Why do you start yelling all the time?" questioned Firdaus after having argued for fifteen minutes and finally deciding to walk out of their bedroom to spend yet another lonely night on the sofa of their sitting room.

Firdaus was too poised to bang doors, but he heard his wife angrily flinging the heavy book in one corner.

On the other end of the floor, Cyrus was blissfully unaware of the argument that his parents had just had. He was meticulously going through the daily finance report which came from their chief accountant, and was simultaneously analysing his personal finances and the ones in his parents' company.

While Cyrus was carefully planning for his own future, his brother Zubin, who, while going down to the ground floor for a late-night snack into the pantry, had overheard his parents' quarrel. He was boiling up with each stride as his well-formed legs stomped down the staircase, more out of habit than the anger that he was feeling.

On the second floor, Farrukh was putting his final polishing touches to his wine holder, which he had decided to place in the library the following day. The loud decibel at which the Sanskrit shlokas played in his headphones made sure that they reverberated his soul.

Sohrab on the other corner was going over the performance of his publishing company, while absent-mindedly doodling a leaf on the margins of the report.

His wife, Sanaya, was going through a sudden epiphany about her ongoing artwork, and the sudden surge of illumination gave her the drive to complete her creation. The pungent smell of weed oozed out of her studio as she smoked her joints and frantically sketched.

Diana had snuck out to the guest house and was pestering Jim by asking him for the nth time, "What were you and Uncle Firdaus arguing about? Do you not trust me with your secret?"

Ignoring her batting eyelashes or her cute smile, Jim replied, "I was not arguing or fighting with him. We were just talking, and I was telling him my observations and discussing a possible business idea. He was not yelling. He just has a booming voice."

"Clearly, he did not like your business idea?" questioned Diana with a peering gaze.

"He will come around and see merit in my idea. Now, enough about him, let us enjoy our moment together."

With the rain pouring heavily and the thunder cracking loudly, the young lovers snuggled and found comfort and warmth in each other's arms.

CHAPTER 10

Little Jacky shall have but a penny a day

Wednesday, 25th January 2023
11:00 AM – 6:30 PM

The following day, with the long hands of the grandfather clock coming uncomfortably close to each other and indicating the time to be 11 AM, the family was assembled in the grand ornate library. Everyone had had a hearty breakfast. The energy would allow them to enthusiastically put across their viewpoints, irrespective of the fact whether the listener was at all interested in the said ideas or had already made up his mind to follow his own strategy.

At 11:15 AM, after making everyone a little more eager, Jahangir along with Bejan, and Shehnaz walked into the library. His flamboyance could have easily made the old Venetians turn green with envy. Even at his age, he was well groomed, in command of his surroundings and, unfortunately of those also who were around him. His silver sukajan jacket had a snake imprinted on the arms while a golden phoenix adorned the backside. His firm, bony hands pinched some of the vanilla-flavoured tobacco and automatically filled the ornate wooden pipe. As he sipped on his pipe and walked up to the fireplace, Jahangir looked like a large cruise ship arriving at the docks. The archaic man knew how to deliver bad news with style.

He settled near the fireplace with the family members all seated around him with varied degrees of nervous anxiety and calmness, per their characteristics. As foots tapped, knuckles cracked, and nails bit around him, Jahangir noticed that Jim, too, had squirmed his way into the library and had silently plopped himself on an independent armchair placed in a corner by the large French windows. He noticed that although some others had squinted their eyes or raised their eyebrows as a silent objection to Jim's presence in a family meeting, no one dared to speak their minds out for fear of upsetting Jahangir or Shirin. Bejan and Shehnaz had made themselves invisible by sitting at the far end of the room, so as to not be directly involved in the discussion, yet they were available for any legal queries that may arise when Jahangir put forward his intentions.

After a final deep gaze and soaking in the atmosphere in the room, Jahangir cleared his throat and began, "As some of you might know, a company in which Dinshaw Finance had invested and purchased a 1% stake has become a unicorn. Consequently, I have come into some more wealth. After conferring with the family lawyer, Mr. Bejan, I have created a new discretionary trust. The newly acquired wealth of seven hundred crores will be jointly held by Shirin and me through that trust."

As Jahangir paused to breathe, a few of the family members lost their breaths, and their soft gasps could be heard around the room. Sohrab whistled like a rustic teenager who, for the first time, may have seen a hot city girl at the mention of the enormity of the wealth.

Ignoring the reactions, Jahangir continued, "After either of us passes away, the other shall be the sole beneficiary of the wealth. After both of us pass away, the money will be held by the trust. The trust will invest the money in the market and in certain real estate projects which I will deem fit. Till either of us are alive, this trust will not distribute any income. However, five years after our deaths, income generated from the trust will be used to give Firdaus, Anahita, Sohrab and Sanaya extra allowances of three lakh rupees each per month. The trust will only bear expenses towards education, general lifestyle and the marriages of the next generation. It'll not pay any gambling debts, divorce alimonies, bail out non-performing assets or invest in any form of business whatsoever. Such ventures, if any, you must partake from your own allowances. When my grandnephews and niece turn thirty-four, each will be paid an extra allowance of seventy-five thousand per month. When they turn forty-five, their monthly allowance will increase to two lakhs, and after fifty, they will get five lakh rupees.

These allowances will be over and above what everyone gets from the current family trust.

The same manner of distribution will continue forever. However, legally, every instrument or trust needs to have an end date. Therefore, if at any point in the future, a generation feels that there are no apparent heirs nor is there a possibility of any heirs being born, then the trust shall dissolve, and the corpus will be split equally between Firdaus, Sohrab and Jim's bloodline."

As Jahangir's words reverberated around the room, almost every eye stingingly looked in Jim's direction as if they would evaporate him just by their deathly stares. Before this information could be processed by the family, Jahangir, reading through the papers in his hands, casually continued, "I forgot to mention that as soon as the trust comes into operation, it would make a monthly pay-out of 1 lakh rupees to Jim."

Diana, who was particularly bothered about the allocated sums, intervened and said, "Grand Uncle, the pay-outs will ensure our comfortable lifestyle but would never allow us to venture into business. I want to move ahead as an angel investor."

"Sweetheart, my intention is for you to have a comfortable lifestyle. I neither want you to gamble away this money nor do I want you to slog through life. Still if your ambitions remain unsatisfied, then study hard, become a professional, amass your own capital and pursue your dreams. This capital does not belong to any one generation. My intention is to secure the coming next generations of this family." Twitching his lips, Jahangir then commented, "Besides, I don't believe any of you have the guts to create and control a vast empire."

"Well, I don't think everyone here agrees with your school of thought, but they are too scared to voice their opinion," commented Sanaya with an air of indifference.

"This is no way to put forward your thoughts. You must not be indignant and arrogant. At your age, you must have the wisdom to stabilize the future of your family," rebuked Shirin while speaking in defence of her husband.

"My daughter worked hard under you and presented the opportunity which allowed you to create such wealth. We should get a bigger share of the pie," said Sohrab, now visibly agitated about the turn of events.

"As I said before, this wealth does not belong to any one generation. And Sohrab, you need the publishing business as a means of stability in your life, as you are a very fickle-minded person," said Jahangir. Then, turning his gaze towards Sanaya, he exclaimed, "I really don't care what anyone thinks. This is how things are going to be."

Everyone's face in the room was white, and it quite matched the pristine snow that was now falling across the Doon Valley and the estate. With a very satisfied and smug look, Jahangir walked back to his room.

Once Jahangir left, everyone stormed out of the library as a show of revolt. Crossing the formal dining, they all subconsciously settled into the informal dining. Jim, Bejan and Shehnaz too had followed the family.

Sohrab, who was the most upset of the lot, angrily barked, "My parents made significant contributions in starting the various family businesses and creating this wealth. It was my daughter who helped uncle garner such wealth. Yet, he has always negated my needs. He calls me fickle minded, but I am just adventurous and try my hands at different things. Anything can turn into a gold mine."

"Well, for anything to turn into a gold mine, you have to be very consistent at it, not to mention the amount of man hours you yourself will be required to put in. A venture that becomes successful without hard work can only be termed as a gamble and not a business," replied Firdaus calmly.

Sohrab's face turned red. He was trying hard to hold back his tears. Hearing Firdaus's comment, he stormed out of the dining room and headed straight for his bedroom.

Anahita pitched in and commented, "You shouldn't be so cold towards him. Uncle is being arrogant and unfair. In the guise of securing future generations, he is starving everyone's ambitions. Anyway, I really don't care about the wealth. What is the point in discussing anything when we don't have any say? I am leaving." Saying as much, she got up, left the dining room and walked straight to the lift situated near Jahangir's room.

Jawahar who was standing in the gallery, noticed that Anahita took the lift to the second floor. Cyrus, who had been quietly observing the situation unfold in front of him, casually commented, "I see merit in Grand Uncle's scheme. But he should have dispersed a little more of the wealth. Maybe we can force his hand somehow."

"Oh! There is absolutely no way he will listen. Besides you have already charted your future plans. You are not going to depend on the family's wealth. Why do you care? I, too don't really care about his distribution plans. I am going to work with mummy," exclaimed Zubin with slight spite and then added, "Maybe Farrukh would plead to Grand Uncle to fund his hobby of carpentry. After all, one does require expensive wood and machines to be able to convert one's talent into a materialistic commodity."

"Why do you keep taking a dig at him? Don't you have anything better to do?" replied Diana angrily.

Ignoring Diana, Zubin calmly walked out of the meeting. His blood, too boiled, but he chose to keep his turbulent perturbations in check. As he stepped out, he noticed the lift had been taken to the second floor. That and the palpable tension amongst the family members made his ears go red. With apparent disquiet, Zubin cynically walked towards the informal sitting room.

Firdaus noticed that Jim was smiling while sitting in a corner. He thought of him as a peeve and was starting to get irritated by his meddling presence. As Firdaus got up to leave, Jim spoke across the room and inquired, "I hope you have thought about my proposal?" He deliberately stressed the last word.

Firdaus felt him getting on his nerves, and while grinding his teeth, yet trying to be polite, he softly replied, "I am still thinking about it." Firdaus then walked to one end of the room and gazed out of the windows.

Farrukh looked at Diana and said, "I was planning to speak to Grand Uncle the previous evening. But my wine holder took longer to complete. I finished it this morning and had just placed it in the library before Grand Uncle addressed us." Then, looking at the thick blanket of snow that was still falling outside, he bitterly added, "I don't think there is any point in speaking to him now."

Sanaya, with her usual indifferent attitude, said, "The previous day, I was thinking about how to achieve my goals and about the roadblocks that I was hitting by not being able to sell my art quickly enough. I felt the need to persevere. But people here seem to be facing roadblocks and difficulties at a whole different tangent."

"You too are a part of the family," replied Firdaus from one end.

"Yes, but I am not so desperate to get my hands on the wealth. Sooner or later, it would come to us," replied Sanaya, who was now getting up and preparing to leave.

"You seem quite sure of yourself and of the fact that the future would turn in your favour," replied Firdaus as he, too, decided to leave the room.

Without reacting to his comment, Sanaya left the room. Firdaus, too, left the room but did not follow her. He climbed the stairs to his unit while Sanaya decided to go for a walk in the brutish, chilly weather. She felt the cold would calm her nerves.

Diana, who was quite upset about the infighting, sadly said, "Father is very upset. I would like to spend some time with him and lighten his mood." She then beckoned Jawahar and said, "I would like you to bring a nice bottle of wine to my room, which I shall then give to him."

"Very well, miss," replied the butler and scuttled towards the door.

At the gate, Jawahar observed Zubin exit the informal sitting and trudge towards the billiards room. Ignoring him, he turned on his heel and stated, "I believe we have a rare red 1993 Gevrey-Chambertin wine in our cellar. It is Mr. Sohrab's favourite. I shall bring it up to your room at exactly 7 PM.

"Thank you," replied Diana as he left the room.

A while later, everyone dispersed.

Given the circumstances, the heated altercations and as a mark of revolt against Jahangir's rules, everyone decided to have lunch in their own respective bedrooms and sitting rooms. Only Bejan, Shehnaz and Jim found themselves eating lunch in the informal dining area.

Post lunch, after the hearty meal had satiated her, Shehnaz decided to interact with the family members individually. She wanted to slyly assess their thoughts and feelings without them realizing about it. The idea made her feel ticklish, and with a slight squeal, she said to herself, "If I am able to peek inside their minds, maybe I could open a doorway to their fears. If fears are put to rest by affirmative actions, then maybe tensions can be eased and altercations avoided. I might just be able to help Uncle Jahangir."

So, with a firm resolve, Shehnaz first walked towards Farrukh's workshop. The snowfall covered her jacket and made her look like a snowman waddling through the snow.

She reached the workshop and observed Farrukh diligently working on his creation. The wood pieces and tools were all neatly organized. On a chalkboard behind him, there was a complete drawing with calculations of the final product that he was going to produce.

"I see that you are very meticulous," remarked Shehnaz feeling impressed by the young adult's diligent and neat style of working.

"I like to plan for everything in advance. Once I analyse everything in my mind, I reproduce the same on paper. Only when I finalize the working sheet along with all the calculations do I actually start working on my creation. The process, at times, causes the workshop to become quite untidy, but I find it de-stressing to sort the clutter."

"So, did you just clean your workshop after Uncle Jahangir's revelation about the newfound wealth?"

"Well, it isn't the best of news, you know. At times, you have an opportunity within your reach that can enhance your future, but the obstinate behaviour of the elder generation just holds us back."

"What would you have done with the money?"

"I don't know. Money has a funny way of being a boon and a bane. It is never enough. I could always upgrade my tools, hire apprentices and build my brand on social media, but then every milestone only has a meaning when it is achieved step by step. Overnight fame and growth are never sustainable."

"You are quite wise for your age," said Shehnaz with a smile across her face.

"It's not age but your experiences and environment that moulds you," remarked Farrukh casually as he picked up his tools again and started working.

Shehnaz got the cue, and she left the young boy to work. She then strolled over to the greenhouse and found Anahita instructing the gardeners about the vegetables that were growing inside the controlled facility. Shehnaz walked up to her and said, "What all do you grow here?"

Anahita turned around at the sound of her guest's voice and took a moment to register her presence. Then, in a cold voice, she responded in as few words as possible, "We grow all kinds of fruits, vegetables and fungi at the estate. We never shop for them."

"How very interesting. You have thoroughly imbibed the farm-to-table concept. How are you doing? How's life?" expressed Shehnaz while placing a hand over Anahita's shoulder casually. Shehnaz had spent time with the Dinshaw family during her early years. She was a regular guest at the estate until the time Farrukh was in his early teens. The kids were young, and the couples were in their early years of marriage with love still lingering in their hearts. So, Shehnaz had in the past, spent a great deal of time with Anahita, Firdaus, Sohrab and Sanaya. Over the years, because of her hectic work schedule, she hadn't been able to make time to visit Dehradun, and so for the past fifteen years, her interactions with the Dinshaws had reduced. But Shehnaz had an inkling of how their minds worked and knew about their inherent natures.

Hence, she was able to sense that Anahita's vibe was of distant coldness. She seemed to be lost in her own thoughts, and so after aimlessly looking into the distant for a few silent seconds, she remarked, "The estate has always grown its own fodder. But of late we seem to be reaping the effects of certain bad implants."

Then, without any provocation, almost as if she was lost in her own world, she continued her rant and stated, "Life has started to become a bit morose. I wish Firdaus wasn't so aloof all the time. Whatever did he retire from business for?"

Before Shehnaz could react to the comment, Anahita seemed to zap out from her zone and quickly said, "I must hurry back to the Mansion. I have some errands to run. I shall see you in the evening for dinner." She then hurriedly scurried off.

The snow now fell in larger chunks and at a much faster rate. The sun was not visible, and the sky was ominously dark. Yet, Shehnaz decided to walk towards the secondary lawn situated next to the library. There, she found Sanaya sitting in the middle of the lawn in a yogic pose. Shehnaz found her behaviour odd, and so she walked up to Sanaya and asked, "Why are you sitting here like this?"

"Oh! I am just cooling my mind off. The snow feels so good. I feel bad that you had to witness so much of infighting. We are generally a cordial lot, but when frustrations mount up then situations get tense. Though it is an unusual occurrence in our house, but it was a long time coming," explained Sanaya casually.

"Why do you say that?"

Sanaya clicked her tongue to indicate her inability to do anything about the situation and then remarked, "Deep-rooted issues, even though suppressed for a long time, have a way of surfacing themselves. But enough about our sullen issues, how have you been doing? How are you?"

"I am well. Progressing through journalism while sticking to one's ethics is tough, but I am surviving. Kicking and floating through the turbulent waters. Why don't we move inside the library?" suggested Shehnaz as the melting snow started to drench her jacket.

The two ladies ventured into the library, where the staff was clearing up Sanaya's art paraphernalia, which was strewn across the carpet.

Looking at the mess, Shehnaz looked at Sanaya questioningly.

The eccentric artist immediately replied, "I had thought of working in the library and had asked the staff to bring my belongings here. But then, after my stroll, I changed my mind and told them to take everything back to my studio."

Though Shehnaz appreciated Sanaya's warmth, she could sense her artistically inclined temperamental brain.

While walking over to the sofa, Sanaya casually asked, "Have you married yet?"

"Oh no. I had a prospect from a cousin of mine, but I honestly felt that marriage would interfere with my career growth. I just didn't want to be bogged down by the additional responsibility. I need space, flexibility and freedom to fly. Marriage can be fun, but it is baggage I don't think I will ever be ready to carry."

"You go, girl. I like the way you think," then, flicking her head sideways, Sanaya slowly commented, "Marriage sure brings a mountain of baggage with itself."

The two spoke casually for about an hour, first in the library, and then they shifted to the informal sitting room. A while later, Sanaya decided to go back to her art studio.

Shehnaz was toying with the idea of working on her next report and had just opened her laptop when Cyrus came strolling into the room. He looked a bit surprised to see Shehnaz there. He sat down quietly across her.

Shehnaz opened the conversation by asking, "How are you? What have you been doing?

Cyrus ran his hands through his curly hair and said, "I am aiming to become an economist. I am applying to universities for attaining my PhD. I also love studying finance and follow the market regularly. I invest some of my own money in the markets. Though unlike Diana and Grand Uncle, I only invest in blue chip stocks. My risk appetite is much like my father's. Cautious and calculated."

Shehnaz smiled. Cyrus then, after careful contemplation, asked her, "How hectic is your life? Journalism seems tough."

"It is when you have to stick to your ethics. These days, anything can be sold as sensational news. I started as a crime reporter and reported about murders and white-collar crimes without prejudice. There is often a lot of pressure to squish stories about scams. Now, as the lead editor, I have a more diverse array of subjects on which I am working. Spot fixing in sports is a big issue in the country and that would be our next revelation. We are working with our sources to expose the corrupt elements of the system."

The two spoke for a while, and then Cyrus excused himself and ambled out of the room softly.

Shehnaz then went over to the pantry, sourced some fox nuts for herself and settled in the informal dining room.

It was 5 PM, and the weather outside was chillingly cold. It was not just the snowstorm but the winds that made the weather brutish.

As she was opening her packet of the fox nuts, from the corner of her eye, she saw a silhouette of Cyrus through the frosted bevelled glass, passing by but not just as quietly.

CHAPTER 11

WEE WILLIE WINKIE

Wednesday, 25th January 2023
6:45 PM – till late at night

In the basement, right next to the staff staircase, was the wine cellar. Adjacent to the wine cellar was the butler's office. At 6:45 PM, the staff was mostly in the kitchen preparing the dinner or around the house making the rooms for the night. Jawahar was going over some expense bills when he heard hurried footsteps entering the wine cellar. Not sure about what he heard, he put down his pen and tried to intently hear for any sound that may arise out of the adjacent room. A few moments later, he heard the door of the wine cellar open again. Staff was not permitted to go inside the cellar without his permission. Besides, he had already decanted the wine they were to serve for dinner that evening. With a sense of unease, Jawahar quickly scrambled outside his office. But the intruder had left, and he could hear the footsteps marching up the staff staircase. Jawahar went inside the cellar and noticed that none of the bottles were missing or had been opened. Looking at the time, he picked the bottle that Diana had requested, locked the cellar and his office and then marched on towards her room.

Shehnaz, who was sitting in the informal dining room and munching on some fox nuts, was reminiscing about her past, when she, Firdaus, Sohrab and some of the distant cousins of the Dinshaw family would play hide and seek in the mansion during their childhood days. She remembered that time with fondness when everyone was simple and easy-going. A faint memory recollected in her brain wherein she hid in the staff staircase as none of the family members ever used that area of the house and that had made her exceptionally difficult to find. Smiling at her ability to disappear in plain sight and wanting to look at her hiding place again with fond memory, Shehnaz walked up to the door leading to the staff staircase.

As she approached the door, she heard someone stomping hurriedly through the staff staircase on the floor above her. When she opened the door, she saw Jawahar standing right in front of her with a bottle of wine in his hand.

The butler looked at her suspiciously and questioned in a polite tone, "Was there something that you wanted, Madam?"

Shehnaz replied, "I wanted to see the staircases where I used to hide as a child while playing with Firdaus and Sohrab. And I just heard someone running up hurriedly."

"I, too, heard someone. Maybe it was one of the younger staff personnel. Now, I must go and give this bottle to Miss Diana."

As the butler went on his way, Shehnaz casually walked up the steps and noticed some snow and mud had fallen on some of the steps and that the snow had just melted into the carpet, making the wet mud stick to the fibres. Shehnaz made a mental note of the layout, and while remembering her past, she slowly walked up the staircase. On the landing of the first floor, she noticed the smudged mud on the carpet, but the trail seemed to end there. As she climbed on to the floor above, she found the carpet to be clean. Ignoring the negligent working of the housekeeping staff, Shehnaz strolled back to the informal sitting area while reminiscing the sweet memories of her childhood.

Brooding while sitting on the ledge of his four-poster bed, Jahangir seemed lost in thought. Shirin looked at him with affectionate concern and said, “Don’t worry. They are young and rash. Your decision is correct and will have a long-lasting positive impact on the future generations of our family. Jamshed, Nariman, and you shared a tight-knit bond. Just like them you too have a penchant for business astuteness. They would have agreed with your foresight.”

“Everyone thinks that I am trying to control their lives or that I am a miser. No one understands my vision. No one has the wisdom to look at the bigger picture. They all just want to live for the moment without ever thinking about the future. During olden times, wars may have allowed the kings to forge great kingdoms, but copious amounts of wealth are what is required to sustain a kingdom,” explained Jahangir in a soft voice. The lack of support from his family made him, for the first time in his life, feel glum.

“Don’t worry, they will come around. Give them some time to process the information,” said Shirin as she wobbled out of the room, wanting to fix herself some hot toddy owing to the chilly cold weather.

Despite his fur lined loafers, Jahangir felt the icy marble under his feet, and the cold suddenly reminded him of the stares that his family members gave him as he had left the library. Switching his thoughts to the recent past events, as a sense of morbidity crept up, he grumpily muttered to himself, “The shy boy Farrukh is very skilled with tools and tackles. I wonder if he tampered with the brakes of my bike. I am also in the crosshairs of Diana and Sohrab now. I wonder if any of them would have the heart to kill me?”

For Jim, fortunes had turned in his favour, and he did not care in the least bit about the uncomfortable atmosphere that now lingered in the Dinshaw estate. He had seen some of the family members piercingly look at him, but their gazes had just bounced off his thick skin and he had just smiled back at them, sheltering himself behind the veil of honour which is bestowed upon guests.

Shehnaz and Bejan, though felt a bit awkward about their presence in the house, were compelled to stay as not only Jahangir held them back but also the weather had now taken a turn for the worse, with an extreme snowstorm enveloping the hill station.

The family members were disconcerted and expressed their agitations differently. Not everyone took the obvious path of agitation and anger. Farrukh was of a reserved nature, and his introverted mind had the habit of processing information silently without expressing his thoughts outwardly. Post dinner, he had planned to walk to his carpentry shed to clear his thoughts. But the snowstorm prevented him to go all the way, and so after a short walk, he had turned back and had now planted himself in the library. The heat emitting from the fire made the library cosy, yet Farrukh felt cold and numb. As he paced around the library to generate some body heat, he regularly pinched his arm or ruffled his hair to remind himself that his brain had not imagined the recent happenings and to keep himself associated with his conscious surroundings.

Cyrus was again working on the financials of his parents' company and his own personal savings. This time around, he created two sheets, one of the existing positions and the other after taking into account the effects and benefits of the new trust which held the family's newfound wealth. Although Jahangir had stated that the wealth would only be distributed five years after both Shirin and he would pass away, Cyrus had calculated those five years from the present time.

Zubin, who was feeling cold, which the red colour of his nose and cheeks indicated, decided to pour himself a generous portion of wine. As his body shivered, he gulped down the wine quickly and tucked himself in bed.

Diana, who had received her desired wine bottle from the butler, now walked across the hall on the second floor. She found her father resting with his head tilted backwards in his sitting room.

Blinking rapidly while biting on his lips, Sohrab looked at his daughter. In a delicate voice, Diana said, "Father, do not be upset at Grand Uncle's decision. The wealth is still in the family."

"Yes, but the way he has divided the wealth between Firdaus and my family seems unfair to me. You, too, should have received a greater share of the pie. Also, he has tied the wealth in such a way that we would only be receiving the interests garnered from the invested principal. We would never be able to enjoy the principal itself. Lastly, I am very upset about the way he treats me."

Placing the bottle of wine on the egg-shaped coffee table in front of the sofa, Diana replied, "Enjoy this rare wine and reconcile with Grand Uncle. Once the reign is in your hands you can always try and find a legal loophole which would allow you to distribute the wealth and dissolve the trust earlier than intended. There is no point fighting with him in the short run or thinking about how he has strong-armed us. We may feel that he has used us, or he may feel that we are not ready for such great wealth, but unless we have the power to do something about the situation, there is no point ruminating about it. We will act only when the rightful opportunity presents itself. Besides, even though I don't agree with the way he has acted, I do believe he has our best interests at heart."

"I see that he has groomed you well. I see wisdom in your words and shall ponder on them. Now, off you go. Get some sleep. Time solves everything, even convoluted family politics," replied Sohrab in a heartening tone. He was calming himself as much as he was reassuring his daughter.

As Diana left, Sohrab gazed at the bottle of wine and cynically muttered, "Opportunities seldom present themselves. Wisdom dictates that prospects must be created and not waited upon."

On the first floor Firdaus was texting rapidly and was getting peeved after every text that he would receive. In his anger and irritation, he was typing faster and in bold capital letters, often before the reply of his previous message could come. Owing to the late hour of the night, Anahita asked with a sense of concern, "Who do you keep talking and texting to all the time? Is something the matter?"

Hearing Anahita's words and taken aback by her observation, Firdaus mentally took a step back and immediately calmed himself. He sensed danger and the possibility of an altercation with his wife. So, to douse the situation, he calmly responded, "Oh no, it is just one of the theatre actor who is acting pricey and throwing her weight around. Nothing that I can't sort out." From his years of experience in business, Firdaus had realized that lies mixed with certain truthful facts always worked. He had been speaking with the lead actress of his theatre company, who was being unreasonably harsh on him. Only it was not in relation to their professional relationship but was about their personal one.

"It is late at night. We should sleep now. I also feel that you should speak to uncle on behalf of Sohrab. I feel he has been unfair in the division of funds. We are all quite well off and it does not make sense to quarrel over a little extra portion of the wealth."

Firdaus did not want to pick a fight with his wife, so he feigned interest in what she was saying. He also got the opportunity to astutely change the subject and divert Anahita's attention away from their recent conversation. Consequently, Firdaus immediately replied, "Yes! I agree with your analysis. Tomorrow morning, before I go for my jog, I shall speak to Uncle."

Then, just before switching off the lamp on her bedside and much to Firdaus's irritation, Anahita inquired, "If that actress is pestering you, why don't you stop casting her? Maybe once she is out of a job, her head will balance evenly on her shoulders?"

Firdaus felt stumped for a second. He did not like the fact that his wife had registered his narrative. He realized that he, too, would have to remember his lies, lest he gets called out on it and caught in his philandering act.

Not wanting to give too much attention or importance to the matter, Firdaus grunted and replied, "Well, if she keeps up her tantrums, I will no longer be able to cast her in my plays."

Not wanting the matter to extend further, Firdaus too, switched off the lights on his side of the bed and prepared to fight his battles another day.

Sleep often allows people to bide time and defer sensitive matters.

The only member of the Dinshaw household who remained unperturbed by the occurrences around her was Sanaya. She, in her care free attitude, continued to paint and sketch. A while later, as she stepped back to analyse her creation, she saw that her mind had made her draw a man on a barren piece of land, walking painstakingly with a huge boulder on his head, which in turn was held over his head by a gigantic hand.

Looking at her own creation, Sanaya smirked and murmured to herself, "Often in life, we unnecessarily carry a burden that is forcefully placed upon us by others. I should show this artwork to Sohrab and explain to the poor fellow that he need not burden himself with his uncle's decision. He has nothing to fret. He is financially secure and our position would be better off if he stops gambling. Besides I have funds to bail him out of his debt, but I can't keep funding his habits all the time. I need to save for the future and for our kids. Maybe I should ask uncle to help him out. If he bails him out, he will ensure that Sohrab stops gambling."

Through the dark, cold night, the wind howled, and snow poured from the sky as if God was generously pouring powder on himself and getting ready for some mischief for the night. Everyone in the family was reserved and lost in their own thoughts. Some were contemplating what they would be discussing with Jahangir the following morning, while some were plotting schemes to deal with their future.

CHAPTER 12

THE KING WAS IN HIS COUNTING HOUSE

Thursday, 26th January 2023
7:00 AM - 12:45 PM

As day broke, snow still fell through the sky, and the sun hid behind the dense cloud cover, making the hill station appear misty, bleak and grey.

At 7 AM, Sohrab slowly strolled down the stairs. Dressed in a warm fleece tracksuit and carrying his windcheater in one hand and the unopened wine bottle that his daughter had gifted him the previous evening in the other, he entered the library. Right in the middle of the room, by the fireplace, sat Jahangir sipping on his pipe and reading a novel.

Sohrab approached him and sat on the sofa next to him. Jahangir noticed that his nephew had crossed his legs by putting the ankle of one foot on the knee of the other, making a four and was actively showcasing a position of power. Contradictory to his characteristic, Sohrab spoke with a sense of composed conviction, "Uncle, I am sorry for lashing out yesterday. I have come to reconcile. Please accept this rare red wine as a token of my apology. I realize the importance of your efforts and sacrifices that you have made for this family."

Smiling, Jahangir put his pipe aside and accepted the bottle of wine. Then he lightly jingled the copper bell, and the sound alerted the butler, who instantly came in. Without looking at him, Jahangir said, "Get me a cork opener." Then, turning his gaze towards Sohrab, Jahangir asked in an exhausted voice, "Does this mean that you would continue to work at the publishing company and try to turn it around?"

"Dear uncle, of all the forms of art created by humans, business by far is the most dreadful and downtrodden practice. I am going to shut the company down effective immediately. Please do not be upset, as I do believe this would be the best decision for all. Enjoy your wine. I am going out for a walk."

As Sohrab got up and collected his windcheater, Jahangir received the electric corkscrew from the butler. Without a sound, the cork popped out, and with the same deafening silence, Sohrab walked out with his head held high. Jahangir poured some wine for himself, relit his pipe and smirked as he mumbled, "Poor fellow. This is the first time he has shown some confidence and resolve, even if it is for the wrong thing. He doesn't understand it yet, but he will have to work per my guidelines till I am alive."

After about three and half hours, at almost 10:30 AM, Firdaus strolled down wearing a pair of faded black jeans and a worn-out red leather jacket that had shone brighter during its prime years. He felt that it was too cold for him to go out for his daily jog, and the hot bath that he had had this morning made him feel warm and cosy.

Casually he entered the library and found his uncle flipping a page of a leather-bound book that he held firmly in his bony hands. Firdaus sat in the armchair opposite his uncle and casually crossed his legs at the ankle, highlighting his vulnerability in the presence of his uncle, whom he considered his superior.

His reflex action, although highlighted by his relaxed, down-to-earth nature, also indicated that he was apprehensive about the conversation that he was about to have and was mentally debating whether he should withhold his thoughts or discuss the matter openly with his uncle.

Finally placing his arms on his lap, indicating his thoughtfulness about the situation and after weighing his words carefully, Firdaus said, "Uncle, I feel that at our position only love and peace are our true wealth. We are all one, and the family must be preserved above all else. If Sohrab wants a greater piece of the newfound wealth, then I would not object to him getting it."

Swirling his glass, then taking a sip of his drink and savouring the strong mix of blackcurrant, cherry and liquorice, Jahangir, with enduring prudence, replied, "Just being alive is not enough, nor does it bode well to give up on oneself. Sohrab needs to stop acting small all the time. There must be something that he can do better than anyone else, other than playing a victim or a damsel in distress. He fails at everything he does, and to top it all, he has taken up gambling. It is not who he is but what he is becoming that irks me. His future seems so uncertain and bleak to me. Leave me alone, and instead of trying to persuade me, try talking some sense into your cousin. He thinks that with his sweet talk and pretentious confidence, he can change my decision. But he is wrong. He must understand that actions speak louder than words."

"I understand your predicament, uncle, but just think about the larger picture. Maybe then you would reconsider your position. It is not a decision that you have to take overnight. Please just observe the situation from a different perspective," replied Firdaus as he got up. He then slowly strolled to the door and halted just for a few seconds in the hope that his uncle might engage with him. But to his utter disappointment, Jahangir believed that silence truly was golden. Moreover, the astute old man knew that since time had a way to solve most problems, all non-pressing issues should be deferred and not acted upon with immediate effect.

As Firdaus left the library, he saw the butler sitting outside by the console table and realized that the silence in the mansion would have allowed the loyal old servant to have overheard his conversation. But he couldn't care about such trivialities right now.

A few moments later, Diana entered the library. She immediately noticed that her father had passed on the wine that she had given him to her Grand Uncle, who had already finished half the bottle. She saw Jahangir salivating and having equal amounts of water as the wine. But ignoring his clumsy hand movements and without bothering to sit, Diana, with a firm resolve, exclaimed in a loud tone, "I realize that one must accept everything just the way it is in life. I do not wish to quarrel, and I have no regrets about my actions and deeds. One must seek nothing outside of oneself. Yet, there is more than one way to climb a mountain. It is not my job to live up to your expectations. I am happy but not satisfied. Knowledge is not enough; I must apply and act upon it. Therefore, my conduct from now on will be as I deem fit. If that leads me to being cut from the trust, then so be it." Saying as much, Diana stormed out of the room with welled-up bloodshot eyes.

After Diana left, Jahangir got up to pace around the room, and he drank a lot of water. A few frequent trips to the loo calmed his nerves, and he settled back on the armchair by the fireplace. All this while, the poor butler kept hearing the door between the library and Jahangir's room open and close and the unmistakable sound of the toilet flush too did not miss his ears. He silently wondered if something was amiss.

Jahangir closed his eyes, tilted his head backwards and tried to take deep breaths. The minutes and the second's hand ticked away on the ornate grandfather clock, and time moved on.

Snow still fell from the heavens above and shrouded the estate in a serene and calm white carpet. The ticking hands of the clock did not tell Jahangir how much time had passed and he could not even tell the same in his present drowsy state.

A light knock on the library door by Sanaya thus went unnoticed by Jahangir as he lay slumped on his chair. Only when Sanaya came and sat opposite him and announced herself a bit loudly did Jahangir stir.

He opened his eyes in a narrow slit and ran his hand down his parched throat. He bent over to his right side and drank some water, but that ignited an abdominal pain, and to calm the sudden burst of cramps, he poured himself some more wine. The divine elixir seemed to ease his pain as it made him feel drowsy. After patiently waiting through his antics, Sanaya finally grew impatient and said, "Uncle, I have come to tell you that I do have the funds to bail out Sohrab from his gambling debts, but I won't be doing it. I want you to step in to stop his habit. If you repay his debts and make him feel shameful, it can compel him to feel responsible and act in a mature way. This can probably put an end to his newfound disastrous hobby." Sanaya's every word felt like a punch in the stomach as not only did Jahangir not agree with her, but also his abdominal cramps had returned. He winced silently, squinted his eyes, moved his hands over his stomach, yet put up a brave face to articulate that he was still in power. From the opposite chair, Sanaya continued in oblivion, "I also feel that you should let go of Sohrab and not control his life. Allow the caterpillar to transform into a butterfly even if the butterfly shows colours that you personally don't approve of."

Staring at Jahangir who had grunted at her suggestions, flicked his hands as she spoke and then placed them gingerly over his stomach and had now shut his eyes again, Sanaya lost her sense of hope. A while later, she got up and left. When she opened the door, she muttered a few words under her breath, which sounded like "obstinate old fool" to the impassive butler sitting by the console table.

A while later Jawahar, who was reading the daily newspaper but by virtue of his job had to keep an ear pointed towards his master's direction, heard the internal door connecting the library to Jahangir's bedroom being slowly shut.

It was unusual for the ubiquitous Jawahar to witness such a disagreement amongst the family members. He had served long enough to realize the long-subdued ambitions and inherent characteristics of everyone, yet his maturity made him aware of his position. He knew it was not his place to judge or comment, for despite all the years of loyal service, he would always remain an outsider. He was an orphan who had carved his own way in life through hard work and determination. He owed all his success to himself. He had observed and imbibed.

The lonely, cold corridor where he sat reflected the mindsets of its occupants and the current family turmoil. He almost had an urge to find a solution to settle the troubled waters but realized that his position was vulnerable, just like that of his true masters. His aimless thoughts converted his urge into a momentary pang of irritation, but his well-trained brain overrode his emotions when he noticed Farrukh arriving at the mud gate. Dusting off the freshly fallen snow from his overcoat and then hanging it to dry and removing his soaked boots, Farrukh entered the mansion. His brown corduroy jacket was laden with sawdust. Ignoring the hint of an inquisitive look on the butler's face, Farrukh entered the library.

Farrukh peered in and saw Jahangir sitting by the fireplace with his eyes closed. He approached his Grand Uncle and noticed the half-emptied wine bottle kept on the wooden console stool beside him. With a disquieted feel, Farrukh moved back, stumbled and pushed down a table lamp set beside the sofa. Regaining his composure, he looked at Jahangir and exclaimed hurriedly and a little too loudly, "Grand Uncle, we must find our own rite of passage. Modern life does not give us a clear path. We all need to face our own obstacles, face different fears and find ways to grow into the best version of ourselves. We cannot just pass life by, we need to live it and therefore set our own limits and boundaries. These days the power to absolve debt is greater than the power to forgive. Therefore, it is my sincere suggestion that you help father out, let him lead his life the way he wants and trust him to make the right choices. You must share the wealth with everyone and not entwine it into trust. I will find my own path through my creative endeavours."

Saying as much, Farrukh quickly left the library. As he left, he saw the butler talking to one of the junior manservants.

Jawahar in a strict tone, questioned, "Have you put the dried firewood in all of the fireplaces? Especially in Master Jim's room. He feels particularly very cold. He is not used to the harsh northern winters."

The young junior staff boy then softy told the butler, "Sir, while I was returning from the garden shed after collecting the dried firewood, I saw young master Jim wandering around alone in the lawn adjacent to the library."

"It is not your place to comment about the actions of the family members or their guests. Go and place the firewood in all the fireplaces. Start from the second floor," replied the butler, as Farrukh's footsteps faded away and the young manservant too quickly darted away to complete his chores.

A while later, a small alarm on Jawahar's phone slowly hummed and indicated to him that the time was 12:45 PM. The butler sent a reminder to everyone to assemble for lunch. Then he entered the library to perceive the patriarch's mood and inquire about his lunch plans.

From afar, looking at the usual slump with which Jahangir generally sat, Jawahar couldn't notice anything out of the ordinary. But as he approached his master, his eyes widened and a cold chill ran through his body. His brain felt numb. He saw that Jahangir had died with his hands folded neatly over his stomach. If not for a painter's knife sticking out of his throat, Jahangir's death would have likely been ruled as a heart attack.

Stumbling on the fallen lamp and then regaining his composure, the butler quickly left the library and immediately ran into the informal sitting room where he knew he could find Bejan and Shehnaz Contractor.

Jahangir Dinshaw

CHAPTER 13

WHEN THE BOUGH BREAKS

Thursday, 26th January 2023
12:45 PM – 2:00 PM

The father-daughter duo was discussing the impacts of Jahangir's decision on various family members and Shehnaz was saying, "I find Anahita oddly reserved and quiet this time around. She used to be very jovial and carefree but I sense a certain degree of reservation and coldness in her attitude, especially towards her husband, Firdaus," when the butler barged in without knocking on the door. His ears were red, and his white face looked like he had seen a ghost. With a shaking voice, he said, "Master has been murdered. You must come at once with me to the library."

Hearing his words, the duo got up and rushed into the library. Shehnaz was the first on the scene; her well-formed legs and well-maintained physique allowed her to take quick strides. But her initial spontaneity, fuelled by the urgency of the situation, died the moment she saw the body. Looking at the lifeless and helpless body of such a dynamic man made her feel sorrowful and impressed upon her the fragility of life.

In that moment, all of Jahangir's elaborate plans seemed so inconsequential. By virtue of her work, Shehnaz had dallied enough around crime scenes and with detectives, so it did not take long for her reptilian brain to kick in. Consequentially, subconsciously, her brain started to observe its surroundings. So, instead of the dead body, which her brain now processed as being a natural part of the crime scene, it concentrated on the layout of the room. Shehnaz noticed that the beautifully painted ballerinas of Edgar Degas were tilted at an awkward angle, indicating that the safe behind it was recently operated. Jahangir's personal stationary was cluttered on his desk. Anger and regret kicked in in equal measures. This was not a normal everyday occurrence for her. Hesitant yet determined, Shehnaz moved around the room.

Bejan cautiously moved towards the body. Although the knife protruding from Jahangir's throat indicated the obvious, Bejan still lifted the body's hand to see if there was life left and whether there was any chance of survival for his dear old friend. After ruling out the possibility and indicating the same to his daughter by shaking his head, Bejan exclaimed, "His hands are neatly resting on his stomach and so it seems he did not put up any fight. Maybe he was drowsy because of the wine and was caught unawares." Looking at Jahangir in such a despicable state made Bejan teary-eyed. Despite their friendship being hinged upon their work, he was fond of the shrewd capitalist. The sudden, shocking, sad news made Bejan feel morose. He was amazed at the quantum of unsatiated greed that could make someone take such a drastic step.

Shehnaz, who was still observing the room, clicking photos of the scene and making a few notes in her phone, heard her father but did not react to his comment.

At that moment, Shirin wobbled into the library and, while breathing heavily with each step, held on to her walking stick ever so tightly. The butler had just woken her up from her catnap and deftly walked in behind her. Shirin's face sunk upon seeing the ashen dead body of her husband. She approached his body and sobbed loudly. Her body shook as she vented in grief. Shehnaz hugged her and tried to comfort her. No words or accusations escaped from Shirin's mouth. She just cried and blew snot into her kerchief. Although Shehnaz found this to be a bit odd, she diverted her attention to the fallen lamp, the half-emptied bottle of wine, the empty glass of water and the blazing embers emitting from the fireplace. Finally, she stared at the victim's stab wound and observed the neat puncture made by the artist's knife. Shehnaz observed an oddity, but before she could voice her opinion, the large library doors swung open like flood gates and the remaining members of the Dinshaw family swarmed into the room. Each reflecting a varying degree of surprise and awe on their face. Everyone took their position around the room, few sat on the chairs at the far end. Though no one stood or sat beside the victim, everyone's curious eyes routinely darted towards Jahangir's slumped body and the knife that protruded from his throat.

Slowly, hushed murmurs started doing the rounds in the room. Amidst the confusion, Cyrus asked the first coherent question in a slightly raised voice, "When was Grand Uncle last seen alive? Who met him just before his death?"

Around the room, the necks craned, and the ears strained as everyone, from their position, tried to look at Cyrus as he spoke.

But before his question could be answered, Firdaus interjected and diverted everyone's attention by exclaiming, "Are the windows open? Did anyone enter the estate? We need to get the entire property swept for intruders."

Innately, Jawahar responded, "Immediately after informing Mr. Bejan and Madam Shirin, I informed the security to close all gates and man all stations. They have even let all of the sixteen guard dogs loose on the property. I checked the windows. They were sealed shut. Just like I had left them this morning." Then, looking at Mr. Bejan, he continued, "I keep all the keys. I do not believe that my keys or these locks have been tampered with."

Shehnaz observed Zubin, who had been staring at the dead body and shaking. Whether his reaction was driven by anger or some other emotion, she could not yet tell. Then she heard him mumble, "Where did this strange knife come from? Who does it belong to?"

Hearing the words, Sanaya approached the body with caution and apprehension. The realization that the knife sticking out of Jahangir's throat was hers gave her a rude, unpleasant shock. She felt the intense gaze of a few prying eyes on her. Then, shaking her head, clicking her tongue in disagreement and taking a few steps back, Sanaya commented, "Everyone knows that this is my knife. Someone has purposely used my stationary to put the blame on me. But I am not stupid enough to murder someone with my knife. Clearly, the killer's ruse has failed."

Bejan instantly responded, "No one has entered the estate. So, it is one of you who has murdered Jahangir." Then, looking at Sanaya, he continued, "You could very well be the killer, and to throw everyone off the track, you could have purposely used your knife."

"Who made you in charge? Where were you and Shehnaz this past hour?"

"Since this morning, Shehnaz and I have been present in the informal sitting. Jawahar is witness to our constant presence there. Even Shirin dropped in to check on us after breakfast. Lastly, we are the only ones who are financially unaffected by Jahangir's decision. Therefore, we have the least motive and are in a position to question everyone till the police arrive."

Shirin's red nose bobbed up and down along with her round head as she nodded in agreement to Bejan's statement. After blowing some more snot, she commandingly said, "I agree with

Bejan's reasoning. He and Shehnaz will question everyone about their whereabouts and actions till the police arrive. And I want everyone to cooperate with them."

Taking the cue, Shehnaz quickly took command of the situation and exclaimed, "We will interview everyone individually in the formal drawing room."

"Oh! All of this is too much for me to bear," exclaimed Diana as her ears turned red, and she slightly swirled before quickly regaining her composure and settling on the sofa. To avoid his sister crashing into him, Farrukh's instinct made him move a few steps back and he stepped on Zubin's toe. Zubin yelped, turned away from Farrukh and stepped onto the fallen lamp. The lamp further unbalanced him, and Zubin fell across the side table, pushing over the bottle of wine and the glass from which Jahangir had been drinking. The bottle and the glass landed into the burning fireplace and shattered as it hit the burning logs. The wine was a good fuel to the fire, and it now burnt as ferociously as Zubin's rage.

As he got up, he yelled at Farrukh, "Are you blind? You almost pushed me into the fire!"

Shehnaz acutely observed the scene and its characters as it played out in front of her eyes. As the young adults were quarrelling, Shehnaz observed that now the weather had changed for the worse. A heavy snowstorm had started.

Owing to the critical nature of the situation, Shehnaz immediately called up her acquaintance in the state's Crime Investigation Department (CID). She tried a couple of times but the call disconnected as the signal dropped. Then, using the landline, she called again. The phone rang, and the Superintendent of Police, Arun Mohan Joshi, picked up the call.

"Hello, Arun, it's Shehnaz here.

"Oh, Shehnaz, how are you? It's been ages since we last spoke."

"I am at my uncle's house in Dehradun," exclaimed Shehnaz, now shouting in the phone as the disturbance in the line increased.

"Oh! You are at the Dinshaw estate. I heard that the family is a bit cuckoo. Is it true?"

"Arun, my uncle has been murdered. How soon can you get here?" asked Shehnaz while straining her ear and holding the big receiver close to her ear.

"Oh my! This is a nasty business. But the weather will not allow us to get to you for another forty-eight hours, at least. The estate is up in the hills, and the snow avalanches have caused roadblocks. We can't even use our helicopter in these storms."

"What should I do, then?"

"Close the house down. Do not let anyone leave. Question everyone in my stead. Take whatever steps you think are necessary, and take care for the killer might–" And the line went dead as the snowstorm severed the connection.

Shehnaz put the receiver down and gazed around the room. Her left ear had gone red because of the heavy receiver that she had pressed against it. All eyes were now on her. Everyone had heard her speak to the police. Regaining her composure, Shehnaz addressed the room and declared, "I am in charge. The police shall arrive in the next forty-eight hours. Till they arrive, the body is not to be moved and nothing else is to be touched. No one is to leave the compound. SP Arun is my acquaintance and I shall question everyone in his stead."

"Why is he taking forty-eight hours to reach here?" inquired Diana, shifting her gaze from Zubin to Shehnaz.

"The snow storms have caused road blocks and the winds will not allow a helicopter to land here," stated Shehnaz while slightly rolling her eyes. She did not like wasting time over things she perceived to be of common sense.

Zubin calmly sat down in an armchair and stared at the fire. His face and ears flushed bright pink, almost like a flamingo.

Was it because of his anger, the murder or something else, Shehnaz again could not say. But she did make a mental note. Her gaze darted towards Farrukh, who looked pale. Probably the poor introvert was upset about the turn of events and the yelling by Zubin had clearly not helped.

Just as Shehnaz was imbibing the scene in the library and observing everyone around her, Firdaus commented, "Let us all move to the informal sitting room and from there, we can go to the formal drawing room one after the other to answer Shehnaz's questions."

A few people made some movement and shuffled around. Sohrab was one of them, and though he immediately hated himself for following the order but doing so had become second nature to him, owing to the grilling Jahangir had given him over the years.

Cyrus, who liked to think ahead, very quickly pointed out, "But what about Grand Uncle? If we just leave him here, he will rot and stink?"

Shirin let out a burst of tears hearing that comment and wailed a bit too loudly for Shehnaz's comfort.

The question was a pressing concern and could not be ignored. So, everyone, including Firdaus, now stopped in their tracks and looked from Shehnaz to Cyrus to Jahangir's dead body.

Cyrus then again asked a pertinent question, almost as if he was a third party and not connected with the occurrences, "Shouldn't a doctor be called? Won't an autopsy need to be performed?"

Shehnaz quickly shook her head in a matter-of-fact way and exclaimed, "The local hospitals are at least thirty kilometres away and the blizzard won't allow the doctors to arrive here anytime soon. Anyway, I shall have Jawahar send out a word to the family doctor, as soon as the phone lines are back up."

It had been around thirty minutes since Jahangir's body was discovered. Jahangir's fair skin looked pale as *pallor mortis* set in.

The body had also begun to cool down. Shehnaz now realized that soon the muscles of the body would stiffen and the body would start swelling as gases accumulate inside. While Shehnaz contemplated her options, a soft fart was heard from Jahangir's body in the eerily silent room. Nobody laughed and the amateur sleuth realized that she needed to quickly make a decision.

To make matters worse, a discussion started about what should be done with the body, and everybody started giving their opinions. Everyone bickered as to why their suggested outlook was the best possible option and wanted to come out on top. To Shehnaz, it seemed that finding the best solution was not the intent of the bickering family members; rather getting their suggestion passed and approved had become the goal.

Sohrab questioningly opened his hands while emphatically suggesting, "Let us open the windows and dowse the fire. The cold air shall slow the decomposition."

Shehnaz just swayed her head disapprovingly. Looking at her reaction and without waiting for her explanation, Sohrab agitatedly asked, "Why?"

"For the very simple reason that when the snow will drift in and melts, it will interact with the crime scene. Any footprints or fingerprints might get washed away, and the melting snow will decompose and spoil the body further."

Then, taking back command of the situation, Shehnaz declared, "This is a crime scene and must remain intact. All the windows and doors will be bolted and sealed. The body, along with the chair on which it sits, shall be transferred to the chiller in the basement. It is a huge cold storage, which was designed to deep-freeze lot of food and vegetables but I believe we can comfortably place the body as it is."

Five minutes later, as Jawahar along with two junior manservants, moved into the library to move the body of the once grandiose Jahangir Dinshaw, the family started trickling into the informal sitting room. Shehnaz made the butler and the servants wait as she diligently took multiple photos of the crime scene and the body with her iPhone.

As the family members started to move out of the library, Firdaus stated, "Given the circumstance, I will ask the butler to discard the prepared lunch. We can all have some sandwiches while we answer Shehnaz's questions."

"Well, I shall stick to my diet. I am to have a feta salad and some leek soup today for lunch. My soul won't be satisfied by a common man's working lunch," expressed Sanaya as she stormed off.

Jawahar (The Butler)

CHAPTER 14

The Saints go marching

Thursday, 26th January 2023
2:00 PM – 3:00 PM

In the informal sitting room, the family members settled on the sofas. Shirin, Shehnaz and Bejan settled themselves on armchairs, indicating that they were in control of the situation. Shirin chose the armchair as at her age and given her health, she felt more comfortable sitting on a sturdy plush seat than getting sunk in a sofa. Shehnaz had crossed her legs, and her posture radiated the fact that she was in control. The somewhat meek behaviour of the family members reflected the guilt that they all harboured. Taking out her diary and pen while addressing the whole room, Shehnaz softly said, "This is a moment of great loss for the Dinshaw family, the Parsi community and the nation in general. Uncle Jahangir was a great businessman and a generous philanthropist."

Rolling her eyes, Sanaya commented, "Darling, we all know about his achievements and shortcomings. Why don't we get on with the business at hand?"

Sohrab tapped Sanaya's hand as an indication for her to remain quiet. But such subtleties often missed her. She questioningly looked at her husband and loudly asked, "What?"

Dejectedly, Sohrab shook his head and looked towards Shehnaz.

Taking the situation back in command, Shehnaz continued, "We all know Uncle Jahangir was murdered. To establish a timeline, I first wish to know the chronology of events. Before his death some of you visited him. Right now, I just wish to know the timing of your visits. Then, accordingly, I shall question you all individually."

Sohrab looked around the room, then ran his hand over his face before finally stating, "I presume I was the first one to meet uncle today at 7 AM."

"I met him at 10:30 AM," commented Firdaus, who was a creature of habit and was always aware about his timings.

"I met Grand Uncle at 11:15 AM," said Diana. As Diana said this, Jim had a disconcerting look on his face. He tried to hide it, but his initial response to Diana's revelation did not miss Shehnaz.

"Well, I also met him sometime late in the morning but before lunch. I generally do not keep a tab of the time, so I cannot tell you when exactly I met him or for how long," exclaimed Sanaya coolly.

At that moment, Jawahar came and announced his presence in the room by giving a slight cough. When Shehnaz looked towards him, he said, "Mr Jahangir is now resting in the freezer. I noted the time when Madam Sanaya visited the library. It was 11:51 AM. A while later, at 12:30 PM, Master Farrukh visited Mr. Jahangir. I believe he was the last family member to have visited him. I went into the library at 12:45 PM to give a reminder call for lunch, which is when I found Master murdered." The slight quavering voice of Jawahar did not go unnoticed. To Shehnaz, he almost looked like he was on the verge of breaking down and crying.

Farrukh silently nodded in agreement to the butler's comments as some of the eyes in the room darted towards him. The stares of his kin made him feel like he was soon going to be behind bars. Farrukh imagined himself doing his carpentry in jail but quickly brushed aside the thought.

"Well, that seems to have settled the chronology of events. Now I shall move to the formal drawing room, where each of you shall come and answer my questions in detail," exclaimed Shehnaz as she got up from her armchair.

After taking a few steps towards the formal drawing room, she turned and looked towards Shirin and asked, "I don't want to bother you, aunt. If you could please answer my question as to where you were this morning?"

"Well, darling, as you know, after breakfast, I came to check up on you and Bejan while you two were sitting in the informal sitting area. After that, I quickly went to the pantry to check on my pickles. Post that, I took my daily diabetes and blood pressure medicines in my room at around 10:45 AM. By 11:15 AM I felt tired and decided to take a nap. I was woken up by Jawahar to this devastating news," finished Shirin as tears welled up in her eyes again.

"And you are sure you did not get up anytime in between?" inquired Shehnaz while looking piercingly at Shirin.

"I am quite positive. I am a sound sleeper," replied Shirin while blowing some snot in her silk kerchief.

"Aunty, why don't you go and lie down for a while. You need some rest."

"I think that is a good idea. I shall escort her to her bedroom," replied Diana as she deftly got up and held Shirin's hand.

Shehnaz then turned on her heel and marched straight into the formal drawing room.

A few seconds later, Sohrab meekly followed her, his head hanging down, almost as if he were a little child who was about to be scolded for being naughty.

Without a second glance, Shehnaz quickly crossed the gigantic hundred-and-twenty-seven-centimetre Bellerby Globe, which royally sat in the middle of the formal drawing room, and planted herself in the most prominent armchair in the room. She motioned to Sohrab to sit across her.

"I will get straight to the point, Sohrab. When did you learn that your uncle's investment had turned into a unicorn?"

"Only when he explicitly told us so. I don't really go through the financial reports that are shared with us," explained Sohrab while slightly shrugging his shoulders.

What was your immediate reaction after the revelation? I did see you go to your room upstairs. You were clearly upset."

"Yes, I was very upset and did retire to my room." Then without any prompting, Sohrab exclaimed, "I gave Uncle the bottle of wine this morning. I offered it as a token of truce between us."

"Where did you get the bottle from? Was it opened when you offered it to him? Did you also sit and have wine with him?" inquired Shehnaz. "My daughter gave it to me the previous night, as I was upset after Uncle's decision about the new found wealth and his comments about me. Diana knows that I am fond of red wine, she must have had the butler get it for her from our cellar. We keep many rare wines in there. It was supposed to be a smooth, light red wine. I left it untouched and let it remain sealed. The butler opened the wine but left quickly afterwards. Uncle poured some wine for himself, but I did not have any of it. I was more concerned about leading my plan into action. After my discussion with Uncle, I left the library and went out for a walk."

"Where did you go?"

"I went to the greenhouse and collected some fresh fruits and vegetables. I spent time talking to our gardeners and going over what we would be sowing in the next couple of months. Anahita guides them, I was just following up with the instructions that she had given to the gardeners. Later, I handed over the produce that I had collected to Jawahar just before he went into the library to announce for lunch."

"So, at the time of the murder, you were outside the house, in all probability coming back from the greenhouse towards the mansion."

"I presume so. Yes."

"What were you discussing with Uncle at 7 in the morning?"

"I wanted to tell him that I do not want to fight, yet I want to curate my own path forward."

"Did he yield to your request?"

"I did not wait for his answer. I almost gave him an ultimatum."

"I hear rumours that you are in debt., mostly from your gambling habits. Also, your publishing business is not yielding you any great results."

Sohrab scorned, stood up, threw his hands in the air and irritably replied, "Yes, I have debts. Yes, I gamble to cheer myself up, to make myself feel better and to feel a little rush of life. Yes, my business is under the water, and I want to shut it down." Then, increasing the volume of his voice, he continued, "Uncle was not in favour of shutting down the business. But you know what, my wife is rich. I have got my own savings. I am rich on my own accord. I did not need to kill uncle to lead my life the way I want to. His life or death is going to have no bearing on the way I conduct myself. I do not need permission from anyone to run my life. Nor do I care for anyone's judgments."

Shehnaz now sternly looked at Sohrab and, in a strict voice, said, "Sit down."

Sohrab immediately followed her instructions.

I have one last question to ask you, "As a family, are you all cordial with each other?"

"Well, except for the fact that Uncle had a very controlling nature and favoured Firdaus over me and that my parents laid the foundations of most of the businesses and trusts which allowed this family to become rich, I would say we are a cordial jovial lot, who on most occasions would get along with each other," replied Sohrab with a hint of spite in his voice.

Shehnaz quietly nodded and scribbled, "Irritable, weak, follower, short-tempered and whimsical," next to Sohrab's name in her diary.

She then gestured to him that he could leave.

After Sohrab left, Firdaus marched in with his head held high. Shehnaz felt that in many ways, he did resemble Jahangir.

Firdaus calmly sat opposite Shehnaz with a poised look on his face.

"What did you discuss with uncle when you met him?"

Firdaus quickly told her all that he had discussed, Jahangir's unrelenting attitude and his final push towards letting Sohrab get a bigger piece of the pie. He concluded by saying, "Uncle was a tough man, just like people from his generation. I just wanted peace in the house."

"What are your thoughts about Sohrab?"

"He is a simpleton and is quite under the thumb of his wife. Not everyone can be ambitious and driven. Business is not everyone's cup of tea. I just wish that his wife's temperamental behaviour had not rubbed off on him."

"Where did you go after meeting uncle?"

"I went for a little stroll near the archery range. I wanted to clear my head. Then I came back and was in my room when the murder took place."

"Did you see anyone outside while you were strolling?"

"No" came back Firdaus's quick response. This was the first time in their conversation he had been quick and blunt.

After a pause Shehnaz analytically asked, "So if anyone would be moving in and out through the library's French windows, there is a possibility you would have seen them and raised an alarm. I presume that you know that no one moved through the windows, yet a while ago you suggested that we should check them?

Firdaus, at first, was taken aback, but his face did not betray his feelings. He quickly recomposed himself and answered, "As I said, I was around the archery range. There is no direct view from there to the library windows. The hedges block the view. And anyway, uncle must have died after Farrukh visited him, so at that time, I was in my room."

"I am not a fool, Firdaus. Uncle could have died at any time before that, and those who visited him after his death may have just feigned talking to him."

"Well, in front of me, he was hale and hearty and enjoying his wine."

"After uncle's revelation, we were all gathered in the informal sitting area. Your initial reaction was quite poised. Where did you go just after the revelation, and why do you think Uncle Jahangir was murdered?"

"As I just told you, I want peace in the house. After our discussion, I retired back to my room. You were there when I left for my room. As far as the murder itself is concerned, it clearly could be for the money. He put all his newfound wealth in a new discretionary trust. After his death, the chairperson of the trust shall be Aunt Shirin. She is soft at heart and can be easily swayed. In fact, I believe we all will be able to persuade her into distributing the wealth immediately."

"I heard that your Theatre company is giving you some trouble. Is it so?"

"We all need money for various reasons. Good theatre requires funding and loyal patrons."

"What do you feel about Jim getting allowances from the family trust."

"He is a small fish. I have bigger things to worry about," replied Firdaus now preparing to get up.

Shehnaz noticed that this was the second time during the conversation that Firdaus had been short and slightly irritable with her.

As she made her notes, Firdaus buttoned his jacket and said, "Oh, I seem to have broken my jacket button. It must have come loose and dropped somewhere."

Ignoring his comment, Shehnaz concluded their discussion by saying, "That would be all for now. Could you please send in Diana?"

"Sure," replied Firdaus and strode back through the drawing room with his head still held high.

Meanwhile, Shehnaz jotted the words astute, confident and shrewd next to Firdaus's name. She then even added, "Has a way of deflecting questions pointed at him. He may be hiding something."

A few moments later, Diana walked in. She seemed reserved and alert. She quickly sat in front of Shehnaz and narrated everything that she had told Jahangir.

After listening intently, Shehnaz asked, "The wine that you gifted to your father, he gifted it ahead to your Grand Uncle. Did that bother you?"

"No. Not at all. In fact, it was I who pushed him to reconcile with Grand Uncle and wait for the opportune moment to make things right."

"What do you mean by that?"

"Well, just after the revelation by Grand Uncle, papa was upset, and I went to his room to talk to him. I told him that after Grand Uncle passes away, eventually, he and Uncle Firdaus would be at the helm and in control, so they could work out a way to dissolve the trust earlier and distribute the monies. Because legally, after the settlor is dead, neither can we cannot bring about any changes in the trust's constitution nor has Uncle Jeh left any provision which would allow us to do so."

"Uncle Jahangir has surely trained you well. By the way, how did he look or behave when you were speaking to him? Did you notice anything out of the ordinary?"

"I was so overwhelmed with emotions that I really did not notice much, but now that I think about it, he was salivating a lot, drinking a lot of water and his hand movements did seem a bit clumsy. Grand Uncle was always conscious about his health and kept regularly having water. At the time, his behaviour did not seem extraordinary to me," explained Diana earnestly.

"I understand," replied Shehnaz, as she scribbled the words intelligent, wise, and emotional in front of Diana's name.

Diana then got up and left, just as silently as she had entered.

CHAPTER 15

Scavenger hunt

Thursday, 26th January 2023
3:00 PM – 4:00 PM

Sanaya entered with some flair. Her heels clacked on the rosewood floor. She casually toyed with the gigantic globe and spun it around, eyeing the countries of the world. Then she crossed to one corner, where a large Daum peacock was majestically placed by the window.

By its side was a bar cabinet. Sanaya opened it, added three cubes of ice and poured herself some whisky. She then slowly swirled the golden liquid, taking in the smoky aroma of the aged oak barrels.

Shehnaz quietly watched Sanaya's antics as she walked over to her. Sanaya sat across Shehnaz and crossed her legs like a princess.

After having a sip of her stiff drink, she said, "I never took you for a sleuth. You seem to be really enjoying yourself."

Shehnaz smiled and replied, "No, I am just trying to find the truth. A murderer cannot go unpunished. I am not trying to play God here. I speak from a position of responsibility and not authority. My intention is not to disrespect anyone here."

"Your marbles seem to be in the right place. What do you want to know?"

"First, tell me all that you discussed with Uncle Jahangir."

Sanaya told her how she wanted Jahangir to step in and put an end to Sohrab's gambling habits. She explained everything very slowly and at times, repetitively, but not with a lot of detail.

"How was Uncle when you met him?"

"Well, I don't notice much of my general surroundings. But Uncle was slumped when I entered the library. His eyes may have been squinted, and he was having water and wine regularly in equal amounts."

"Was he in some apparent pain?"

"Well, I don't think so. I surely didn't realize if he was. He didn't say anything to that extent," replied Sanaya coldly.

"Where did you go just after the revelation? For a while we were all discussing the matter in the informal sitting room. Then your husband, Sohrab, got upset. Did you go to console him?"

"Darling! First of all, *we* were not discussing the matter. *You* are a family *friend*. The family was discussing the matter for the decision of the old man was impacting only the family members. And no, I don't follow my husband around. I went out for a walk, and the chill helped my mind cool down. Later I retired to my studio, next to my bedroom and was toying with ideas for my art."

Ignoring the acrid part of her reply, Shehnaz pressed on, "Where did you go after meeting Uncle this morning? What did you do?"

"Again, I was in my studio creating art. I spend a lot of time there. I may have been smoking some weed, too. I don't exactly remember."

"How often do you smoke weed? Were you stoned enough to murder uncle?"

Sanaya smirked, gave a small laugh, and replied, "I am never that high. I just smoke enough that it unlocks the creative side of my brain."

"How did your knife come to stick out of Uncle's throat?" asked Shehnaz, now keenly eyeing Sanaya.

Sanaya again smirked, gulped down her whiskey and said, "Darling, if you cannot be a sleuth, then at least act the part. Do you honestly think that I would use my stationary to kill someone?"

"Well, you could have purposely used your stationery to throw everyone off the track?"

"I paint and sketch all around the estate and often leave behind my stationaries, which are then collected by the staff and kept back in my studio. A couple of weeks ago, I was practising art on the lawn outside the library. Anyone could have gotten hold of my knife. Besides, I was never dependent on Uncle's trust monies, nor was he ever able to control me. His life never had a negative bearing on me. On the contrary, we were distantly fond of each other. We never spent too much time together but appreciated each other's virtues and skills from afar."

"Who in the family is not fond of you? Who do you think could have framed you?"

"Well, it is I who am not fond of most of the family members. I am generally a bit reserved and aloof."

Then, after pondering for a while, she continued, "To be honest, Firdaus is shrewd enough to do this. But of late, he has retreated into a shell. He has lost the charisma that he once had. He now prefers his slow life. Anahita could be a suspect. She is a silent worker, and owing to her work, she has mastered the skill of long-term planning. She has the ability to envision the future. But I could not tell you about Anahita's motives. It could be Sohrab, too. With me out of the way, a third of my family wealth would go to him. The rest would go to my children. Or it could be Shirin."

"You think Aunt Shirin would kill her own husband?" remarked Shehnaz, clearly sounding surprised at Sanaya's thinking

"Well, she is not very fond of me. She may not have killed Uncle, but she is sly enough to plant evidence against me."

"You seem to think that everyone has got motives to act against you?"

"Everyone has motives to act against everyone. You need to figure out who had the guts and the impatience to act upon their feelings," said Sanaya as she got up and left. She was an eccentric artist in every way, for it was her brain that decided when her questioning ended.

As Sanaya left, Shehnaz jotted the remarks, "shrewd, cunning, intelligent, reserved, cold yet seems to lack motive", against Sanaya's name.

After Sanaya, it was Farrukh's turn to come. He came in slowly. His face was pale and ashen. It looked like he was in a haze and had probably cried since the incident. He nervously came and stood across Shehnaz.

Only when she beckoned him to sit did he actually take a seat across her. His mannerisms were being acutely noticed. With a straight face and in a solemn tone, he regurgitated everything he had told Jahangir.

Shehnaz listened to him patiently, without giving away any of her feelings. After he had finished, she asked, "Where did you go after meeting Uncle?"

"I went back to my room and was there till Jawahar broke the news to us."

"Did Uncle like the wine holder that you created? Was he appreciative of your work?"

"I... We didn't get a chance to speak about it. He occasionally did appreciate my work, but of late, he seemed very reserved and kept to himself," replied Farrukh in a defensive voice.

"Do you agree with the way he has distributed the wealth? I have seen the wine holder you have made. It is indeed very good, but the materials and the wood look expensive,"

"Well, no, I don't agree with the distribution, and I cannot think of anyone who actually does. In fact, after the revelation, I was so disturbed that I tried to go to my carpentry workshop to cool off and meditate. Carpentry is my way of meditation. But the brutishly chilly weather forced me to come back to the mansion. I then spent time in the library before retiring back to my room," replied Farrukh in a matter–of–fact way. Then he continued, "The things I build are good because I use the best of raw materials and machines. They cost money. I do sell some of them online. But we all could do much better with money in our hands. Not everything in life needs to be scaled into a million-dollar business."

"What did you observe about the crime scene? What do you think caused Uncle's death?"

Hearing the question, Farrukh's eyeballs immediately darted towards the top left corner of his eyes. He pondered a little before replying, "He was stabbed in the throat. Other than that, I cannot tell you much."

"You were the last one to visit him. So, I would ask you again, what did the library look like when you entered?"

"I did not notice anything," came Farrukh's quick reply as he started tapping his leg in the hope of killing time faster.

Shehnaz, couldn't yet contemplate whether Farrukh's nervous pangs were because he was lying or that he was feeling intimidated by the whole situation. Silently observing on, she questioned further, "So nothing was out of place?"

"No."

"What about the lamp that was fallen on the ground? Don't you think it is weird that Uncle was murdered while he was sitting on his armchair, yet when we arrived in the library, the lamp looked like it was toppled over, and his stationary was strewn across the carpet?" pressed Shehnaz while pensively looking at Farrukh.

"I…I did not notice any lamp fallen on the floor."

"Don't you think it was rather convenient for the wine bottle and the glass from which Uncle was drinking to have fallen into the fire?"

"I…I don't know what you are talking about," replied Farrukh, looking visibly confused.

"Diana felt dizzy after looking at uncle's dead body. She swirled, but instead of holding her, you moved out of the way and stepped onto Zubin. He tumbled onto the fallen lamp and pushed the wine bottle and the glass into the fire. Either you stepped onto him purposely, hoping that he would crash into the wine bottle and the glass, or Zubin purposely overreacted. What do you think happened?"

Tears flowed from Farrukh's eyes. His face welled up and flushed pink. His ears turned red. Desperately trying to control his emotions, he replied with a hoarse voice, "You are cooking stories. Diana had a natural reaction, and I had a reflex action to her reaction. Nothing about my actions was premeditated. I am done with this."

Farrukh got up as a mark of revolt.

As he was preparing to leave, Shehnaz said, "I am not saying you killed Uncle Jahangir. But you are hiding something. Who are you trying to protect? You must know that I will get to the truth."

"You are unnecessarily being delusional," replied Farrukh angrily and left in a haste.

While Farrukh's sobs and deep breaths echoed around the formal drawing room, as he left, Shehnaz noted the words, "introvert, shy, lacks confidence or is feigning so, self-aware but is hiding something. He seems to be lying" against Farrukh's name.

Post his interview Farrukh rushed to his mother's art studio. He could hear the loud beats pouring out of her headphones and the slight smell of weed. He softly crept up to her and touched Sanaya on the shoulder. With a start, she turned around and exclaimed, "Jee…kid, you startled me. What's up? Has the newbie sleuth done interviewing you?"

Farrukh understood that his mother used weed to calm herself down. He did not judge her for that. Though, he did wish she found other, better-coping mechanisms like yoga, meditation, or practising Tai Chi. Ignoring the slightly inebriate state of his mother, he emphatically and with a lot of caution stated, "Mum, I want to discuss something about Grand Uncle's death."

For a few moments, Sanaya stared at her son intently, then, for no apparent reason, gave her widest grin and said, "Oh! I am done discussing that morose man and his death. I need some peace and me time to let the steam off. Can we do this some other time, sweetie? I am sure you must have questions about the will and the disbursement of the wealth. But I assure you that you will be taken care of, and you have got nothing to worry about."

"But I am concerned about…" exclaimed Farrukh before realising that his mother had swivelled her chair around and increased the volume of the music she was hearing. She did not even wait for his response or question. Dejectedly and with suppressed fear, Farrukh walked back to his room. He desperately wanted to hide.

After Farrukh left, Bejan came in. Looking at him, Shehnaz said, "I am so tired after trying to decipher everyone's intentions and statements."

"All those who visited Jahangir have given you their statements. Have you been able to deduce anything yet?"

"It is too early to tell. They all seem guilty and conniving enough to have done it. The image I had of them from my childhood days, seems to have long gone. These are some very convoluted adults who seem to have taken their mid-life crisis a bit too seriously," explained the amateur sleuth while turning the pages of her diary.

Unknown to her, Bejan had come into the room to check upon his daughter. He felt scared for her, given the fact that his daughter was intending to find the one person in the house who had already taken a life and may do so again if he or she felt threatened.

Shehnaz closed her eyes and tried to think of the events that had unfolded since her arrival at the Dinshaw estate. The silence of the room was occasionally broken with Bejan, opening the bar cabinet and pouring himself a generous pour of the nutty Oloroso. From the corner of her eye, she questioningly gazed at her father. It was not the most convenient time to raid your host's liquor collection. The situation could have become slightly awkward if one of the family members would have strolled in. But she knew that her father was in shock and was finding ways of coping up with the untimely gruesome death of his friend. In an attempt to include him, she asked, "Who do you think is cold and calculative enough to commit murder?"

Bejan had drifted into a world of his own. The question slightly jolted him, and after some thought, he said, "But I don't think any of them are capable of murder. Why do you think one of them did it?"

With a sigh, Shehnaz replied, "Papa, there were no intruders. There couldn't have been any in this snowstorm. One of them did it. It is extremely apparent."

"Isn't it always the butler?" remarked Bejan while moving towards the armchair next to the fireplace. The strong fragrance of the sherry originating from the fermented Andalusian grapes soothed the nerves of the archaic Barrister. While looking at the pristine white snowfall outside, the cosy fireplace and the rich red sherry in his hands, he seemed to have drifted again in a world of his own. Bejan felt he was too old in life to now be bothered by the travesties of modern times, and the sudden death of his friend had forced him to think about his own life.

Bringing him back from such vague thoughts, Shehnaz suddenly sat up and said, "Thanks for the tip, papa, for I haven't interviewed that very important character. The butler has been observing the whole thing from the beginning." She then got up and rang the intercom bell.

Farrukh Dinshaw

CHAPTER 16

SING A SONG OF SIX PENCE

Thursday, 26th January 2023
4:00 PM – 5:30 PM

A few minutes later, a soft knock, followed by a softer cough, was heard in the room. The omnipresent butler, Jawahar, deftly walked in.

Jawahar silently approached Shehnaz and asked, "Was there something you required, Madam?"

"I want to question you about the events that unfolded before uncle's death."

Jawahar was momentarily taken aback and for a few seconds the feeling showed on his face. Shehnaz caught it and inquired, "You were not expecting me to question you?"

"I knew you would question me, but I never thought that you would get to it so early." Then, regaining his composure, he continued, "Very well, Madam, what would you like to know?"

"Would you like to sit down?" asked Shehnaz while beckoning him to the sofa across her.

"That is something I cannot do."

"Very well. Since when have you been working for the Dinshaws?"

"I have been working for them for the past seven years. I was in a lot of debt. I was a manager in a posh restaurant which Madam would visit whenever she was in Delhi. I was at a very low point in my life when Madam took me under her wing. She gave me enough advance with which I could pay off my debtors and settle my family afresh in Dehradun. As I learnt and took over more responsibilities, she elevated me to the status of the house butler. Their older butler retired of old age, but she called him back and had me trained in all the required skills. Madam Shirin ensured that I was highly paid and she saved my family and me from definite doom. I shall always be in debt of this family, especially Madam Shirin."

"What is your routine?"

"I get up at 4 AM and ensure that the first shift of the staff is ready. The staff starts preparing for the breakfast and starts cleaning the common areas. Everyone in the house takes their morning tea or coffee at different times, so I maintain a chart of their preferences."

"What are their preferences?" interjected Shehnaz.

"The first one was always Jahangir sir at 5 AM, followed by Shirin Madam at 6 AM.

Earlier, both Firdaus sir and Anahita Madam would have their coffees together at 7:30 AM. But, recently, Mr Firdaus has shifted to tea and has it at 7 AM, whereas Anahita Madam continues her earlier routine. Their kids, masters Zubin and Cyrus, have their coffees at 7:30 AM.

Sanaya Madam has her coffee at 8:30 AM, and generally, Sohrab sir tries to match her schedule unless he has to travel to Delhi in relation to his publishing company's work. Master Farrukh has his tea at 6:30 AM, he is an early riser and an early sleeper. Miss Diana gets up at 8:30 AM but is often up till late in the night. On most days, I am able to retire for the day at 10 PM."

"Announcing lunch and dinner, coordinating everyone's schedule and maintaining the estate can be a tiresome job. But let us get back to the pivotal point of our conversation," said Shehnaz and then immediately asked,

"What can you tell me about uncle's death? Where were you at the time of his death?"

"This past week, Jahangir sir had gone to Delhi. After he came back, he seemed anxious. Then a few days ago, he fell off his bicycle, but thankfully did not injure himself and escaped with only a few minor scratches. After that he seemed more disturbed than usual. Quite often he would retire alone to the library and sit there for hours. At times, he would make copious notes, then tear them away and start again. He had increased his daily intake of black coffee to three cups in a day. To cater to his erratic needs, I would mostly sit on the console table outside the library and would retire as late as 12 at night. Over the past week, I have coordinated my activities mostly from the console table, it had become my working desk."

"Did you specifically hear or see anything earlier today?" pressed Shehnaz while taking notes of her own.

"Well, after Madam Sanaya left at 12:01 PM and before Master Farrukh came in at 12:30 PM, at exactly 12:06 PM, I heard the door between the library and Madam Shirin's room open. There may have been a very slight sound that came from the library that sounded like a wail. But Jahangir sir had been wincing since early morning, so it may have been him. A few minutes later, at 12:25 PM, I heard the door between the rooms shut again."

"Is Aunt Shirin a sound sleeper?" inquired Shehnaz, now thinking ahead.

"Yes, she is a deep sleeper. I know what you mean. It is possible that someone could have either climbed through

Madam Shirin's window and accessed the library or came in and left through the bedroom door that opens into the hallway."

"Wouldn't you have seen the person leaving through the main bedroom door?"

"No. I sat facing the main door of the library. My back was towards the other half of the hallway. The hallway is long and carpeted, so if someone was careful enough, they could have tiptoed out," explained the butler earnestly.

"The previous evening, we bumped into each other at the staff staircase when you were carrying the wine bottle for Diana. At the time, I told you that I had heard someone running up the stairs hurriedly, and you agreed. Could you elaborate on that?"

Jawahar was always alert. He did not need to strain his brain to recollect the memory from the previous day, though much had happened since then. He quickly narrated to Shehnaz how he thought he had heard someone move in the wine cellar beside his office but upon inspection, had found no one.

Noting down the points, Shehnaz continued to press on, "When Farrukh left the library, did you notice his expression or his behaviour?"

"At that time, I was talking to one of the junior manservants. He had just informed me that Master Jim was roaming outside the library. I castigated him for opinionizing about the family members and told him to place the logs in the fireplaces around the mansion. Therefore, I did not notice Master Farrukh when he left the library."

"What can you tell me about Jim since his arrival at the mansion?"

"Master Jim is easy going. He does not have any intemperate requirements. The day he arrived, he played tennis with Sohrab sir. After that, he has been spending a lot of time with Miss Diana. I saw them at the archery range and then later going for a walk." Then, after a bit of deliberation and thoughtful consideration, the butler added, "Though they seem to have developed a liking for each other, Miss Diana walked back alone. A while later, I saw Master Jim and Firdaus sir walking back together. For some reason, Firdaus sir seemed a bit disquiet about something, but I cannot really say what it was." Then, looking at Shehnaz's expression, Jawahar added, "The only reason I told you this was because you are investigating the murder of a person whom I held in high regard. I am just trying to help."

Shehnaz's expression eased, and she casually replied, "Thank you, Jawahar. You have been helpful. That shall be all for now. Could you bring in some coffee for me please and tell Jim to wait. I shall call him myself shortly."

"Very well, Madam," replied the butler and softly walked out of the library.

As the butler walked out, Shehnaz scribbled the words, "observant, seems loyal, sharp memory and motive yet unclear" against his name.

Bejan, who had been listening obscurely to this conversation, now removed himself from the shadows and settled on the sofa. After taking a sip of his red wine, he asked Shehnaz, "Now, what do you think about the crime? Have you made any headway?"

"Before I answer your question, I would like to ask you one. What are your thoughts on the crime and the crime scene?"

"I really don't think I can help you there, darling. I am a corporate lawyer, not a criminal one."

"Okay. I will throw an observation at you, let me know what you think."

"Go on then, don't keep an old man waiting," came back Bejan's eager response.

"The death was immediately discovered. Unless they are all lying about having interacted with him. This seems unlikely as even the butler heard him shuffling about and wincing through the morning."

"So, what it connotes is that firstly, it highlights that the murderer did not get a lot of time to calm down or hideaway.

Ideally, the murderer should still be feeling some form of adrenaline rush. And secondly, since the crime was found out almost immediately, the murder does not look premeditated, but rather an act done on impulse," explained Bejan. He then got up and paced around the drawing room silently.

After a few minutes Shehnaz said, "There are a few other aspects about this whole situation that have been irking me. I shall now first go and check the crime scene again and then go downstairs and check upon uncle's body."

Saying as much, Shehnaz got up and went to the library. There, she again intently observed the crime scene. She saw Jahangir's stationary that had been scattered across his table and also on the table by the fire. She then walked to the safe hidden behind the still tilted ballerinas of Edgar Degas. She found the safe to be locked and muttered to herself, "Whoever operated it last knew the numbered combination for it. The safe was not cracked open."

Then she walked up to the fallen lamp. Shehnaz bent down to see the lamp, and then she tried to consciously trip on the lamp, just as Zubin had. Next, she checked the fireplace. From here she collected the burnt bottle and glass of wine, out of which Jahangir had been drinking. While bending over, she observed that some of the wine had spilt onto the carpet, and a tiny amount was also still present on the marble beneath the armchair.

Shehnaz quickly collected the fibres from the carpet and soaked up the wine on the floor on a tiny cotton ball. Shehnaz carefully placed the soaked cotton ball in a small plastic bag. She had used a pair of tweezers to handle everything so as to not contaminate anything.

Her handbag at times, acted as a multipurpose tool kit and had the capability to house almost anything. She generally carried around a small grooming kit, though today, the cotton balls and the tweezers were being used for a very different purpose.

Just before exiting the library, Shehnaz walked to the centre of the room and from there, looked outside towards the lawn and the hedges that covered the archery range. She closed her eyes and imbibed the scene for about thirty seconds, and then, while nodding her head, she left the library.

Next, instead of taking the elevator, she took the stairs to the basement. She walked quickly to the freezer. There, she carefully observed Jahangir's body. She first noticed the puncture wound where the knife had entered his throat. Next, she saw that his fingernails had become opaque. The slight discolouration of hair and apparent hair fall from the eyebrows and the scalp suggested that early signs of *alopecia* had set in. Not wanting to touch the body, Shehnaz used a stick lying nearby to slightly lift Jahangir's shirt. She saw that small oval bumps or *discoid eczema* had started forming on the body's torso. In one of her initial cases as a young beat reporter, she had observed the forensic team on the ground handling the body and connecting the signs and symptoms to possible causes of death. The symptoms of Jahangir's body were something that she had seen before, in a case she had reported on years ago. Now, Shehnaz had an inkling. Throwing the stick on a side, she rushed back to the library.

Once in the library, Shehnaz rang the intercom for the butler.

After about five minutes, the butler came in.

Before he could ask anything, Shehnaz, in a frenzy of excitement, said, "You know I have a theory, but to test it, I need a rat or some kind of a guinea pig."

"I am sorry, madam. I do not follow?"

"I just need some kind of a live animal."

"Well, we only have dogs here. No one keeps any other pet. Would any of them do?"

Shehnaz let out a small grunt before replying, "Desperate times call for a desperate measure. Are any of them very old or very small?"

"We don't have any small dogs, but one of our Australian Koolies is very old."

"In that case, I would like you to get that dog here to the library and give him some food and water."

Fifteen minutes later, the old Koolie was brought in and fed some food. Just as the butler was about to give the Koolie some water, Shehnaz stepped up and dropped the wine-soaked cotton ball into the water. Using the forceps, she ensured the contents of the cotton ball dissolve and mix well with the water.

The next fifteen minutes saw the library be filled with the painful wailing of the old dog as he succumbed to the effect of the ingredients dissolved in his water.

Before Jawahar could react, Shehnaz said, "Take the dog out and preserve his body in storage outside. Maybe in the barn. Do not tell anyone about this. It is now very imperative that I speak to the remaining members of the family."

But before the amateur sleuth could rush back to the formal drawing room, her father, Bejan, called out, "Stop there, what in God's name are you up to. You killed their dog, for Christ's sake. I need to know what's going on in your mind."

Shehnaz stopped in her tracks, turned and slowly walked back to her father. Placing an arm on his shoulder, she explained, "From what I have just observed, there was not a lot of blood that had spilt from Uncle Jahangir's stab wound. From all my experience as a crime reporter, I can confidently say that such a thing can only happen if the injury was inflicted after the person had died. Therefore, someone saw Uncle Jahangir dead and then, as an afterthought or on an impulse, stabbed him with Sanaya's knife. It seems someone deliberately wants to implicate her. So, the stabbing does not seem to have been pre-planned. Someone maliciously stabbed him, not to kill him but to implicate Sanaya."

"How twisted is that, but then what exactly caused Jahangir's death?" inquired Bejan.

"If my theory about the stab wound is correct, which I really do believe it is, then either Uncle Jahangir died of a natural heart attack or his heart attack may have been induced somehow. To me, the latter looks more plausible."

"Why?"

Well, firstly, because when I observed uncle's body, I could see discolouration of his hair, hairs from his scalp and eyebrows had started to fall off, and there were bumps on his torso. These factors hint towards poisoning."

Then, flipping through the pages of her diary and while thinking hard about the facts in front of her, Shehnaz continued, "Secondly, Diana stated that uncle "was salivating a lot, drinking a lot of water, and his hand movements did seem a bit clumsy". Sanaya also added that uncle was slumped when she entered the library. His eyes may have been squinted, and he was having water and wine regularly in equal amounts."

Also, Jawahar had heard someone in the wine cellar that is located next to his office. So, prima facie, it seems as if the wine was poisoned."

"But why would someone poison Jahangir's wine? What do you think is the motive?"

As she was flicking through the pages of her diary, a complex web of occurrences formed in Shehnaz's mind. She had the ability to remember the minutest of details, and now she was trying to join the dots. She closed her eyes and remembered everything that everyone had told her. Then it struck her like a bolt of lightning and Shehnaz softly replied, "Nobody poisoned Jahangir's wine."

"What do you mean? Then it was the knife that killed him?" inquired Bejan, now totally confused.

"No. The wine was poisoned, but that bottle was not meant for Jahangir, it was meant for Sohrab. Someone knew that Diana was about to give her dad a bottle of wine, and the perpetrator induced the poison, believing as much. But nobody could have thought that Sohrab would gift the wine to uncle. This is not a planned murder but rather an accidental one," explained Shehnaz, now sitting up straight on the armchair.

Shehnaz then got up and declared, "I must first speak to all those who are left and then announce my findings to the family."

"Do you think that would be wise? The killer is still amongst us?" inquired Bejan, looking at the extreme blizzard outside and silently cursing the fact that he was trapped in a house with a killer on the loose.

"That would be imperative, father, for the killer has missed their target, and I want the killer to know that I have caught on this mistake," replied Shehnaz with a smile.

She then rung the bell and after a few minutes, when the butler showed up, she requested him to send Jim.

CHAPTER 17

DAME, WHAT MAKES YOUR DUCKS TO DIE?

Thursday, 26th January 2023
5:30 PM – 7:00 PM

Jim walked in with the confidence of a classic middle-class man who has some to lose and some to gain but always exhibits as if he has nothing to lose. The smile on his face even made Shehnaz forget for a second that she was investigating a murder.

Jim realized his place in the world and so sat right in the middle of the sofa, across Shehnaz's armchair.

"So how can I help you?" inquired the young lad with a false smile that only engaged his thick lips but failed to encompass his round face.

To showcase her position, Shehnaz pushed back her shoulders and spoke with a sense of power, "By telling the truth. Start by telling me about your whereabouts at the time of the murder and then about your equation with the Dinshaw family?"

Jim interlaced his fingers as he pondered for a while and then said, "I don't really know when Grand Uncle got murdered.

But this morning, I got up around 8. The weather at that time was cold, yet the estate looked so pleasant that I went for a quick stroll.

A little after breakfast, at around 11 AM, I went to the archery range. Till then, the weather had not turned so dastardly. But just when the snowfall and winds increased, and we had decided to come back in, we were informed about Grand Uncle's death."

Shehnaz noticed that Jim had unconsciously said "we" towards the end of his sentence, indicating that he may have been with someone at the time. But for the moment, she decided not to interrupt and let her suspect speak.

Without much thought and still continuing with his flow, Jim continued, "Well, you already know that my maternal grandmother, Nina, was Grand Aunt Shirin's sister. I have always been coming to this estate since my childhood days. I love it here, away from the hubbub of Mumbai. I get along with everyone. I am an easy person."

I hear that you have been getting along pretty well with Diana. What is your equation with her?"

The few extra blinks of Jim's eyes told Shehnaz that her suspect was feeling a tad bit nervous. As she jotted this down, Jim, still portraying his usual demeanour, stated, "Yes, we have been getting along really well. We have known each other since our childhood days, but this was the first time I actually was able to spend quality time with her. Though we have very different tastes, given the fact that she has always been exposed to the finer aspects of life, whereas I never had such opportunities, we have been able to find a lot of common ground to talk about.

"How so?"

"I make the effort to read and research a lot on varied topics. I talk to a lot of people to understand their perspectives. I am a social butterfly," said Jim, while slightly laughing self-deprecatingly at the last bit.

"Do you feel a sense of lack in your life?"

"No. But I am ambitious," came back Jim's curt reply as his smile faded off. This was the first time he had given a curt reply.

Without wanting to push the topic, yet noting her suspect's antics down in detail, Shehnaz moved forward and asked, "How do you think the other members of the family contemplate about your inclusion in the trust? Has someone said anything to you?"

Regaining his smile, as if he was back in his element, Jim replied, "Other than the death stares I got when Grand Uncle disclosed his intentions, nobody has actually said anything to me. I suspect Uncle Firdaus and Aunt Sanaya don't really care much about my inclusion. They seem to have a lot of money of their own. Diana looked happy for me. I am pretty sure the brothers, Zubin and Cyrus, and their mother, Aunt Anahita, were upset."

Then, while trying to reassure himself, Jim declared a bit too confidently, "But now nobody can do anything about it. The fate of that wealth seems to have been sealed."

"You just said that Diana looked happy for you. She is wealthy and smart. I have been told that you two have been going on long walks around the estate?" Shehnaz's insinuation did not miss Jim. He was a bit healthy, but the extra fat did not suppress his intelligence. Crossing his hands over his chest and after letting out a mild grunt, Jim replied, "Yes, we go for walks around the estate. I am fond of her and have fallen for her. I would not twist words; her wealth is an added bonus, but that is not *why* I am in love with her. I am capable in my own right, you know."

Not forgetting the actual motive of the questioning session, Shehnaz now pulled the conversation towards her investigation and in a stern voice, asked, "I have been informed that from one such walk, Diana returned alone. Later, Firdaus and you were seen coming back together, and Firdaus looked quite disquiet. Do you have anything to say about the matter?"

Jim became a bit defensive as he sat up straight on the sofa and the raised eyebrows and the shaking of his legs demonstrated his inner shaky feeling. While trying to curb his involuntary actions, he replied, "I was discussing a private matter with Uncle Firdaus. It is of no consequence."

"What is this private matter?" asked Shehnaz now more sternly.

"I was giving him a business proposal. I thought it would be profitable for me. But uncle hasn't yet come around to it."

Jim's usage of the word "me" and not "us" while discussing the profitability of the said venture was not missed on Shehnaz. Earlier during their conversation, he had used the word "we" while affirming his location at the time of the murder. Looking at Jim's reaction and body language, the amateur sleuth decided that it was time to turn on the heat. Jogging her memory, she remembered that Jim had a disconcerting look on his face when Diana had mentioned that earlier in the day, she had met Jahangir at 11:15 AM. Shehnaz also remembered that Firdaus had given her a curt reply when they had spoken about Jim. And lastly, by his own admission, Firdaus had revealed that after speaking to Jahangir he had gone towards the archery range.

Culminating the data in her head, Shehnaz decided to attempt a tightrope walk. She lied when she said, "I have been told that after Firdaus met uncle Jahangir, he met you at the archery range. Someone observed the two of you talking from the library. What is cooking between you two?"

A streak of annoyance flashed over Jim's face which he tried hard to hide by feigning confidence and by trying to keep a straight face. Yet his annoyance was apparent in the louder decibel of his voice when he replied, "You are unnecessarily being pushy. There is nothing to know about. I am trying to convince him for a business deal. I just want to make some money. The venture seems profitable to me."

This was the second time Jim's rattled mind mentioned the venture being profitable to him alone.

Shehnaz tried to push the questioning further and probed, "Is the venture going to be profitable only for you?"

It took a while for Jim to contemplate Shehnaz's insinuation, after which he really got flustered. Throwing his hands in the air, he declared, "I really don't know what you are talking about. It is just a simple deal. I really am tired of this interview. If there is nothing more, then I would like to excuse myself."

Jim got up slowly. He was unsure and somewhere believed that Shehnaz was going to shout at him and pull him back down. But Shehnaz did nothing of the sort. She was going to be patient. She still had an ace up her sleeve. As Jim left, Shehnaz wrote the words "opportunistic, eager to please, ambitious, motive- not yet clear" against his name.

A few minutes later, Anahita walked in. Her fair complexion was enhanced by the black silk scarf that she had stylishly knotted around her neck. Her almond eyes darted around the room and imbibed the atmosphere in there. She noticed Bejan, who was quietly standing by the window, hardly making his presence felt in the room. She did not stoop while walking, her well-developed legs and rounded hips ensured that her strides were quick and sure-footed. But unlike Sanaya, Anahita's persona reflected calmness. Though, Shehnaz felt that the calmness in Anahita was not that of a yogi but of a hunter waiting for its prey.

For the first time since her arrival, Shehnaz felt unnerved, and Anahita saw this.

With an attempt to take back control of the room and the situation, Shehnaz began the inquest by asking, "Where were you at the time of the murder?"

"I am an artist in my own right. But unlike Sanaya, I am not quite eccentric. I began my day as usual. After breakfast, I went up to my veranda and covered all my bonsais. I moved some of them inside as the weather turned for the worse. Then I went to my music room and started playing the Piano. That is the time I usually think about a lot of things, including the designs of my upcoming projects. On most days, I have a mimosa to kick my brain into action, at times, I even have a red wine. Though curiously enough, it is Jawahar who serves me my drinks, sharp at 11:30 AM. But this morning, he had it sent up by a manservant, who claimed that the butler was busy."

Shehnaz gave a forced laugh and said, "I saw what you did there. Very slyly, you tried to create doubt in my mind against your butler. But let us move on for now. Tell me, are you happy about your architectural ventures? Are the projects profitable?"

Ignoring Shehnaz's earlier comment, Anahita replied, "Every building or house that I create is one of a kind. I never replicate my style. Plus, I only do the designing work. The clients have to get the projects executed by their own agencies, so it is less of a headache for me. The ventures are profitable, but of late Firdaus has been spending a lot on his theatre company. He even spends a lot of time with the troupe. Last evening, he was complaining about his lead actress throwing some tantrums. He was thinking of firing her, but I don't know much about his ventures. I just wished that he would take his retirement more seriously and spend some more time with me."

"What do you think about the way Uncle decided to disperse the newfound wealth? Do you agree with the allocations?"

"Well, at the moment, we could all foster better with some liquidity. I know Sohrab has started gambling, and his wife refuses to bail him out. Poor guy, I really feel sorry for him. He tries so hard to fit in. Just the other day, he was trying his hand at botany, but he harvested poisonous mushrooms instead of the edible ones. I don't know where his mind is, as nothing seems to last with him. I wonder why he fails at everything he does and what his kids would do now?"

Again, Shehnaz smirked and let out a laugh and said, "I like how you keep slyly implicating others, but when I asked you about your opinion about the disbursement of funds, I really wanted to know about its effect on you and your family. Will you please highlight that?"

"Oh! But it wouldn't have much of an adverse effect on us. We are not exactly hand to mouth."

"Did you know that Jim is trying to get into a business venture with Firdaus?"

"Poor boy, I wonder what has got into him. Though Firdaus did seem quite riled up by Jim's idea. I really don't know what they are planning."

Then, looking intently at Anahita, Shehnaz said, "I am told that some of your Bonsais are poisonous. Why would you grow something like that in your home garden?"

"Life is poisonous. Just like the water surrounding a ship does not drown it, likewise, the poison would have absolutely no effect unless someone is stupid enough to ingest it. Besides, the rare breeds that I grow fetch me a lot of money from collectors around the country. And money has a way to make you dance to its tunes."

Shaking her head, Shehnaz said, "Do you have any opinion about how Uncle Jahangir died?"

"I thought you were playing the sleuth, or are you now tired of acting the part. I really don't care who stuck the knife in his throat, all I know is that he could have been a better human. He created enough trouble while he was alive, and now, even after his death, he has all of us dancing in the web that he created through his trust. When did my life become so convoluted?" replied Anahita while adjusting her butterfly frames. Then, without much of a pause, she continued, "I think what he did with Sohrab and his daughter Diana was unjust. He could have given them an extra bit of the pie. He could have distributed at least half of the newfound wealth amongst us and of that, given a greater share to Sohrab. In fact, after uncle's revelation, I went to Sohrab to tell him of the same."

"And you would have been okay with that?"

"We are not vultures. We are just pressed for liquidity at the moment," explained Anahita.

"You do realize that for someone who does not know how to manage their finances, they would always be in a tight position. Financial astuteness is a necessity, not an option."

"Of course. Why do you think I take five to seven projects a year? It is hard work, you know."

Shehnaz realized that either Anahita had a very blithe personality or that she was feigning it. Her callous, calculative comments made Shehnaz feel that her suspect may be hiding her true self.

Noting her observations down and writing the words "calculative, sympathetic, shrewd" against Anahita's name, she pondered about the characteristics of her suspect.

As Anahita stood up and prepared to leave, Shehnaz got an impulsive gut feeling. One which arose after she wrote the word "sympathetic" for Anahita. And so, immediately, Shehnaz asked, "How bad do you feel for Sohrab? Do you feel bad enough to kill the one person who kept him under a tight leash and implicate the one who also seems to pity him and add to his misery?"

Anahita turned on her heels and responded with some flair and acridity in her voice as she hissed back, "Be careful, Ms. Contractor. Do not let an adventurous zeal sway you. You are alluding towards something that I consider very sick. You are a sleuth, so use facts to guide you. As far as my feelings about Sohrab are concerned, then I would like you to know that I do feel very bad about the situation he has been in. Do you know it was his parents, Nariman and Alaya, who laid the foundations for this family, including the trusts and the various businesses? And look at him now, he is lost like a dog without a bone while everyone praises Firdaus."

Saying as much, Anahita stormed out.

Next came Cyrus. His curly hair, bulging prominent nose, on his lean figure made him look like a typical Parsi gentleman. The large white polka dots on his red shirt and the twinkle in his eyes showcased his mischievous personality. He was tall, but despite his long legs, he walked slowly. He came, casually sat across Shehnaz and waited for her to begin. He was not an eager beaver.

Shehnaz, while trying to study his personality, began with her standard question, "Where were you at the time of the murder?"

"I don't know when Grand Uncle was stabbed. I woke up this morning at my usual time, around 7:30 and had my coffee. After I freshened up, I was going through my applications to various universities to which I have applied to pursue a PhD in economics. Post breakfast I was going over some papers related to our companies and investments."

"You were reviewing the financials of your companies and investments?" interjected Shehnaz.

"Yes."

"Were you reviewing the details of the investments held specifically by your family branch or of the entire Dinshaw family?"

"Both. Since the previous evening, I had been reviewing the projected gains that our family would make after the new trust starts paying its dividends."

"But that trust will only payout five years after both Uncle Jahangir and Aunt Shirin's death. Did you factor that in?"

"Yes. I calculated those five years from the present time, just for ease of calculation."

Shehnaz raised her eyebrows slightly at that remark and purposely ensured that Cyrus saw her reaction. Then she slowly asked, "And you were informed of uncle's death while you were reviewing these papers?"

"Yes. I was in my room when a manservant informed me about the murder," without feeling the silent pressure that his interrogator wanted to put on him.

"Do you agree with Uncle's disbursement of funds and the way he has tied up everything in trusts?"

"I understood Grand Uncle's point of view and the merit of securing the future generations. Though he could have helped everyone a little by distributing the funds partly. But then the money is never enough. Lastly, I don't see the point of mulling over a situation which now cannot be reversed."

"You are eager to branch out? You seek to become an economist to get away from your family and have a routine meticulous life? You see the trust funds only as an added bonus?" said Shehnaz, as she threw a barrage of observations cum questions at Cyrus.

"Yes. All of it is true."

"You seem to be a man of few words. At a young age you have learnt to control yourself. You don't seem to be eager to share your opinions."

"Unless my words have meaning, why must I break the silence."

"Who do you think murdered uncle Jahangir?"

"My guess is as good as yours. Also, Aunt Sanaya keeps leaving her stationary all through the estate, so it could have been anyone of us."

"By implicating everyone, you wish to save everyone. But you see, unlike you, some of them do seem to have had explicit motives to murder." Then, changing the subject in a flash, Shehnaz inquired, "Are you and Zubin alike in everything?"

"No. He is hot-headed and shrewd. Other than the fact that we look the same and have the same built, we are nothing alike. The only advantage is that we can share each other's wardrobes at times, but that is about it. Our tastes and thinking are very different."

"How do you feel about Jim's inclusion into the trust?"

"As I told you earlier, there is no point in discussing about something that we cannot change. These issues are not grave enough for me to murder. Now, will that be all?"

"Not quite. What do you feel about Sohrab and his children? Are you close to them, or is there animosity amongst you all?"

"We are a family. And like every large family, we quarrel and argue, but if we started killing each other over disagreements, we would soon be out of members to kill."

"So, you all disagree and argue a lot?"

"We pick on Farrukh. He is a shy reserved man and so it is fun at times. But the mathematical calculations that he keeps doing for his carpentry has made his mind sharp enough for him to be a silent striker."

Continuing on, Cyrus explained, "Uncle Sohrab himself is always so miserable that we don't need to do anything. His life has been a tightrope walk between following Grand Uncle's orders and trying to impress his wife. He seems to have lost his own identity. Though I don't portray my anger as overtly as Zubin, I, too, am unhappy about Uncle's pity-seeking behaviour. He keeps going to mummy in the guise of being helpless and seeks active appreciation and approval for everything. It is irritating, to say the least." At this point, Shehnaz realized that Cyrus had a very passive-aggressive way of expressing himself. He knew the art and value of restraining himself.

Then, after thinking for a moment, he added, "Diana is intelligent. I wonder if she felt spiteful enough to take such a drastic step, especially after how Grand Uncle side-lined her."

Shehnaz let out a small laugh. With a smile she said, "I see that you have your mother's quality of diplomacy and slyness. So, you clearly have a distaste for your cousins and don't mind seeing them go to jail?"

"Only if they have committed a felony."

"Would you say you hate Sohrab or his family?"

"Oh! No. Hate would be a strong word. This is a big house, and we all like our individuality and privacy."

"I understand. Could you now please send in Zubin."

"Sure," responded Cyrus as he got up and quietly left the room.

As Cyrus walked away, Shehnaz wrote the words, "Diplomatic, cunning, sly, shrewd, intelligent, foresighted and motive not apparent," against his name.

After Cyrus had left the room, Bejan said, "That boy sure does move very silently." His comment made Shehnaz jump for she had forgotten that her father was standing by the window. The astute lawyer had been quietly lingering around just to ensure his daughter's safety.

Before she could respond, Zubin walked in.

Like his brother he too was tall and lean and had curly hair. Like Cyrus, he had piercing blue eyes. His feet stomped as he brisk-walked from the door towards the sofa. Zubin looked like a man who was always in a hurry. His hand unconsciously seemed to have rotated the Bellerby globe, almost as if his brain was working in an overdrive and wanted to constantly do something. Zubin exuded an uneasy persona.

He sat not across to Shehnaz but diagonally to her on an armchair. He sat up straight, and his torso leaned forward as if he was ready to leave.

"Why don't you relax and sit comfortably so that we can have a proper conversation," remarked Shehnaz.

"Let us just get it over with," replied Zubin hotly.

Shehnaz noticed the apparent lack of confidence, which was being covered up by an obvious show of temper.

Unfettered by his antics, Shehnaz started her inquest, "Where were you at the time of the murder?"

"I was in my room studying mummy's past architectural projects."

"Who told you about uncle's death?"

"A manservant informed me. I suspect he had first informed Cyrus and then come over to my room."

"What do you think caused uncle's death?"

"Well…I…I am not a doctor. How could I tell you how he died?" replied Zubin now going a little white in the face.

"So, you don't think it was the knife that killed him?"

"The knife…Why, of course. Yes! It was the knife that killed him," replied Zubin with a sense of relief.

"Why are you so uneasy? Are you trying to hide something?"

"No. I just cannot stand blood and death."

"Ah! But there wasn't a lot of blood spilled from the stab wound."

"I did not notice that; I was in a haze myself."

"You got very upset at Farrukh when he stepped on your foot, and in the process, you tumbled onto the lamp and pushed the wine bottle and the glass into the fire. Do you have something to say about that?"

"That boy Farrukh is so slow in life. He would have merely used me as a cushion. To avoid that I stepped away from him, but he stepped onto my toe and I lost my balance. I don't know why that lamp was thrown across the floor but that caused me to crash into the wine bottle and the glass," explained Zubin in a booming voice with apparent anger flushing his fair face pink.

"Clearly, you are not fond of your cousins, especially Farrukh. What do you feel about Sohrab?"

If the Renaissance masters ever wanted to use the right shade of crimson red, they could have lifted the colour off from

Zubin's cheeks. That's how much they had flushed with anger. In a fit of rage with apparent irritation in his voice, he replied, "For no evident reason mummy feels for him. He keeps acting pitiful around her and has of late, even taken up botany. He is absolutely useless at everything that he does. The previous day, when Grand Uncle had revealed his plans about his newfound wealth and had castigated Uncle Sohrab about his lifestyle choices, mummy had gone and consoled him."

"How do you know that Anahita went to console Sohrab?"

"Because I saw the lift carrying my mother go to the second floor. I am not so dumb. I understand what is going on."

"Why doesn't Sanaya console Sohrab?"

"Because she is too busy chiding him about his inabilities and rubbing the fact that she is independent into his face."

"Judging by your anger and irritation, do you believe that Sohrab is trying to woo your mother?"

"I don't know, and I don't care. But I know for a fact that my mother wouldn't ever be impressed by a failure," replied Zubin while gritting his teeth and rolling his eyes.

Zubin had now stood up. The anger had made his body temperature so hot that his skin crawled. He no longer was able to sit still.

"How are relations between your parents? Do they fight, or are they in love?"

"That is none of your business."

"When I am investigating a murder, everything is my business. So please answer the question."

"They are a healthy couple. And like all couples, they love each other and at times fight with each other." Then, throwing his hands in the air, Zubin rhetorically asked, "So what? What's the big deal about it, and how is their relation relevant anyway?"

To throw him off the track, Shehnaz softly responded, "You are right. It is not relevant. I am sorry I pried into your personal life."

Hearing as much, Zubin now turned and started walking back.

Hardly, he had taken a few steps when Shehnaz loudly stated, "You know, I asked your mother about this, and she vehemently rejected having any feelings for Sohrab. How does that make you feel?"

The colour from Zubin's face drained. His anger subsided. He turned around and, with a know-it-all attitude, responded, "Isn't that what I just told you? Uncle Sohrab is a failure." Then, in a jiffy, he turned and started to leave the formal drawing room.

But just as he had taken a few more steps, Shehnaz pressed on, "The night uncle revealed his plans, you were having wine in your room. Do you often drink alone? I know of this as the manservant who delivered you the bottle told me the same." "Such a big mansion, yet we get no privacy. The helpers are everywhere. Yes, I was drinking wine, as I was feeling very cold. I had ventured out before the grand revelation, and the cold set inside my body. I was shivering," muttered Zubin as he left the room.

Meanwhile, Shehnaz noted the words "hot-headed, immature, impulsive, self-centred, egoistic and narcissist, yet motive is unclear" against his name.

After studying her notes thoroughly, she called in the butler. Jawahar announced his presence with his usual soft cough. Looking up from her diary, this was the first time Shehnaz properly imbibed the butler's personality. She noted his crisp black suit, starched white shirt with old-style barrel cuffs and his clean-shaven face. She realized that the butler, too, was made to look rich, almost as a reflection of the pomp and flamboyance of the Dinshaws' existence on Earth. She wondered if the butler's condition was a way to showcase the family's old money. Pushing aside her thoughts, she told Jawahar, "Please tell everyone to gather here."

"Very well, madam," came the quick response.

As the butler walked out, Shehnaz couldn't help but appreciate his deftness. He had been quick to provide the whereabouts of every staff member, most of whom could be seen on the CCTV cameras working in the kitchens. They also had strong alibis while being present elsewhere on the estate. Therefore, other than the butler, all the general staff had been completely ruled out as suspects by Shehnaz.

Jim

CHAPTER 18

Can I get there by candle light?

Thursday, 26th January 2023
7:00 PM – 8:00 PM

Bejan Contractor, who had been silently standing in one corner and was now on his second glass of wine, brooded on his life and journey with Jahangir. The bleak weather outside made him reflect at the fleeting nature of life. He thought about all that Jahangir had achieved over the years, the plans that he had made not so long ago for the future of his family and how in a split second, everything in the house had changed. As the thoughts raced through his mind, people started slowly trickling into the formal drawing room.

Shehnaz had made everyone come to her to highlight the fact that she was still in charge of the situation. Zubin and Cyrus arrived together. Although Cyrus silently sat on the sofa, Zubin created a scuffle. His persona ensured that his presence was felt in the room. As he plopped himself on the sofa, he remarked, "Why have you called us all back? I thought we had all given our statements."

Before Shehnaz could respond, Jim and Diana arrived and seated themselves together on the sofa. Although a lot many seats were clearly available in the room, the young lovebirds chose to stick together, as if they were physically clinging onto their feelings, which would otherwise run away.

"Patience is a virtue that you could do well with, Zubin," remarked Shehnaz to his earlier comment.

In the next five minutes, Sanaya and Farrukh came in. Then Sohrab trickled in and he was quickly followed by Anahita. Then Shirin wobbled in, and finally Firdaus came and sat in the armchair across Shehnaz. Jawahar, too, was told to remain in the room.

Everyone's eyes darted from one to the other. They all were trying to assess the level of guilt in each other and make themselves feel secure. Shehnaz noticed this uneasiness amongst the attendees.

Finally breaking the silence, she said, "You know life is a series of comedies and tragedies. In fact, for God, some tragedies may also play out like comedies as he sees the best laid plans of us mere humans go for a toss. I am sure God must be enjoying seeing the outcome of the current turn of events."

"Are you trying to mock us at our time of grief?" inquired Anahita.

"Oh, please! Do not feign your emotions. Throughout the interviews that I have just conducted, everyone has tried to hide some fact. Some tried to mislead me by showing anger and irritation, while some others tried by causally placing the blame on others," explained Shehnaz, now looking directly at Anahita.

"But after a thorough analysis, I have now come to a definitive conclusion."

"So, you know who stabbed uncle?" inquired Firdaus

Ignoring the interjection, Shehnaz continued, "Uncle Jahangir's death was not a classic murder." As soon as Shehnaz made the statement, whispers and opinions started floating around the room.

Diana inquired, "But then what about the knife that was sticking out of his throat."

Sanaya asked, "But then how did he die?"

"Please settle down and allow me to explain," said Shehnaz in a little raised voice. A few seconds later, the murmurs died down and everyone intently looked at the young sleuth.

Shehnaz continued, "I have come to understand that Uncle Jahangir was not the intended target. Therefore, his death is an accidental murder."

Again, the room erupted, and questions started floating in. This time, Firdaus asked, "But then, who was the intended target? And how exactly can someone stick a knife into the wrong person?"

"The knife!" said Shehnaz in a loud, commanding voice and the commotion again died down, allowing her to continue, "was not the murder weapon. Uncle died of poisoning. I examined his body. The signs indicate poisoning. I even collected a sample of the poison from the broken wine glass and bottle. Not all of it was destroyed by fire. I put the same wine in one of your dog's food. The dog is dead," explained Shehnaz coldly as she gazed intently at Farrukh. The young boy felt uncomfortable and purposely looked away.

Shehnaz then continued, "However, the poison in the wine was meant for Sohrab. The killer did not know that Sohrab would offer the same wine as a gift to uncle Jahangir."

"Then what about my knife?" inquired Sanaya.

"The victim was stabbed after he had died. The lack of blood from the stab wound, along with my now-tested theory of poison, proves as much."

"So, someone wanted to implicate me. I am clearly innocent," explained Sanaya with a sense of obvious relief in her voice.

"Not quite. You may have had poisoned your husband's wine, and after realizing your mistake, you may have purposely stabbed Uncle Jahangir to throw us off your trail."

Sanaya just shook her head and kept mum.

"I haven't yet figured out who wanted to kill Sohrab. But I shall soon arrive at that, too. The killer is still amongst us, and I have purposely exposed the flaw in the plan. The killer should realize that we are not far behind."

"So, my life is still in danger?" inquired Sohrab, visibly shaken.

"Unless you were the one who poisoned the wine, of which there could be a strong possibility as you yourself never had a sip from it, you should feel scared.

In a fit of anger caused by a culmination of fear and irritation arising out of Shehnaz's comments, Sohrab got up and left the room.

Zubin, who until now had been quietly observing the snowfall outside and had thus retreated into obscurity by sitting aloof in a corner by the large ornate French windows, suddenly turned his red face around and exclaimed, "Diana! You had been doing some business with Grand Uncle. He then side-lined you. You were the one who gave Uncle Sohrab the wine bottle, which he then gifted to Grand Uncle Jahangir. Did you tamper with the wine?"

Zubin's face flushed bright pink now. Anger was visible in the tone of his voice. The room, which, till now, was silent not in the memory of the departed but for the sheer reason of no one wanting to get into an altercation, now broke into pandemonium.

From the other side, Jim loudly expressed his disapproval by stating, "Don't even dignify his questions by replying, Diana. Zubin is unnecessarily hurling baseless accusations. When two people work together, there are bound to be disagreements between them. Grand Uncle had his perspective, and Diana had hers, that does not mean that either was bloodthirsty for the other."

To this, Cyrus replied, "There is a point in Zubin's analysis, you know. There is circumstantial evidence against Diana."

Diana opened her mouth to respond, but Farrukh put his hand on hers to stop her and sternly replied, "You brothers always pick on us. A tragedy has occurred in the family. We must stand together. Besides, Ms. Shehnaz may have deduced the entire situation incorrectly. It is possible, in fact, that Grand Uncle was indeed stabbed, so stop throwing baseless accusations around."

Shehnaz shook her head and kept mum, for she did not want to retort to all the opinions that were flying around the room like a headless chicken in an Asian market.

Anahita, who had been flipping through the pages of a coffee table book in one corner of the room, now looked up. Her oversized Chanel butterfly eyeglasses made her look like a school principal.

With a commanding voice, she said, "Enough! I don't want either of you boys throwing around any wild ideas or theories. You will all sit silently in the room." Then, grinding her teeth slightly, she continued, "Get your idle minds to do something. We already have an adult playing sleuth in the house, we don't want anyone else playing as her assistant." In a jiffy, the room quietened; no one even whispered. Anahita slowly delved back into her book.

Slowly and steadily, everyone left the room. Shirin waddled a bit towards the door, then turned around and, looking at the butler, exclaimed, "Could you fix me a hot toddy? The winds are blowing with such fury that they rattle my windows and their continuous howl cause a ruckus, which does not let me sleep. I think the toddy should work wonders."

"Very well, ma'am," replied the butler and retired from the room as Shirin waddled away.

"What do you think will happen now?" inquired Bejan, looking at the pristine yet thick snowstorm outside. The snowfall was so heavy that it looked like the weather Gods had decided to put a shroud over Jahangir's body.

"Well, not another murder, I hope," replied Shehnaz, with quivering lips, as she silently observed Shirin waddle away.

Sorabh Dinshaw

CHAPTER 19

Some like it hot

Thursday, 26th January 2023
8:00 PM – 9:30 PM

The clock struck eight. The snowstorm continued to blow heavily and the howling wind made everyone's hair rise. Everyone had left the formal drawing room and while some had retired back to their rooms, some others were lingering around.

Sanaya, ever aloof, had retreated into her studio. She lit another joint and inhaled the pure, finely cut weed of the mountains. The quick successive drags ensured that her mind became numb to the problems around her. With the effect kicking in, she picked up her paintbrushes and began splashing around the canvas. The strokes of deep red seemed to reflect her mental state of agony and anger.

Her visibly shaken husband, Sohrab, had chosen to remain in areas that were frequented by the public. Hence, he did not retire back to his room, instead, he lingered around the library and the informal sitting areas. Remaining in solitude was not an option for him. His uneasiness was not missed upon by

Anahita. She casually walked up to him and offered him a glass of a single malt.

Sohrab quickly gulped the double shot and said, "You know, ideally, I should be feeling scared, but weirdly, all I am feeling is a sense of calm."

"Don't worry, Sohrab. Hopefully, the police will be here soon, and this matter would be behind us all."

Sohrab did not reply, just nodded his head. Whether he understood her point of view or he was contemplating something else, Anahita could not point out at the moment.

On the first floor, Jim had entered Firdaus's unit. Through his personal sitting room, he had marched in unannounced into his bedroom.

"Hello uncle, I hope you have given some considerable thought to my proposal," inquired Jim with a sense of urgency in his voice.

Firdaus, who had been trying to fix his phone network by continuously restarting his device, was so engrossed in the activity that he had not noticed the intrusion into his privacy. But when the unmistakable squeaky voice fell on his ears, Firdaus looked up angrily and yelled, "What are you doing here. How dare you barge into my room like that? You think I really care about what you think you know? Go tell the world, let's see if anyone cares?"

Firdaus's voice boomed and although his speech couldn't be heard word for word downstairs, yet it did become apparent that Firdaus was screaming at someone.

Shehnaz, who, till now, was silently listening to Sohrab and Anahita's discussion, got up and made an instant move towards the first floor. Looking at her, they both too got up and started towards the point of action.

The three of them hurriedly tumbled one after the other, like small kids eager to see some performance.

Looking at them all, Firdaus's face turned even a brighter shade of red and he threw his phone on his bed. But before he could say anything, Shehnaz said, "What happened? I hope all is well?

"Nothing, we were just having a casual discussion about possible business ventures," replied Jim.

"I think we are all shaken up and are feeling a bit flustered. We must all go down," suggested Shehnaz.

"Well, then Jim shouldn't keep pestering my husband," pointed Anahita coldly.

"I am not pestering him. I am just trying to save him from a huge loss," replied Jim as he stepped out of the room, swaying his head in irritation. Sohrab, Anahita and Shehnaz all heard Firdaus grunt and saw the scowl on his face.

"Come. Let's have a drink together," suggested Shehnaz, beckoning Firdaus.

Sohrab, who had just been a silent observer of the entire show, moved out of the room. Firdaus followed him. Shehnaz was about to follow Firdaus when she turned to look for Anahita. She saw Anahita looking at the screen of Firdaus's phone. Colour from her face seemed to have been wiped out. As her hand scrolled through the phone screen, Anahita's face looked paler and turned yellow.

"Are you not coming?" probed Shehnaz with a hint of concern in her voice.

"You go ahead. I have some work," mumbled Anahita without looking up and continued scrolling through the phone.

Shehnaz looked at Anahita intently for a minute, then silently walked out of the room. As she was moving towards the lift, she heard Diana's voice from the floor above.

Diana vehemently stated, "I am not being able to shake off the feeling of being cheated and, in a way, humiliated. You know Farrukh, for so many years, I worked diligently under Grand Uncle. I accomplished everything that he told me to do. Yet, in the end, he never understood me. First, he shut down our finance firm, then he tied all the wealth in trusts, and lastly, the distribution was also done equally between ours and Firdaus uncle's family. Sometimes I feel, I should have curated my own path and not given so many years of my life to such a man."

"But you learnt a lot under him," replied Farrukh.

"Yes, but see how frustrated I am today. Oh! How I wish I could go back in time and change so many of my decisions," sighed Diana.

"I just feel bad for father and how he is routinely treated," added Farrukh.

The elevator bell dinged, and Shehnaz quietly got in. When she reached the ground floor, she found Jim and Sohrab in the informal dining room having a light-hearted conversation.

Shehnaz was now feeling tired from the day, so she poured some vodka on crushed ice, added a slice of green chilli and some lemon juice in her drink and swirling the glass around, she proceeded towards the formal drawing room. Just as she was about to push the door open, the door was pulled from inside, and Firdaus stepped out. He looked like he had had a few drinks in quick succession and stumbled out as he was tipsy. Loosely holding his own whisky glass in one hand and an antique sixteenth-century flintlock pistol in another, Firdaus angrily wobbled out of the formal drawing room.

"Where are you going?"

"To my sitting room. I am going to write a letter to our lawyers and set some things straight."

"Why do you have an archaic pistol in your hand?"

"I will bludgeon that boy Jim with the pistol's handle if he tries to unnerve me again," replied Firdaus hotly and then staggered off as his legs tottered unsteadily.

Ignoring Firdaus, Shehnaz, with apparent tiredness, stepped inside the formal drawing room. Her hand tightly held the vodka glass from its bottom, subconsciously indicating her cautious nature. She settled near the fireplace, which had been rekindled. The snowstorm outside had picked up its pace and the fast-flowing wind ensured that outside the mansion, visibility wasn't beyond a few feet. The heat from the fireplace opened up the wooden furniture and a heavy woody cum smoky aroma filled the room.

The spirit kicked in and Shehnaz felt her nerves calming down. Yet her mind kept trying to join the dots and find the apparent loophole. She kept thinking about the chronology of events and her mind raced to scrutinize everything that it had learnt over the course of the interviews. After a few large sips, her mind went into an overdrive. In a flash, she recollected everything Farrukh had told her. But before she could act upon her gut feel, Bejan walked back into the room. He, almost as a reflex, poured some wine for himself.

Then, after quietly moving back to his favourite spot by the window and while looking out at the massive snowfall, he softly stated, "Darling, you say that Jahangir was poisoned, but if that were the case, wouldn't his wine's odour, colour and taste have changed? And Jahangir had a flair for quality. He was a self-proclaimed connoisseur. Then how come he did not notice anything odd in his wine."

Hearing the words and realizing their importance, Shehnaz sat up with a start. She could feel the slight buzz of her alcohol waning off as her brain kicked into action. Drawing from her vast experience as a crime reporter and now as an editor, she exclaimed, "You are right Father. I had been wondering if Anahita's rare bonsai flowers or the poisonous mushrooms that Sohrab had found in the greenhouse were used to murder Jahangir. But clearly those substances would have altered the wine greatly. Only very spicy and rich food could have camouflaged the bitter taste and the foul odour of these poisons. And uncle had been consuming a very controlled diet of fruits, light club sandwiches and sautéed vegetables."

"Yet you have proven that Jahangir was poisoned through his wine. How? How can a poison be odourless and tasteless?" inquired Bejan with a perfect bamboozled expression on his face, which was highlighted by his round eyes popping out of their sockets and his thick eyebrows climbing up his forehead.

Shehnaz got up and paced around the room in silence. She gulped down her vodka and poured herself another one. The pang of the green chillies in her drink stimulated her mind even more. She tried to surf the internet for answers, but the networks were down. Walking around the grand drawing room, her eyes spotted some old parchments displayed in a glass casing. Shehnaz noticed that the paper had a slight greenish tinge to it.

She muttered, "Maybe the parchments were earlier exposed to dampness. There is an obvious suggestion of moss being formed on them." The moment Shehnaz had uttered these words and her brain pictured the green moss, she knew which poison had been used. The colour green had triggered her memory and reminded her of the poison which was named after the Greek word for a "green twig." Nodding her head, Shehnaz approached her father and softly said, "The killer is a very intelligent person. A very old poison, also called as the "inheritance powder or the poisoner's poison," has been used to commit this crime."

"What is its name?"

"Thallium. It's odourless, colourless and tasteless. It is often used as a rat poison, and the killer could have easily found a bottle of it in the garden shed or around the greenhouse."

"You seem to have cracked the means with which the crime was committed or the murder weapon. Now you need to figure out the motive and thus highlight the killer."

"I believe the answer lies in the characteristics of these people. I wonder if my hunch is correct? Was Uncle Jahangir's an accidental murder or was he the actual intended target? If he was not the target, then who is annoyed enough with Sohrab to have tried to kill him and at the same time stupid enough to have missed their target. Clearly, the killer does not seem to be a thorough planner.

"Earlier, you had gone back to the library. What did you learn from the murder site?" egged Bejan while trying his best to probe his daughter's brain cells.

Shehnaz hummed a little in an attempt to jog her memory. A lot had been going on since her arrival at the estate, and it was proving a daunting task for her brain to keep track of all the information that she had assimilated either by her own observation or by virtue of being told via the interviews that she had conducted. After stressing on her mind, Shehnaz confidently replied, "You know the one thing that has been tingling my mind is the incident when Zubin tripped over the lamp and pushed the wine glass and bottle into the fire. The entire sequence from the time when Diana felt dizzy and swayed has been playing in my mind frame by frame. And for that particular reason, I tried to trip over the lamp myself."

Bejan raised his eyebrows suspiciously and quizzed, "And pray tell what did you learn by conducting this thorough exercise?"

"What I learnt was that it took me a lot of effort to reach the wine bottle after tumbling over the lamp. Though Zubin is taller than me and has longer arms. But I wonder if the force from Farrukh was hard enough for him to have actually thrown the wine bottle into the fire or did Zubin put in some extra effort on his own. My mind finds both of them guilty."

Then, looking out at the thick yet beautiful white snow falling from the heavens above, Shehnaz's brain reminded her of another important observation, which she was quick to voice out, "I also stood in the middle of the library, a little away from the central mantelpiece above the fireplace. Looking out towards the archery range from there, I realized if looked from a particular angle, one can observe the people in the archery range but from most other angles, one's view would be obscured by the hedges."

CHAPTER 20

When she hollers

Thursday, 26th January 2023
9:30 PM – 11:00 PM

While the father-daughter duo was discussing their suspicions and observations, loud argumentative voices were faintly heard. It was clear that two people had fought, and the shrill in one of the voices highlighted the fact that somewhere in the house, a woman seemed very upset.

The apparent anger in the woman's voice made Shehnaz feel as if solving the murder was now the least of her problems. She thought that probably someone had upset Sanaya, and she would soon bury someone alive. Thinking as much she stepped out of the formal drawing room and was closely followed by her father, Bejan. Bejan found it safer to remain a bit behind owing to the continuous verbose and angry sentences spoken by the female.

As Shehnaz ventured ahead into the hallway, she realized that it was Anahita who had been shouting. Straining her ears, a bit, she realized that the meek defensive voice was of Firdaus.

A few minutes later, Firdaus came storming down and hurriedly entered the informal sitting room. He was still tipsy, and his feet wobbled a bit. His ears were red, and his cheeks were drained of colour. While grinding his teeth, he held Jim by his collar. Before the esteemed guest could comprehend the situation, let alone object, he was dragged to the formal drawing room.

Shehnaz and Bejan, who had now moved into the informal drawing room, looked on with dumbfounded expression. For Shehnaz, the day didn't seem to end. Sohrab, who had been venting out his own problems to Jim, looked equally lost.

From the formal drawing room across the hallway, Shehnaz could hear Firdaus yelling, "Are you happy now? You have accomplished what you wanted?" Then, in a sneering voice, she heard him continue, "You can now forget about your beloved business venture." After that, Firdaus's voice dropped, and Shehnaz could not hear any more of their conversation.

A few minutes later, Jim came back to the informal sitting room. His face was red, and though his face did not reflect any shame that he might be feeling, it surely did reflect a feeling of loss that one would face when losing out on money at a business venture.

Then, Anahita came down the stairs yelling at no one in particular, but everyone understood that Firdaus was the intended target.

"You are an insensitive fool. You have ruined everything for me. Don't you feel any responsibility towards your children? How could you have been such a selfish prick?"

Continuing her monologue, Anahita entered the formal drawing room, and the argument between Firdaus and her began again.

Following the uncommon commotion and the raised voices, the younger generation of the Dinshaw family, Diana, Farrukh, Zubin and Cyrus all came down. They were all dressed in their night suits and looked visibly sleepy with bloodshot, swollen eyes.

Sanaya was nowhere to be seen.

Everyone except the arguing couple settled in the informal sitting room as if they had gathered to see a late-night matinee show.

"Where is Sanaya?" inquired Shehnaz.

"She is in her studio. I saw the light coming from under the door and heard mummy moving about," replied Farrukh earnestly. Diana, too had seen where her mother was, but she was not too eager to make any more statements.

A while later, everyone heard the door to the formal drawing room open and Firdaus storming out as best he could, given that he was still tipsy and now had another glass of whisky in his hand. It seemed he had developed an urgent need to douse his sorrows.

Anahita, instead of going back to her room, went to the informal sitting room and angrily hissed at Jim, "You are such a low life. You think you can blackmail your way to being rich. We welcome you into our home, treat you respectfully and this is how you behave? You should be ashamed of yourself. How low are your morals?"

"Oh, aunt, please. I understand that you are upset, but there is no point in venting it out on Jim. You and Uncle Firdaus have hoarded most of the family wealth for yourselves. Yet you talk about morals?" expressed Diana in an irritated voice. It was out of character for her to behave like that and speak so harshly, but given the developments of the past few days and Anahita's tone, she could no longer contain her agitation.

Jim now found a voice and replied defensively, "I was just trying to make some money and capitalize on the opportunity in front of me. It was uncle who had been misbehaving." Saying as much Jim walked out of the room.

But Sohrab, shaking his head and looking straight at his daughter, spoke in a stern voice, "Diana, you must not speak to Anahita like that. It wasn't her who has tried to control my life nor has she been responsible for my failures. Yes, it is true that my parents laid the foundation for the various family businesses and trust and from which Firdaus has gained undue advantage, but that isn't Anahita's fault. All she is saying is that as our guest Jim should have behaved in a more rational way. Though I still don't understand what was he blackmailing Firdaus for?"

Anahita just shook her head in disgust and left the room. After she left, Jim re-entered the room and sat in one corner and started talking in hushed tones to Diana. Diana was feeling overwhelmed, she also felt shocked as to why her father castigated her and had taken her aunt, Anahita's side.

A few minutes later, not wanting to hear anymore of Jim's frivolous comforting statements, Diana got up and stormed out of the room.

During this time, in the other corner of the room, Zubin had started accusing Sohrab. In an angry voice he yelled, "You are unnecessarily trying to gain sympathy from mummy. What are you playing at? It seems you are the reason of rift between my parents."

Hearing her son's accusations and rude tone, Anahita re-entered the room and now started scolding Zubin. She hissed in anger and said, "No, he is not the reason for the rift between Firdaus and I. Your anger gets the better of you. You don't realize what you say and do when you are angry. You need to get a grip on yourself. Show a therapist if you must. You imagine things and then boil up inside. Your behaviour is going to be detrimental for you."

While Anahita was scolding her son, Sohrab left the room.

Shehnaz had been observing the entire commotion and her head now swirled as the family members quarrelled with each other. It seemed that everyone had their own agenda and was upset about something.

Gazing around the room and imbibing all the ruckus, Shehnaz noticed Farrukh sitting quietly in a corner by the window. His face was not even turned towards the room where all the action was. He seemed to have been merely enjoying the heavy snowfall that was shrouding the entire estate in a thick white veil. His presence caught Shehnaz by surprise. It was almost as if he had been hiding in plain sight. A slight pang of irritation hit Shehnaz, and she cursed herself for missing out on the clandestine presence of Farrukh and she cursed Farrukh for being such a sly silent personality. Walking up to him, she tapped him on his shoulder and sat beside the young adult.

Then, in a soft voice Shehnaz said, "I know you lied in your interrogation. I know you are hiding something. You were the last person to have seen uncle Jahangir alive. Who are you trying to protect?"

"I…I am not protecting anyone. I told you this earlier also. You seem to have some misconceptions. I have got nothing to hide." Replied Farrukh in a quivering voice.

"Your mother, Sanaya, visited uncle before you. Is that whom you are trying to protect? Does this mean that your Grand Uncle was dead when you entered the room? Did he mean nothing to you?"

Again, tears started welling up in Farrukh's eyes, and he shook as he muttered, "You don't understand. My mother is innocent. She is not the temperamental being everyone points her out to be. She is a very loving and caring person. She did not stab Grand Uncle."

"Darling, I know she did not stab Grand Uncle. But did she spike the wine with the intention of killing your father?"

Farrukh closed his eyes, then, with a hint of irritation, replied, "My mother would never do something like that. She loves father dearly. If you are a sleuth, then you would understand the importance of peeling the layers of the characteristics of a person in order to understand that person better. My mother is an established and recognized artist. She has an inflated ego and an air of arrogance around her. Moreover, she comes from money. Even a reasonably established artist in our world is eccentric, then why is her eccentricity the only highlight of her personality. She is much more than what is projected about her."

"Very interesting. So, you are confirming that when you entered the room, your Grand Uncle was already dead, and someone had already stuck a knife in his throat? The shock of that scene is what made you suddenly move back, causing the lamp to fall on the carpet?"

"I...I don't know what you are talking about," explained Farrukh as the colour drained out of his face and tears started flowing out of his eyes. As Farrukh got up to leave, Shehnaz caught his hand in irritation and said, "For God's sake, kid, I am trying to solve a heinous crime here. At least nod your head if you can't muster up the strength to affirm my views."

All Farrukh could muster up to do was the great Indian head wobble, wherein he wobbled his head diagonally from side to side. In the general Indian society, the interpretation of this head wobble is deciphered by the person who is listening to the conversation by analysing the context and by looking into the eyes of the speaker simultaneously. However, here Shehnaz was in a fix, for Farrukh quickly ran away, and his tears-filled red eyes were not in a state to emote anything further. Now, just by analysing Farrukh's earlier reply, she would have to deduce the context of his head wobble.

Shaking her own head, Shehnaz went and sat on the sofa. That is when she saw Sohrab and his wife, Sanaya, walk in hand-in-hand as if they were entering a prestigious red-carpet event.

Her eyebrows shot up, and her jaw fell as she saw the scene unfold in front of her. In her mind, Shehnaz wondered if the antics of the family would ever stop. She muttered under her breath, "Don't they get tired?"

Sanaya looked visibly stoned, and Shehnaz could smell weed off her, despite standing at a considerable distance. Sohrab was sweating and the heat reflected on his face for it had turned red. With some difficulty, he half nudged-half dragged Sanaya to the nearest sofa and planted her there.

Looking at Shehnaz's puzzled expression, Sohrab explained, "I found her in the pantry, gorging on some chocolate chip cookies. All this weed makes her feel hungry at odd times." Shehnaz could see crumbs of the cookies sticking to Sanaya's red woollen sweater and could smell chocolate mixed with weed on her breath. Oddly enough, she also noticed Sanaya holding onto an empty packet of chips.

"You all do realize that a murder has been committed in this house. This behaviour is very unbecoming," expressed Shehnaz while disapprovingly shaking her head. Then she rang for the butler, who till now had been sitting outside and hearing everything silently. He was not allowed to form opinions and was expected to ignore all the idiosyncrasies of the family members. He announced his presence by his usual cough, to which Shehnaz instantly replied, "Could you please arrange some green tea for Sanaya. It would help to flush out the intoxicants from her body. At least those that have been infused by the weed."

The butler nodded silently and left.

Shehnaz then sat on the sofa, put her head back and tried to relax. Sohrab walked to the bar cabinet and poured himself an elixir of golden liquid brewed and aged in the highlands of Scotland.

CHAPTER 21

Stick, stock, stone dead!

Thursday, 26th January 2023
Sometime between 10:00 & 11:00 PM

Firdaus had thoroughly scolded Jim but had gotten it back from his wife at double the intensity. He had then stumbled angrily out of the formal drawing room. The fact that he was drunk and had been slurring and mumbling did not help. He unconsciously reached the billiards room. His tired and frustrated mind started arranging the billiard balls. He continuously fumbled with the cue stick and was hardly able to hit any ball with any proper force. After a few desperate attempts, his frustration mounted up even more, and he gave up and sat in a corner.

Thoughts about his life journey and all the wrong decisions that he had taken started playing on his mind. Firdaus put his head back on the sofa and stared at the ceiling. He then closed his eyes. A few moments later, a voice called out his name and Firdaus opened his eyes. His vision was blurred, but he recognized the voice. In his drunk state, Firdaus slurred, "You…you never understood…"

At that very moment, Firdaus saw a pair of hands enveloping his face with a plastic bag. He tried to struggle, but his sluggish brain was not exactly being efficient in sending the correct signals to his body parts. His hands moved but in the wrong direction and too slowly. It was easy for the attacker to hold him down. His blood pressure started rising, and he could feel his heart working overtime as it pumped out more blood in anxiety and fear. Survival instinct kicked in, and his legs started kicking, too. But the alcohol running through his veins disrupted the proper instructions being dispatched by the brain. As he tried to desperately gasp for air and forcefully breathe, the plastic got stuffed in his mouth and nose, choking him further. The oxygen present in his blood cells and lungs started getting consumed rapidly. The lack of oxygen increased the level of carbonic acid in the brain. This made his brain even more foggy. Firdaus's feeble attempts to struggle put him into a death spiral. Energy and life started getting sucked out of his body. Flashes of life played in front of his eyes as his regrets bore heavy on his mind. A few quick minutes later, the level of carbonic acid in the body reached to such high amounts that the PH level of the blood started dropping. Finally, synapses, the brain structures that allow the neurons to transmit electrical and chemical signals to other neurons, stopped working. Firdaus's mind became unconscious as his blood pressure and heart rate began to drop. The reflex of his body that triggered breathing also stopped. His body went slack. In the next few minutes, the neurons of his brain start to die, and a few seconds later, there are not enough live neurons left to resume life.

Firdaus Dinshaw

CHAPTER 22

PETER PIPER PICKED A PECK OF PICKLED PEPPER

Thursday, 26th January 2023
11:00 PM – 12:00 AM

Sanaya was drinking her green tea, and Sohrab was talking in a low hushed voice to Anahita. Diana and Jim were sitting in one corner and lost in their own conversation. They were so engrossed that they did not really care about their surroundings. Cyrus and Zubin had retired back to their rooms a few seconds ago. Shirin had been sleeping. The butler, Jawahar, after giving the green tea, had gone back to sitting silently by the console table, awaiting further instructions. Shehnaz and Bejan had been discussing about who could have murdered Jahangir.

A while later, Anahita called the butler and asked, "Has Firdaus gone back to our room?"

"No, Madam, I had seen him go to the billiards room."

"Could you fetch him. Tell him I want to talk to him and so he must come up to our room at once."

"Very well, Madam."

As the butler left, Anahita got up to leave the room.

Sohrab yawned and also got up. He, too, looked tired and drained out. He nudged his wife, who seemed to be popping in and out of sleep. She would drift into sleep, and when her head would get too comfortable and fall too low, it would jerk automatically and for a fraction of a second, she would lift her head up and look at the world with her tired red eyes. Sohrab tried to lift his wife up and put one of her arms around his neck. By this time, Anahita had reached the lift.

Suddenly, everyone heard Jawahar yell, "OHHH! Oh my God. Oh God!"

With a start, everyone made a move towards the source of the sound. Sohrab dropped his wife back on the sofa, and she slid back without any protest or resistance.

Anahita was the nearest to the billiards room and was the first to arrive. A split second later, Sohrab, Shehnaz, Bejan, Diana and Jim arrived.

Shehnaz saw in the dimly lit room Firdaus's body slumped onto the sofa. She entered the room and switched on the lights. The sadness of death felt by her heart was quickly metamorphosed into astute alertness by her brain's reptilian survival instinct. Again, Shehnaz almost subconsciously started observing the surroundings. She fervently started taking photos. As she scrambled around the small room, what she noticed first was that some of the litter, like some chocolate wrappers, a water bottle, a torn sleeve of a packet of chips and an empty bottle of wine, from the dustbin was strewn across the carpet. She beckoned the butler to check the bin. Jawahar silently shook his head. She moved closer and found the plastic bag lining the bin to be empty. She asked Jawahar to take it out. As he did so, she observed some other litter below the plastic bag inside the dustbin.

Next, Shehnaz moved closer to the body and saw that Firdaus's eyes, face and neck had purple splotches. There was a slight discolouration in his skin. Drawing from the countless crime documentaries that she had seen and crime scenes that she had visited during her early years as a beat reporter, Shehnaz knew that a lack of oxygen caused the red blood cells to turn blue. Using a pencil, she lifted the shirt and found blue spot marks clearly indicating that the blood vessels around the heart had broken due to high inter-vascular pressure.

Horror-stricken, Shehnaz moved a few steps back as she realized that Firdaus had just been murdered. The world swirled around her as it hit her that she was in the midst of some very cold and calculating killers. She suddenly lost confidence and had an urgent desire to get out of the Dinshaw estate.

Shehnaz turned and noticed Anahita's thin eyebrows were drawn up in the inner corners, and the corners of her mouth were drawn down. Her face expressed the sadness and the sudden unexpected devastation that her soul was feeling. Tears fell from her eyes as she remembered all the fights that she had had with Firdaus over the past two days, and regret gripped her mind.

While sobbing, Anahita stammered a few times, blew her nose, caught her breath and then finally managed to say, "Did he get a heart attack? Was it because I fought so hard with him? Oh! Has it all been my fault?"

Shehnaz felt angry at the suggestion. She herself was so fearful of the killer that her fear transpired into anger. Did the killer actually think her to be so stupid that she would not immediately pick up on the obvious signs? The mere mention of another possibility irritated Shehnaz, and she quickly replied, "Darling, please! It is quite apparent that your husband was murdered. He died due to asphyxiation."

"Oh!" replied Anahita with a very apparent surprised look on her face.

Shehnaz did not even bother to reply. She just looked beyond Anahita and saw Zubin and Cyrus standing at the door motionless.

Cyrus was visibly shaken and started relentlessly crying. He couldn't hold back his tears. It hurt Cyrus deeply to look at his father, who in his eyes had always been a magnetic personality in such a dishevelled state.

Zubin, who although had always been closer to his mother, stumbled backwards and kneeled down on the floor. He covered his face with his left hand and tried his best to control his tears. He was always conscious about expressing his emotions publicly.

Behind Anahita, Diana emoted surprise as she cupped her mouth with her hand and her eyelids opened wide. Her quick blinking eyes reflected her distressed state of mind.

Jim, who was standing beside her, had his mouth open in an apparent show of fear. It was reinforced on Shehnaz how tall and heavy Jim was as he continuously shifted his body weight from one leg to the other. Unconsciously Jim then bit his lip, which indicated to Shehnaz that her suspect was feeling anxious. For a fleeting second Shehnaz thought she saw Jim's face betray the expression of guilt and regret as his eyes narrowed, his head tilted to one side, and then quickly shook disapprovingly.

Behind Jim, Sanaya was standing stone cold. Her face was expressionless, and her breaths were quick and shallow. Sanaya's eyes stared blankly into the room. Shehnaz was not sure whether the eccentric artist was faking her behaviour of being stoned or was she actually high.

Beside her, Sohrab was standing with a dumbfounded expression. A look of disbelief was apparent on his face, which quickly changed into one of taut. A pang of irritation flashed, and a scowl formed on his face. Narrowing his eyes, Sohrab remarked, with gritted teeth, "Why is it always the butler who finds the body?"

"Why are you being so edgy? What is wrong with you? It is part of his job to roam around the house and tend to everyone's needs," remarked Bejan. The butler just looked on silently. He realized that at a time like this, emotions would be running high, and silence could truly be golden.

"Or put people out of their misery," muttered Sohrab under his breath.

"What did you say?"

"Nothing. I just feel that he found the body too soon?"

"How do you know when he was murdered?"

Taken aback by Bejan's comment, Sohrab replied angrily, "Just a while ago, we heard the argument between him and Anahita. And then he left the drawing room. I thought he had gone back to his room. I did not know he was sitting in the billiards room."

"What makes you think that he was murdered in this room? He could have been murdered elsewhere, and the killer could have dumped his body here in the hope that it would not be discovered soon?"

Flustered, Sohrab's face went red, and agitatedly, he replied, "I…I don't know what you are talking about." Then, throwing his hands in the air, he went back to the informal sitting room.

Shehnaz looked towards the butler and asked, "How is the weather outside? Have the storms subsided yet? Can we contact the police now?"

"No, Madam, the storms are fierce as ever. The phone lines are down. I am sorry, but we'll have to wait. As per the predictions of the weather forecasts that I had read a week earlier, though they are usually wrong, the storms would subside tomorrow onwards, and the weather should clear out in a day or two. We can only hope for the best."

"After two murders, I don't exactly know what hoping for the best would now result in. Anyway, we now need to move the body down to the freezer. Firdaus needs to be parked next to Uncle Jahangir."

"We would have to transfer him onto a chair."

"Do it. But don't disturb the crime scene any further."

"Very well, Madam."

"After you are done, I want everyone, including yourself, assembled in the informal sitting room. Everyone except Aunt Shirin. Do not disturb her just yet. Let her sleep."

"Yes, madam," replied the butler in a mechanical way and entered the billiards room to complete the task at hand.

CHAPTER 23

A HUNTING WE WILL GO

Friday, 27th January 2023
12:00 AM – 3:00 AM

A while later, all the designated people had assembled in the informal sitting room of the Dinshaw Mansion. Shehnaz and Bejan looked around and found that most of them clearly showcased fear and guilt on their faces.

Shehnaz broke the silence by stating, "Clearly, the police cannot be contacted right now, so by the powers vested in me earlier by the Superintendent, I'll be investigating this murder also. Following people are my suspects - Jim, Diana, Anahita, Sohrab, Sanaya and the butler Jawahar."

"Why aren't Zubin and Cyrus suspected?" inquired Diana

"They had retired to their room much earlier, but more so because I don't suspect them of being capable of killing their father. They have no motive whatsoever," explained Shehnaz.

With apparent anger in his voice, Zubin was quick to respond while looking in Diana's direction, "Why isn't her brother, Farrukh, a suspect."

Farrukh, who was already looking pale and sickly since after the first murder, hearing the comment, sank further in the sofa, and his skin turned yellow. Almost as if the accusations alone would cause him to develop severe jaundice.

Before Shehnaz could reply, Sanaya, who till now had been sitting rigidly like a statue, softly slurred while looking at no one in particular, "My son is not capable of murder."

Shehnaz's face betrayed her feeling of being surprised as her left eyebrow shot up. Recomposing herself, yet making a mental note of the comment, Shehnaz said, "Firstly, I don't owe anyone any explanations. But just to satisfy your query, I would like to tell you that this entire evening, Farrukh has been present in front of my eyes. In fact, after Firdaus left the formal drawing room, Farrukh and I had been engaged in a conversation in this informal sitting room, which is just across the hallway. So, in all probability, when the murder took place, we must have been engrossed in our conversation."

"But weren't we all in front of you and having an argument in the informal sitting room?" inquired Anahita.

Shehnaz smiled and replied, "Except the butler, all of my suspects kept going in and out of the room. You see, I am a very observant person and that is precisely why you all are my suspects. The killer might be smart, but I am not a fool who can be swayed by mere facial expressions."

Nobody replied.

Considering her position of power, Shehnaz continued, "Again, we'll follow the same principle. You will all come one by one to the formal drawing room and give your statements. I would like to begin with Anahita."

The amateur sleuth then got up and walked out to the formal drawing room.

A few seconds later, Anahita, who had been bursting into tears every now and then, got up and walked towards the formal drawing room.

Shehnaz wanted to appeal to the humane side of Anahita. She understood that a lady who had been wronged and betrayed could have a lot of fury inside her. She thus offered her suspect some wine and allowed her to settle down in silence.

In the next few minutes, Anahita took big gulps of the wine, cried some more and blew enough snot in her kerchief that it was now soaking wet.

Shehnaz observed in silence. She saw that through all the drama, Anahita would quickly glance at her and then again bury her face in her napkin.

After a painful ten minutes, Shehnaz said, "I understand that Jim had been blackmailing Firdaus. Earlier, Jim had found his way up to your room and had gotten into an argument with Firdaus. Later, you went through his phone. And recently, when you came down the stairs yelling at the top of your voice, I heard you. I infer from all of this that Firdaus was having an extramarital affair. Is it true?"

"Yes. That piglet of Firdaus's theatre, the one with a thin voice, wooed him. That pathetic actress was the main lead in our plays. I now realize that despite being such a shitty actress, the only reason she was being repeatedly cast was because of her affair with my husband. What she lacked on the stage, she clearly made up for in bed," fumed Anahita. Then, without any further prompt, she continued, "And that useless boy Jim somehow found out about it and had the nerve to blackmail him. If he had any sense of righteousness, he should have come straight to me, but the conniving worm that he is, he preferred to slither around and blackmail."

"Was this the first time that Firdaus has had an affair, or has he philandered in the past?"

"No, this is the only time. At least, that is what I know and suspect. But I don't know what to believe anymore."

"What did you plan to do the moment you found out about the affair? I saw the colour drain from your face while you were going through his phone earlier."

Anahita grunted a little and bitterly said, "The first thought that crossed my mind was that I should kill him. Not that I did, though. But I was just so angry with him for cheating on me. I don't know why he did it. We were so happy together."

"So, you didn't plan on taking any action other than yelling at him?"

"I honestly don't know. Everything happened so fast. It has been too sudden for me to process. But if he had continued to deny and falsely apologise the way he did throughout our argument, then I would have definitely divorced him."

Then, after a slight pause, Anahita said, "Or maybe I would have given him a second chance, for old time's sake. Who knows?"

"You would have given him a second chance?" inquired Shehnaz, looking very puzzled

"If he would have apologized sincerely… then yes, I would have. But if, after that, he would have gone back to his philandering ways, I would have poisoned him myself," explained Anahita.

"You know, I strongly suspect he was suffocated to death. I checked his body and the signs were all there. Plus, he was very drunk, so the attacker wouldn't have required a lot of strength."

"Are you suggesting that Firdaus was suffocated by a pillow or something?"

"Yes, I suspect, the plastic bag of the dustbin. Do you suspect anyone, Anahita?"

"I believe it was that boy Jim who, out of frustration, murdered my husband."

The choice of words used by Anahita got registered in Shehnaz's mind. After pondering over the statement for a while, she said, "Very well. You may go. Please ask Jim to come in here."

A few minutes later, Jim walked in. Shehnaz noticed that his brown leather jacket, which he wore over a pair of distressed blue jeans, looked relatively new. Shehnaz knew that only people with new money or the upper middle class ever overtly dress well to showcase their newfound wealth and status in society. For those who have been generationally rich, clothes are a routine part of their life and lifestyle. They don't dress up while going to the movies or even for any fancy restaurants. They are casual about these things. The rich generally dress up for important events like fundraising or other PR activities. And inferring from such experiences that Shehnaz had had by virtue of moving around in the most elite social circles of the country, she gathered that Jim was trying hard to climb the ladder. He was not there yet, but his behaviour and mannerisms indicated that he was desperate to reach there.

This time, Jim sat in an armchair and not in the middle seat of the sofa. He confidently faced his interrogator and even crossed his legs one over the other in a figure-four lock. He exuberated aggressive dominance and confidence via his posture and body language. Shehnaz noticed the difference in his attitude from the last she had interrogated him. She was mature enough to be not flustered by Jim's passive aggressiveness. She made the young boy wait in silence for a few minutes while she observed him. Jim stared back for the initial minute or so but then he started moving his leg as nervousness crept in.

That was the moment Shehnaz realized that she had reeled her prey in. Capitalizing on the moment, she began by asking, "You were blackmailing Firdaus about the affair that he was having with his theatre actress?"

"Yes. I caught them in the green room when I had seen the play in Delhi," came back the confident response.

"Funny that you should blackmail one member of the family while trying to court another?"

"I thought that I would make some big and quick buck. They have so much, why shouldn't the prospects of my life improve? But alas, that was not to happen. My bad luck."

"Your bad luck? You are still alive."

"Yes, but Uncle Firdaus died at a very inconvenient time. If only I could have extracted a few rounds of payments from him. You must know that I had absolutely no motive to kill him. His death has resulted in a direct loss to me."

"Or did you kill him when he refused to pay up?"

"He kept stalling me and buying time. But I think he was on the verge of paying. I did not spill his secret to Aunt Anahita, for which he wrongly blamed me. Though I suppose the sound scolding that he got from her was well deserved," expressed Jim with a hint of agitation in his voice. Then, after a break of a few seconds, he continued, "You know, I hadn't grown frustrated enough with him that I would have killed him."

Again, Shehnaz registered this comment in her mind. She then continued with her inquest, "Does Diana know about your side business of blackmailing people and of your opportunistic behaviour?"

"She just learnt about it when Aunt Anahita was yelling at me about my morals. This is what we were talking about in the informal sitting room while you were talking to Farrukh. I tried selling to Diana that the blackmailing was an error of judgment on my part but she is not buying my excuses. It seems I have lost everything. All roads which could have led me to money seem to have come to a dead end."

Shehnaz was surprised by Jim's revelation and was quick to ask, "So you were wooing her just for her wealth?"

"She is rich and intelligent. It is a good combination to have. But what difference does it make now? As I said, I have lost it all."

"No, you haven't. Uncle Jahangir did make a provision for you in his new trust. And this actually gets me to my next point, why do you need money so desperately? You have your life in front of you; you can work hard and earn your way up the ladder?"

"Money buys freedom. It's always convenient to have it in large amounts. And I am not getting any younger. Age catches up with all of us."

"You are very sly," said Shehnaz with a vulpine smile.

Jim got up. Taking a long breath, he said, "Yes, I am, but I am not so frustrated with life that I'd go around killing people. I am shrewd, and I tried my hand at a shortcut. It didn't work out for me, but I know my limits."

Shehnaz felt a pang of irritation hearing Jim's comments. Her brain kept giving her signals and tried joining the dots but she kept looking for more solid evidence. She silently told the voice in her brain, *it cannot be as simple as analysing the characteristics of the people. I need some more concrete proof.*

Her brain immediately responded by stating, *Observe, you fool and you would have all the evidence that you would require right in front of you. The individualities of the people are what highlight them. And that differentiates between a killer and a bystander.*

Brushing aside her thoughts, Shehnaz called in Sanaya.

This time, Sanaya did not enter with her usual flair. Her heels didn't clank on the floor, her hands did not disturb any piece of furniture, and her brain did not demand any alcohol at the moment. She softly treaded towards Shehnaz, took off her Louboutins and sat cross-legged on the sofa. She took a pillow and placed it on her lap, then with a slight giggle, she said, "Don't you feel a sense of thrill? Since you arrived here, you have witnessed two murders. Are you enjoying being a sleuth?"

"We don't have time for your insensitive remarks. Where were you this evening?"

"I am still a bit stoned, though your green tea did help a bit. Since it has been snowing so heavily for the past two days, and I have mostly remained cooped up in the house, I really have lost the sense of time. I remember being in my studio working on my art, and the next thing I knew was that Sohrab opened the pantry door, and I was standing in a corner sweating profusely. He gave me some cold water to drink, and I remember telling him that I was feeling hungry. He sourced out some nuts and cookies from the pantry shelves and handed them to me. He also handed me a packet of chips. A few minutes later, I think he walked me to the sitting room, where you all were gathered," explained Sanaya, in a slurry speech, while regularly throwing her hands around in an attempt to express herself better. She sounded unsure about her own memory.

Shehnaz got up and walked around the room for a few minutes, then she walked up to Sanaya and said, "Why don't you put your head back, close your eyes and relax a bit."

Sanaya followed the instructions. Her mind was tired, and she was in no mood to fight.

A few minutes later, Shehnaz whispered into her ear, "Recall the time when Sohrab came into the pantry. Remember everything and break every instance frame by frame. Play it all in your head in slow motion."

Sanaya's brain kicked into motion and tried to recreate the situation scene by scene.

"Now, try to explain everything to me again. Frame by frame. There is no hurry."

Sanaya's eyes were red and droopy. After an apparent delayed reaction, she lifted her head and incoherently said, "Sohrab busted into the pantry. I was standing there feeling hungry. He gave me a packet of chips. Then I told him I was feeling hungry, and he sourced some cookies and nuts for me, which I ate. Then he brought me to you. That is about it."

"Okay, I understand," said Shehnaz. She then requested her father, Bejan, to walk Sanaya out of the room.

As Sanaya got up, Shehnaz asked her, "Why do you do weed?"

"Oh, it is just to channelize my creativity. I am not depressed or frustrated."

Shehnaz's brain picked on Sanaya's comment and tried to connect the dots to find the missing piece of the puzzle. Yet, Shehnaz wanted to be thorough. She wanted to complete the interrogations. Next, she called upon Diana.

Diana came and sat across Shehnaz in the armchair.

Shehnaz quickly got to the point and began by asking, "I guess now you know that Jim was blackmailing Firdaus. What is your reaction? How do you feel about it?"

"Well, a person's deeds highlight his character. Clearly, Jim has a lot to work on in that area of his personality. I have told him that in this lifetime he can forget about me. I also warned him that I would be telling Grand Aunt Shirin of his deeds and to our lawyers in the hopes of striking his name off from our newly formed trust."

"So, you were not in on the blackmailing plan?"

"Absolutely not. I am intelligent and can work hard. I don't need to resort to such menial activities to make money. I am rich; I just have greater ambitions."

"You also seem frustrated. I heard you complain to your brother Farrukh about the unequal distribution of the newfound wealth. You feel you were not given your due?"

"Yes, I do feel so, and that adds to my frustration. First, I was unfairly used by Grand Uncle, and then I fell for a guy who resorted to blackmail at the first opportunity that he got. I am irked by the fact that he fooled me and that I could not read his mind and character earlier. After reading so many people during my journey of investing in start-ups and having studied psychology, it frustrates me that an average boy could have so easily taken me for a ride. I should have seen beyond his obvious charms. I was so overwhelmed and confused that I even defended him against Aunt Anahita. Something that I shouldn't have done," explained Diana while shaking her head in utter disappointment.

Squinting her eyes a little and while still shaking her head, she continued, "I am frustrated, but that does not mean I killed Uncle Firdaus. I was earlier in my room, and post the argument, I was mostly in front of your eyes, giving a piece of my mind to Jim. Besides, I wouldn't have the strength to strangle uncle."

"He was drunk and couldn't have put up a fight. Even you know that. Besides, I never said he was strangled. Asphyxia can be caused by a pillow or even a plastic bag."

"Maybe, I wouldn't know anything about it. As I said, I have standards and don't need to stoop so low to get what is rightfully mine. If I would have to beat someone, it would be a war of wits, not fists."

"Very well, could you now request your father to come in please?"

"Will do," replied Diana as she got up and scurried away.

Sohrab entered casually with his hands inside his pocket and the top two buttons of his shirt open. The light grey suede jacket added a level of ombré to his ensemble and personality. As he walked in, Shehnaz was first reminded of Firdaus and then of the great Jahangir Dinshaw. Looking at his demeanour, Shehnaz smiled and asked, "When you walked in, you reminded me of Firdaus and Uncle Jahangir."

"I am my own self. I do not emulate anyone. The dead – may their souls rest in peace – were legends in their own right, but that does not mean that the living have to exist under the weight of their shadows."

"You are now the head patriarch of the family. How does that feel?"

"We are not the British Monarchy. The murders have placed added responsibility, if anything, on my head."

For a few silent moments, Shehnaz silently judged Sohrab. He shifted in the armchair and then crossed his legs.

"Who do you think killed Firdaus?"

"Isn't it the butler who always does it? He found uncle this morning and by night, he seems to have struck again."

"Both the murders were committed by different people. Besides, the butler lacks motive. You were the target for the first murder. The butler wouldn't have missed you for the second time."

"Ah! Yes, your theory about me being the actual target of the first murder. Well, couldn't someone have killed Firdaus believing it was me?"

Shehnaz understood the slight insinuation that Sohrab had just made towards his wife, Sanaya. She was the only one who was stoned enough to confuse one person for another.

Still, Shehnaz kept a straight face and pressed on, "You don't think it could have been your daughter, Diana or Anahita?"

"Diana is not the kind to murder. She is shrewd and intelligent. Besides she knows that she has got nothing to gain by killing Firdaus. Uncle's Will and, by extension, the new found trust would still operate the way he intended for it to. As far as Anahita goes, I think she is smart enough to have not acted on an impulse."

Shehnaz pondered over Sohrab's choice of words then said, "You are right. Firdaus's murder has not been committed for monetary gains. And given the short window in which the murder has taken place, it really seems like an impulsive decision."

Then, changing the topic, Shehnaz asked, "Your wife is temperamental. Did she have a reason to kill Firdaus or kill you?"

"I don't think she had any beef with Firdaus. She may harbour many reasons to kill me, given that I am a constant underachiever and a disappointment to her. She detested the fact that I never stood up to Uncle Jahangir and failed at all my business ventures. The fact that I occasionally gamble also does not help."

"Are you frustrated with your life, Sohrab?" asked Shehnaz as she compartmentalized all the information in her brain.

"Aren't we all? Life has a way of throwing us off balance. It feels like I am struggling to keep my head above the water. People often say that money buys freedom, I can tell you that it does not buy you dignity and self-worth. If anything, you are required to prove yourself all the time. After a point, all you want is a routine, peaceful life."

Shehnaz got up and walked to the bar cabinet, and poured some whisky for herself and Sohrab. They drank in silence. A few minutes later, Shehnaz asked, "Sanaya was overtly implicated for the first murder. Does no one in the house like her?"

Sohrab let out a small laugh and replied, "She is a difficult personality to live with."

"So, do you know who the killer is?" inquired Sohrab in a tense voice.

"No," lied Shehnaz and continued, "I will present my findings to the police and let them decipher the clues."

Sohrab left the room as Shehnaz rung for the butler.

Jawahar stood patiently and waited for his interrogator to begin.

Shehnaz eyed the visibly tired butler carefully, then asked, "Earlier, you said that you had seen Firdaus go to the billiards room. So, you must have also seen who went thereafter in the room?"

With a peaceful aura and a sense of calculated calmness, the butler expressed, "Unfortunately, no, madam. There are two console tables at which I sit. One is opposite the library, along the formal drawing and dining room wall. I sit there when the family is gathered either in the library, the formal drawing room or is eating in the formal dining room. The rest of the times, I sit at the console table, which is next to the informal siting and near the mansion's entry. Since everyone was gathered in the informal sitting area, I obviously just had to sit there."

"Then when and how did you notice Firdaus going into the billiards room?"

"After the discussion between Mr. and Mrs. Firdaus ended (Shehnaz liked how the butler called Anahita's yelling and Firdaus's apologetic pleas a "discussion") I saw Master Firdaus exiting the formal drawing room from the door which faced the main entry of the mansion. He looked drunk and had a drink in his hand. I was concerned lest he tried to climb up the steps to his bedroom and would stumble and fall. So, I followed him from a distance. I saw him enter the billiards room and slam the door shut. I gathered that he would not have liked to be disturbed, so I let him be. I turned back from the end of the hallway and saw Mrs. Anahita enter the informal sitting room. I could then hear her scolding Master Jim. After which, I could hear the arguments flowing around."

"Did you, by any chance, know when Sanaya entered the pantry?"

"Ah! Yes. In all probability, she would have entered the pantry right about the time Mrs. Anahita was scolding Master Zubin."

"How can you be so sure?"

"We have an old-style lift with scissor doors, which clank every time someone opens or shuts them. The lift itself makes considerable noise as it moves. So, it is my educated guess that Madam Sanaya would have arrived into the pantry at that time."

"Does Sanaya have a violent streak in her? Does she get aggressive while she is under the influence of weed?"

"No. She is never that incoherent. Some people may feel that she is arrogant or sarcastic, but she genuinely has a good heart. She never speaks about her charitable endeavours, so everyone just sees her eccentric side."

"Do you get anything from the trusts? Did you have any issues with Uncle Jahangir or Firdaus?"

With the same chillingly calm demeanour and expressionless face, Jawahar said, "No. Neither did I have any issues with the dead, nor do I get anything from the trust funds. I don't even expect to. I work for them. They give me a hefty salary and they have trained me over the years. If anything, I am grateful to this family."

"Do you suspect anyone?"

"I am just a humble servant working here. I am not at liberty to form opinions or judge people," expressed Jawahar with his hands neatly clasped in front of him. Shehnaz analysed his body language and understood that the butler was feeling vulnerable and anxious. She thought that he could be withholding some information, which she felt was his list of suspects. Shehnaz realized that the confidence that the butler was exhibiting was a feigned one.

"Okay, thank you. I would like you to now escort my father and me to the guesthouse outside. The storms have died down, and it is no longer snowing. Hopefully, the weather will open up tomorrow."

"Very well, madam," replied the butler as he prepared to lead the way.

Once the butler had left, Bejan told Shehnaz, "Every soul that resides in this house has a unique characteristic, and that is what you must explore. You must delve into their idiosyncrasies and traits to find your answer."

Shehnaz nodded silently and retreated back to her room.

That night, though Shehnaz had figured out everything that had transpired in the Dinshaw estate, sleep escaped her as her mind couldn't fathom the extremities to which a human mind was capable of going. It was not the first time in her life that she had seen dead bodies or was around a crime scene. She had reported about murders as she had spent her life being a crime reporter and had always analysed crime scenes, but this was the first time she had seen how frustrated minds could cause members of a family to turn on one another.

A few hours later, despite her mind feeling heavy and needing sleep, Shehnaz for the last time, went over her notes and details. She played everything chronologically in her mind and settled on her conclusion.

CHAPTER 24
A Pig in a wig

Friday, 27th January 2023
9:00 AM – 3:30 PM

The morning rays filtered through the sheers and basked Shehnaz's room in a warm golden hue. The snow outside, too, reflected the sun rays and the estate looked pristine white with faded golden light reflecting all around. A swarm of crows, a murder, flew out, circled around the outhouse and settled on the perch outside the mansion.

Some traditional minds would say that the presence of crows indicated the arrival of guests and visitors at home. For Shehnaz, however, the opening up of the weather was an indication that the police would soon be here. The phone lines were still down owing to the ferocity of the storm and the snow that had fallen over the transmission towers and lines.

Shehnaz looked at the previous weather forecasts, which claimed that snowstorms would begin again late in the evening.

'It was 9 AM. Maybe things could still turn around for the better,' thought Shehnaz. Just then, a soft knock was heard on the door. Her father entered and inquired, "What are you planning on doing now?"

"Oh! Father, I cannot be bothered anymore. Let us enjoy our tea and this beautiful morning."

Till after breakfast, none of the Dinshaw members saw the father-daughter duo. Upon inquiry, the butler informed the house that they were busy discussing their findings and had requested not to be disturbed. They had also had their breakfast in the outhouse.

At 11:30 AM, two helicopters were seen descending down on the far side of the grand lawn of the Dinshaw estate.

Superintendent of Police Arun Mohan Joshi, along with five other police officers, descended from one helicopter, while from the other, a team of plain clothes officers were seen hurrying down onto the lawn. The police team had started moving through the snow-covered lawn when two small golf carts reached them. Each of the carts had a snowplough attached to them, and they could thus easily manoeuvre around the estate. As soon as SP Arun sat in the golf cart, he asked the caddy, "Where is Shehnaz Contractor? Could you take me to her immediately?"

"She is in the outhouse. We will escort you there."

SP Arun met his friend Shehnaz and the well-renowned lawyer Bejan Contractor. They had a quick twenty-minute chat, which culminated with the SP stating, "I would first like to inspect the dead bodies and get my forensic teams to start working on them. Then I would need all the family members, including the butler, to be assembled in a room."

So, a few minutes later, the police team, led by the Superintendent, marched into the basement to observe the bodies of Jahangir and Firdaus Dinshaw, which were *chilling* in the cold storage.

Fifteen minutes later, the entire Dinshaw family, along with SP Arun, Shehnaz and Bejan were assembled in the large ornate formal drawing room.

The Superintendent sat in one of the armchairs, sipping a cup of hot tea. Except for the five inspectors standing outside the drawing room or the team in plain clothes undertaking the forensic analysis of the dead dog, Jahangir and Firdaus Dinshaw, nobody could have guessed, looking at the seemingly casual atmosphere in the drawing room, that soon arrests would be made for the murders.

Placing his cup and saucer back on the centre table and dabbing the tea drops dangling on his handlebar moustache with a white napkin, SP Arun looked around the room. The obvious, palpable tension did not reflect on anyone. So, looking at Shehnaz, he said, "Since I have arrived, you have not told me anything. You insisted that every member of the household must be present and so we are all gathered here. I believe that you have made some inquiries into the murders. Do you know who the culprit is?"

Everyone looked at Shehnaz with subdued enthusiasm. No one wanted to show their eagerness, but the eyes twinkled, the breaths were held, and the hairs raised as anxiety took over those who called themselves part of the Dinshaw household.

After a painful few seconds, Shehnaz said, "Yes, I know who all committed the crimes."

Instantly soft murmurs started around the room as people softly asked either each other or to themselves, "How can she be so sure?" "What is the basis of her confidence?" "Why did she not tell us the previous night?"

SP Arun turned around and glared at everyone in turn. That action alone made the room fall silent once more.

Sitting upright on her chair, Shehnaz first explained the existing financial layout of the Dinshaw family. How, the existing trust earns and distributes its monies. Next, she described about the venture that had turned into a unicorn and had allowed for a new trust to be formed. She then elucidated the workings of the new trust. Lastly, she concluded by saying, "But neither of the two murders were committed for money."

"What do you mean?"

"Let me explain, Jahangir Dinshaw was not the target. Almost nobody gained anything by his death. His death was an accidental murder. It was committed by someone who wanted to target Sohrab."

"What do you mean almost nobody gained anything?" inquired the SP, sounding surprised by Shehnaz's choice of words.

"Well. Diana was hurt by the way she had been treated. It is in her nature to get even. Killing is not her style of revenge. My mind wandered to the fact that Diana may have poisoned the wine and then given Sohrab the idea to gift it to Uncle Jahangir. But this would be a risky proposition. She is wise enough not to take that kind of a risk with her father's life. Therefore, she was not the one who poisoned the wine.

Jim is opportunistic, but he has had no arguments or fights with Uncle Jahangir. In fact, it was in his interest to remain in his good books. More so, Since Jim had no quarrels with Sohrab, he was ruled out as a suspect.

Anahita deals in rare poisonous plants, which made me believe that it could have been her. But she is far too thorough in her conduct and replies. The wine in which the poison was mixed was gifted ahead. Something which a thorough killer would have taken into account.

Next, was Sanaya, who mostly lives in her own bubble and is incapable of seeing the world around her. Although she tried very hard to sway and confuse me, I saw through her antics. She did not need Jahangir's money, nor did she care about his distribution strategies or the trust funds. But she was worried about her husband's rising gambling debts, and she disliked his callous attitude towards life. She wanted him to succeed and egged him on. At times, she even belittled him. She seemed frustrated with Sohrab. But she was not frustrated enough to have poisoned the wine. If Sanaya would have to murder, she is the type who would have either shot or stabbed her target. She acts on impulse and is not a long-term planner. Therefore, her using a unique poison like thallium did not sound plausible to me."

"But then who targeted Sohrab and why?"

"I asked myself those very questions. When I interviewed everyone, I understood that Firdaus wanted peace in the house. He was everyone's favourite and wanted to maintain his position, even if it meant him giving a larger piece of the newfound wealth to his cousin Sohrab."

"The wealth that came in the family was due to my daughter's hard work. It was not his to give me anyway. I demanded what was rightfully mine," interjected Sohrab angrily.

"I do not want any of the family members to interject. If that happens again, I'll have that person locked up in the adjacent room," said SP Arun while turning his bald head in Sohrab's direction.

Then, looking towards the amateur sleuth, SP Arun said, "Continue."

"So, as I stated, Firdaus had no motive to kill Sohrab or uncle Jahangir."

Now Shehnaz got up and spoke in an affirmative tone, "Sometime during the interviews, it struck me that it could have been Sohrab himself, who could have drugged the wine and is pretending that someone is trying to kill him. But then later, it dawned on me that firstly, he wanted to prove his worth to Uncle Jahangir, therefore he wouldn't have killed him. And more importantly, the killer had heard Diana tell the butler, Jawahar, that she would be gifting the rare wine to her father. Now, just before Jawahar was about to finish his work, the killer entered the wine cellar and poisoned the wine by injecting thallium through the cork. Then, the killer hurriedly rushed upstairs through the staff staircase. Unknown to the killer, I had just opened the door to the staff staircase to reminisce about my old days in the mansion. It was where I used to hide while playing hide and seek. Jawahar told me about the disturbance that he had heard in his wine cellar but had found no one to be there. When I went up the staircase, I found botched footprints and traces of mud and snow all through the steps up to the landing of the first floor. But the steps going up towards the second floor were clean. Therefore, I thought it couldn't be Farrukh. On the contrary, the poor introvert thought for the longest time that his mother had stabbed Uncle Jahangir. Later, when I revealed that he had died of poisoning, he, in his terror, believed that his mother must have done it. You see Uncle Jahangir was dead by the time Farrukh visited him the previous morning. The moment he realized that his mother had visited Uncle Jahangir before him, he assumed that the killer must have been his mother. But it wasn't her. Analysing Farrukh's personality, I understood that he is meek. He does not have the guts to kill, much less plan a murder."

"Then who did it?"

"Well, obviously, it couldn't have had been Aunt Shirin who poisoned the wine, for she is not that quick to move.

Then, for a moment, I thought that Jawahar could have been lying about the disturbance in the cellar and the smudged footprints on the steps could be unrelated to the murder. But alas it was not so, Firstly, because the butler wouldn't risk poisoning a substance that he himself was delivering. Secondly, he had nothing to gain by killing either Sohrab or Jahangir."

Then, looking at the corner of the room, Shehnaz said, "It was only after I carefully analysed Cyrus's interview that I was sure about who the killer was. The reason for this murder has got everything to do with personalities and characteristics. The killer did not like Sohrab's behaviour, nor did he like him getting sympathy from his mother, Anahita. He thought of him as a failure and blamed him for the rift between his parents."

Everyone's head turned towards Cyrus, who was standing still in a corner. Cyrus looked confidently back at them and said, "I did not poison the wine. Just because I made certain calculations about the new trust's payouts from the present time, it does not mean I poisoned anyone. Nor do I care about Uncle Sohrab's sympathy-gaining behaviour."

"It is not you, darling, but your identical twin, standing right behind you, who has committed this crime," explained Shehnaz.

"I did not kill anyone. Your theories are all bogus. You are just shooting arrows in the dark. You have no proof," yelled Zubin while protesting to the allegations.

"How can you be so sure?" inquired Cyrus, looking horrified and ignoring his brother's angry rant.

"You see, not everything about the two of you is identical. He walks with a stomp. The same stomping sound I heard when I was near the stairs, as the one which I heard when Zubin entered the formal drawing room to be interviewed. And just before that I thought I had seen Cyrus's silhouette walk past me when I was in the informal dining room munching on fox nuts. But the man walking by was not as discreet as Cyrus. In fact, it was Zubin. Also, he was the one who was served wine the previous night by one of the manservants, because he had walked out to the gardening shed to get his hands on thallium. He was impulsive enough to plan a murder just after hearing Diana's comment about gifting her father a bottle of wine. And lastly, in the heat of the moment, he told me all that he thinks about Sohrab," explained Shehnaz emphatically.

Then, pointing a finger at Zubin, she continued, "If only you had the patience to understand your surroundings, you would have realized that your mother was not having an affair with Sohrab. She just liked talking to him as a family member.

And she felt like that because your father wouldn't give her any time. He was busy philandering with his theatre actresses. You unnecessarily tried to kill your uncle, and your hot head never allowed you to think your plan thoroughly. You accidentally murdered your Grand Uncle."

The room fell silent, and Zubin's numbness was palpable. Zubin just silently stood there for what seemed like an eternity. He did not even bother to deny the charges anymore. A few minutes later, he angrily yelled, "Just because I stomp my feet while walking, you reeled me in so I would vent about Uncle Sohrab. You linked it to the fact that I had been served wine the evening before Grand Uncle's death. You picked on the minutest of the details and brought it all together."

"You need to treat your mind and get your dots connected properly," thought Shehnaz, not wanting to voice her opinion.

"But then what about Sanaya's knife that was sticking out of Jahangir's throat?" inquired Bejan

"Ah. You see, a lot of people here don't like Sanaya. But the only one who could have done it is Aunt Shirin."

At this point, the old lady gave out a squeal, almost like a child who gets caught while playing hide and seek.

"How did you deduce that?"

"I had my suspicions from the very beginning. First was when I saw you crying after learning about Uncle Jahangir's death. Your reaction looked very artificial to me. You did not portray the initial shock one does when one learns of the death of a dear one. Especially with whom you had spent so many beautiful years together. Hence, you already knew that he was dead and had allowed the initial shock to pass over. I know this because Jawahar heard the door open and shut after Sanaya had visited Uncle Jahangir, but before Farrukh had come in. When Farrukh had visited, he saw uncle dead with a knife sticking out from his throat, but when Sanaya visited uncle, he was still alive. Next, there was not much blood from the stab wound, which reinforced my theory that he was stabbed after he had died. Lastly, sometime back, you requested Jawahar to fix you some hot toddy so that you could sleep better. You said that the wind rattles the windows and that disturbs your sleep. Whereas earlier, both the butler and you had lied to me about you being a sound sleeper," explained Shehnaz earnestly.

"Well, I just wanted to teach that moody girl, throwing around her opinions and weight everywhere, a nice lesson. I thought some years behind the bars would set her mannerisms right," justified Shirin as a pang of jealousy and hatred crept up in her towards Sanaya.

"Some years? They would have hanged me from a pole! What is wrong with you?" screamed Sanaya, her irritation showing on her reddened face.

Sympathetically, Shehnaz softly mumbled, "Aunty, it is not Sanaya or Anahita's fault that you couldn't bear children or are not creatively active."

"Yes, but they could show respect for all the sacrifices we have made for the prosperity of this family. It is unbecoming of them to be so thankless all the time," retorted Shirin as her lips twitched and curled.

SP Arun turned around again. This time, the bickering went on for about a few minutes before the room fell silent again.

At that moment, he looked at Shehnaz and beckoned her to continue.

Shehnaz took the cue and explained further, "To deduce who killed Firdaus, I had to deep dive into the mindset of all my suspects. The moment I entered the billiards room, the first thing that caught my attention was not the dead body but the litter that had been strewn on the floor. Some of the litter was also present at the bottom of the bin, and the plastic bag was replaced over the bin. This told me that the killer had hurriedly entered the room to capitalize on the opportunity. In a haze, the killer looked for a murder weapon and settled on the bin's plastic bag, threw out some of the trash, emptied the balance in the bin and then suffocated Firdaus by holding the plastic bag around his face. The more I linked the dots, the more it became clear to me that the killer always wanted to kill Firdaus, so the murder was a premeditated one. But, the method lacked thorough planning. There was a streak of impulsiveness in the capitalization of the opportunity of finding the victim in a helpless state."

Then looking at Anahita, Shehnaz continued in a sombre tone, "My first suspect was Anahita. She had just found out that her husband was cheating on her and had a massive altercation with him. In fact, for quite some time their marriage had been on the rocks and they had been fighting often. She is an architect and maintains a collection of bonsais. Both these activities require thorough planning and a lot of patience. She understands the value of taking one step at a time and of being accurate in everything that she does. Now, the crime scene did not reflect on such mannerisms. Secondly, if she wanted to kill her husband, she could have done so at any point of time earlier or much after the police had concluded Uncle Jahangir's death. You see, she is not a risk-taker at all. Killing her husband right after her public argument with him, especially when another murder is being investigated and the police are due to arrive soon, is not something someone as meticulous as she would have done. So, I ruled her out."

Shifting her gaze towards the next suspect, Shehnaz continued, "Jim is an opportunistic person. For him, it would have made sense to keep Firdaus alive. His frustration stems from his lack of financial status and where he wants to reach in life. He sees life as a balance sheet, and so the loss of reputation that he may have suffered by trying to blackmail Firdaus, in his books, has been written off as a loss incurred while trying to capitalize on a unique opportunity. He is driven by money and so without there being an absolute financial gain for him, he wouldn't have risked killing Firdaus."

Flipping through her notes, Shehnaz shook her head and said, "I found no change in the butler's mannerisms and behaviour. His conduct was always the same. He had absolutely nothing to gain from the murders, and so he was never a serious contender for the hangman's noose."

"But Diana; she felt frustrated about the way she was treated and side-lined. She felt used by her Grand Uncle. Yet it was she who had shrewdly advised her father, Sohrab, to patch things up with Uncle Jahangir. She understood the value of buying time and striking at the right moment. Therefore, a calculative mind like hers wouldn't take the risk of committing a murder when one is already being investigated."

"Then who would take such a risk? Who was incoherent enough to kill Firdaus?" asked SP Arun.

"I like your choice of words. You see, Sanaya is mostly high on weed and does not necessarily remember everything. She is moody and temperamental. Her observation of her surroundings and of people surrounding her are very bad. Though she did not really care for uncle Jahangir's wealth, she did not like the way her husband was treated by him. Nor did she like the fact that Firdaus was favoured over her husband. The crime scene was overtly made to look like the crime had been committed on an impulse, something a temperamental person like Sanaya would do. But the killer made a fatal mistake by trying to evidently implicate Sanaya. When Sanaya walked into the informal drawing room, accompanied by her husband, I could see cookie crumbs fallen on her cashmere jumper and I could smell weed and chocolate on her breath. Yet she held an empty packet of chips in her hand. The same packet whose torn sleeve was found at the crime scene."

"I don't understand," stated the Superintendent with a bewildered expression on his face.

Unperturbed, Shehnaz continued, "When I interviewed Sanaya, she stated that when Sohrab found her in the pantry, he had given her cold water to drink. After which, she told her husband that she was hungry. At that point, he sourced out some nuts and cookies for her. Initially, Sanaya stated that Sohrab also gave her a packet of chips. But when I asked her to relax, recall the incident and repeat everything to me frame by frame, she said that Sohrab came into the pantry and handed her a packet of chips, and *then* she told him that she was hungry. After that he sourced some cookies and nuts for her, which she ate."

Shehnaz then stood up and exclaimed, "You see, Sohrab entered the pantry and gave his wife an empty packet of chips. At that point, she told him that she was hungry, and he gave her those cookies and nuts. Therefore, there were no crumbs or evidence of Sanaya eating those chips. She just had the cookies, whereas the packet of chips had been given to her by Sohrab, who is the actual killer.

He is the only one who has the profile of being a risk taker. His gambling habits have attuned his mind into taking undue risks in life."

"But why did he do it?"

"Ah. Yes. That is the most interesting part. The motive for this murder, too, wasn't money. Since I arrived here, I observed each and every character. Before Uncle Jahangir's death, father and I discussed extensively with him about how the trusts operate, about the individual sources of income of the various members and where they spend their money. I realized that all his life, Sohrab had been controlled by his uncle. He kept doing different things because, just like a small child who is hungry for attention, he too wanted to grab everyone's attention and affirmations. Except, he kept failing at everything that he tried, and *that* added to his *frustration*. If one really analyses, it would become apparent that his gambling habit is just another way for his mind to grab everyone's attention. The fact that his parents had laid the foundation for the various family businesses added to his irritation. More so, as he was side-lined by being made to stick in a non performing publishing business. Sanaya, his wife, is eccentric and wants to control him. She also keeps reminding him that she is independent in her own right, both financially and otherwise in life too. That is why he eagerly spoke to Anahita and found solace there. He craved for a conversation with the one human who wouldn't judge him or pity him but would talk to him for who he is.

Lastly, everyone, including uncle, favoured Firdaus. His opinions were valued. So, when his daughter, Diana, was not given her due by Uncle Jahangir, he felt even more frustrated. He felt that he was always at a disadvantage. The side-lining of Diana, seemed like the last straw on the camel's back, which spiked Sohrab's vexation so much that he couldn't keep it in any longer. All of this led to building up of frustration and spite and that caused Sohrab to murder Firdaus."

All this time, while Shehnaz was speaking, Sohrab's mind had "zoned in." His brain had entered a trance like state and had blocked out every other noise and presence in that room. The chirp of the birds outside or the sighs of the family members, nothing was heard by his brain. His brain was in a peaceful, deep meditative state, a state which one reaches during clinical hypnosis to tap into and solve the past traumas of one's life.

When Shehnaz had finished, SP Arun had walked up to Sohrab. He did not react immediately. But when he placed his hand on his shoulder and gave it a light squeeze, Sohrab slowly snapped out. His brain felt dizzy and drowsy, but he was at peace. There was no irritation or anger on his face. Looking at him, the Superintendent asked, "Do you have anything to say?"

Sohrab smiled and said, "No. I am at peace. My brain doesn't hammer anymore."

EPILOGUE

After the arrest, both Zubin and Sohrab were taken to remand and placed under judicial custody. On the day of their hearing, while they were being transported to court in the rickety old police van, they observed the world outside through the fine grilled mesh of the matador. They felt hope moving out of their mind. They saw some homeless children playing on the pavement, beggars on the road, a man pushing a fruit cart and a couple fighting in the car nearby – everyone's life seemed better off with their freedom.

The police van soon reached the court. The two culprits noticed some other convicts in chains and handcuffs. There were a few more cases ahead of them, and the anxiety killed them. They needed the suspense to be over.

Soon, their case was called and the defence put forward their final submission and the prosecution highlighted the evidence against them. Although the defence said that the evidence was circumstantial, the prosecution was able to prove beyond reasonable doubt that the evidence strongly highlighted the motives behind the poisoning and the murder caused by asphyxia. The judge awarded a fourteen-year sentence to the culprits.

Shirin's act of stabbing Jahangir was illegal and, in principle, should have been considered as an attempt to obstruct and misguide the law. But Shehnaz chose not to disclose her actions or her name in the chargesheet. She understood the old lady being piqued at Jahangir for not being able to have children, and that had made her stick the knife in his throat. All that anger that she had kept bottled up for so many years burst out in a pang. Shehnaz had sympathy for Shirin and was cognizant of the latter feeling incompetent in front of her daughters-in-law, which had made her plant evidence against Sanaya. Yet, Shehnaz felt that given the present state of the family, the matriarch had been punished enough and should not be tormented further.

The Judge, though, directed Shehnaz to pay a fine and donate to dog shelters for killing the dog and using it as a guinea pig. "A life is a life," the judge had sternly remarked.

At the Dinshaw estate, Sanaya moved to her parent's house along with her kids, Diana and Farrukh. Sanaya had never developed the emotional depth or maturity to forgive anyone. She preferred to live in her own world, without any disturbances from outside forces. The move from the Dinshaw estate was due to this reason and not because Sanaya felt anger towards Shirin or had, in a way forgiven her and yet wanted to maintain distance. It was simply because she wanted to live in her own world. They were still a part of the Dinshaw family trusts though and received their quarterly allowances. Sanaya never visited her husband in jail, though she did allow her kids to go and meet him. She found pleasure and peace in her art. For a short while, the art patrons shared reels and memes about her husband being in jail, which gave her art a momentary push in the market. Not that she ever needed or cared about such frivolous two minutes of fame.

Diana started her own investment company and began her journey as a venture capitalist. She knew more than her peers, yet she had much to learn. She invested in companies that operated in the food, pharmaceutical, and defence sectors. Her deep understanding of these sectors allowed her to confidently analyse the upcoming market trends in these areas of the economy. She regularly visited her father in jail and compassionately understood his side of the story. She felt sorry for him and thus regularly discussed about her professional growth and achievements with him.

Farrukh continued with his carpentry. He created bespoke pieces of furniture and regularly collaborated with big designers. Through his mother's fame in the art circles, he created a niche for himself. He loved his peaceful, slow life and found his mother's home to be less daunting. For a long time, he underwent therapy to be able to get over the death of his Grand Uncle Jahangir and how easily Shirin had been able to stab her dead husband of more than fifty years, just out of spite for his mother, Sanaya. He also felt broken about the fact that his father, out of sheer spite, had murdered his uncle. Unlike Diana, he couldn't fully comprehend his father's perspective and thus found it difficult to forgive him.

Jim went back to Mumbai. Though Diana had informed about his blackmailing antics to the lawyers and to her Grand Aunt Shirin, Jim was still a part of the new family trust. Shirin had exclaimed that she was not going to overturn her husband's wishes and was not going to turn her back on family; however, they may have behaved. Jim's weekly apology letters fell on Diana's deaf ears and she was having none of it. So, he continued his mediocre existence in the hope of another opportunity, a knock on his door that would allow him to overnight change his status.

Within the estate now, only Anahita and Shirin stayed and were promptly served by the omnipresent butler Jawahar and the battery of manservants.

Cyrus had moved out and was working as an economist for the Indian government. He stayed in New Delhi and would often visit his mother and Grand Aunt. Most evenings, Cyrus felt lonely and pondered on how a house full of people was destroyed to bits because of the sheer misunderstanding on his brother's part. He felt angry towards Grand Uncle as compared to his Uncle Sohrab, for he believed that had Jahangir allowed Sohrab to live the way he had wanted, he would never have become so frustrated. The frustration led to spite that triggered Sohrab into killing his father. It was an occurrence which, in Cyrus' mind, could have been avoided.

It is evident that discontentment and the never-ending need for lavish desires can trigger the greatest of disasters. For want of a nail, a kingdom was lost.

SCENE - DO NOT CROSS CRIME SCENE - DO NOT CROSS

Word Search Puzzle

A MURDER IN DEHRADUN

R B M W M R Q L W N P O I S O N E P D Y
D O V Y S D A P C K K C M B H E A R S T
W L J H Z I I L I B R A R Y G N A E U K
E A A G C C S A N A H I T A A D A S A W
C D H E K G E V K S M Z D I L H V P D R
N U A S T J E N Y M O Y D H F R G E R D
A U N J N A Z X Z I Y H K G K Z N C I J
T Y G E H I T T L J Q N R I H U E T F I
I X I R M J D S S P U G D A S Q R M F G
R Q R J E E O Y E I C B Z S B R U R S O
E C S L F L L S L S T I E K O R A U A D
H J I I S I T L L B A R I F D U R P Y F
N H N K M N I U L A Q C A E M Y Y N G K
I K F A I N I A B E A Q R U C S U C S G
D Y F X E H C R Q K M D Z I W D D O D B
S E T L D K D Q I W D U Q Z A N H E H S
Q N T G M X X W D H B B G R M T O K O D
J O O A B Y S P F I S X H T M X S E V M
Y M I B O P G F N E W E F O M S N G M W
B I U S A N A Y A C D N A J E B X Y V A

Words to Find:

ANAHITA
JAHANGIR
ARTIST
JIM
STAIRCASE
POISON
DIANA
RESPECT
DINSHAW
FIRDAUS
SANAYA
DOG
SHEHNAZ
ESTATE
ZUBIN
BEJAN
KNIFE
BLACKMAIL
LIBRARY
INHERITANCE
SHIRIN
FAMILY
SOHRAB
FARRUKH
MONEY
BUTLER
MURDER
CYRUS
PARSI
DEHRADUN

Find all 30 words hidden in the grid above.
Words can go in any direction:
horizontally, vertically, diagonally, forwards or backwards.

MY CONFESSIONS

1. The moment that twisted my mind the most:

....

2. A character I suspected the most (and why):

....

3. The line or dialogue that stuck with me:

....

4. If I were part of the story, I would be:

....

5. One clue I noticed early on that made sense later:

....

6. My rating out of 5: 💧💧💧💧💧

....

7. Describe the book in three words:

....

8. Would I recommend this book to a friend?

(Why/why not?)

....

Loved this book? ❤

Then you won't want to miss what's next.

Turn the page for an exclusive early chapter from Siddharth Maheshwari's new thriller.

TWISTED TANGLED AND TRAPPED

One murder. Three confessions.

CHAPTER 1

PAINT THE TOWN RED

ANIRBAN CHATTERJEE

I am that man who has a semblance with every irritating character in your life. I have a squeaky voice, capable of jolting your soul, which can be heard every time I move my extremely prominent jawline. The same jawline that is a part of an oblong clean-shaven face and on which sits a mop of neatly oiled up hair, always parted on the left side and cut in a neat mushroom style. I use the same cologne every day, and the odour is now a part of my personality. I am that fellow whom, when you see or hear, you naturally want to beat up. Not that anyone has, but I have gotten into a few scuffles. I would like to believe that any such contest of fists that may have occurred has always ended in a draw.

I am a little jumpy, so I like to stick to the familiar routine. Surprises upset me. Therefore, I always visit the same restaurants, where I know the environment, the food, the servers, and even the time it would take for each dish to be prepared. My strong sense of survival, and not particularly my habit, is what makes me sit at the same tables in the diners. My mind scans for the exits every time I visit. The quick reassurance helps calm the nerves. I like to observe the world from a remote corner without making my own presence felt. Though I am well known and respected, I ensure that outside my working hours, I do not get observed easily. I feel more secure with this side of my personality. The other is just to exhibit to the world. You must be thinking that I am a spy, a detective, a member of the military intelligence or worse, a stalker or a murderer. Well, I am neither of those, nor am I a whistleblower working in some large, corrupt organisation. No, I just have a strong sense of survival because I am a journalist. I am a member of the fourth estate in the largest democracy of the world – India. And I assure you that I did not choose my profession keeping my surname in mind.

I come from humble beginnings; my parents were primary school teachers in the small hill town of Kalimpong, West Bengal. Their income wasn't much; life was simple yet strict. So, I have had to create my own path, and the struggle has left a bitter taste in my mouth and memories. I have done everything possible to become successful. After many risky shortcuts and astute calculations, yet with ample hard work, I rose from being a beat reporter informing the world about crime to now being a prime-time reporter and editor-in-chief of one of the leading news channels of the country. At this stage in life, I don't chase or create stories. I just ensure that I am the first to know about them. And I achieve that by any means possible, it could be blackmailing, giving bribes, pleading to someone or if required, generating self-pity. I am like that spider on the wall who likes to quietly ensnare the unassuming flies, or in this case, humans.

Now, you may not like me, but you cannot ignore me. Not because I shout, insult the guests or debate during prime time, without actually caring for the outcome, but because I always smile and ask questions even if it makes the other person uncomfortable. I report only what is factual or at least what I believe is a fact. I am on a constant quest to find the truth. Though these days, everyone seems to be running around with their very own version of it.

My perfectly aligned teeth, coupled with my jawline, create the most devious smile, which I showcase while being on prime time. I also constantly nod my head. I nod not to show that I am understanding your viewpoint or that I am sympathising with you; I don't *actually* sympathise. I nod my head to stop myself from falling asleep because of your boring personality.

My reports on crime are not mere front-page news, which the nation gobbles up with their morning tea; they are mathematical deductions taken seriously even by the police.

I am not a sleuth, but I have a method, and that method is like an equation, which, if deduced correctly, will have a definite solution. Therefore, I always strive to be technically correct, backed by theoretical knowledge, but I may or may not always be practically appropriate. In my profession, I can enjoy the freedom of being technically correct and can observe the world in either black or white. Practicality would involve me running the risk of evolving empathy for the doers. It would compel me to look at their side of the story and show understanding. But I never empathise.

For the next ten minutes, I sit silently and enjoy my tea cake and a strongly brewed English breakfast tea. I ponder the questions that I would be asking the investigating officer and make a note of the things that I should notice when I enter the crime scene. The case is too sensational for them to let the junior field reporters anywhere near the crime scene. I...Well, I have a certain clout and a way of handling situations. Soon, I shall be granted access.

The café owner is an inquisitive Parsi man with a prominent nose that has a penchant for sticking itself where it does not belong. He knows why I am here and has seen me making notes.

Looking over my shoulder, he says, "I know it's the son who did it. The young blood these days has no sense of restraint or patience."

"Now, why would you say something like that? The lad has not even confessed. It's the others who have. Isn't it so?"

"Yes. But I fear they are all trying to protect him. The police will soon see through the ruse. The lad is a pretentious, good-for-nothing chap. Just keeps idling and throwing his weight around."

"How do you know so much?" I enquire with genuine curiosity, ignoring the fact that the café is right across the road from the building where the incident has occurred.

Excitedly, almost as if waiting to tell the story, the Parsi replies, "Last evening, the family in question called for some food from that Chinese restaurant down the road. The delivery boy from Zomato is a friend of one of my staff members here. He told my staff that while delivering the food, he heard the father-son duo arguing intensely. The fight seemed to be about the latter being kicked out of the father's upcoming film. It seemed like the father was unwilling to back his son; maybe he did not believe in his talents." Then, after a slight pause, during which he took a deep breath to fuel his excitement, he continued in his slight nasal voice, "That lad is surely weird if you ask me. Always wears dark glasses and waves at the passersby, even when they are not looking in his direction. He has a need to snaffle attention."

I just shake my head, get up, settle my bill and move out of the café. I light a cigarette and take in a few quick drags before tossing it and squishing its butt under my heel. As I cross the road, I know for a fact that I will be stepping into the biggest story of my life. A scoop whose exclusive coverage would be the dream of any news channel. The sensation is about the brutal murder of a high-profile individual but the zest for the front-page news is added by the fact that three individuals have confessed to the crime. The building in question here is Coral Heights and I have to reach its thirteenth floor. A lot of media personnel and some members of the extra enthusiastic general public are jostling at the main gate of the compound. The constabularies are trying their best to keep them at bay. But these average minds will always be at the mercy of others; they want someone else to give them a chance. I just carve my own path as I go. Since I had handsomely bribed the guard and some of the constables, I was ushered into the compound from the rear gate.

In every crime, the spotlight always falls on the killers. We generally try to understand the flaws in their personalities and blame their irrational behaviours or their twisted psyche on some childhood trauma or a fractured past that they may have faced. We find reasons to justify their monstrosity to ease our minds. It spirals into a classic, nature versus nurture debate about the criminal.

But there is a flip side to this narrative. The victims are often seldom understood. They are mourned, pitied and quickly reduced to mere statistics. They just receive the much-needed sympathy, but no one tries to understand their characteristics or the flaws in their personalities that made them the target. What was it that made them the prey in this game of life and death?

I will tell you about the victim. The pesky, conniving filmmaker, who has gone ahead and gotten himself murdered, was a sly fox. Initially, he worked hard and backed a few good projects, but then quickly learnt the tricks of the trade. He started using his smooth tongue to entice financiers to put a large chunk of money in his projects. That way, he diluted his own risk. He would make these financiers occasionally dine with the actors and get them invited to the actors' fancy parties, which would satiate these investors and keep them starstruck for at least a year. The movies were made under the banner of his own production house, where none of these investors had a direct stake. They were on board only for a specific project. So, once the movie was made, his production house quickly sold the rights to the distributors, the OTT platforms and the TV broadcasting channels. His company also sold the music from the movie. The financiers, therefore, only got the normal profits from the sale of rights and a marginal piece of the pie if the distributors made extraordinary profits. However, through his production company, he ensured that he got a share of the profits which the distributors were earning. Therefore, he always made maximum returns and came out on top. He made his capital using his investors' money and sold them the story that he was their gateway into the movie business.

He was careful never to make sequels of his successful films so that, after a few years, his production house could sell the rights of that story to other production houses at a premium.

He was a marketing genius and during his early years, understood the vitality of public perception in his business. Therefore, he bought awards, critics, reviews from my fortunate friends in the media who had the mundane job of reviewing the repetitive works of similar-looking actors on celluloid.

Yet, everyone praised his business acumen and lauded the projects that he backed. He had amassed a good fortune, and for the past decade, he had been producing only three films a year. This shrewd strategy allowed him to reject projects and that made his market value go up even more. At times, he would reject a director with a good story and at times, he would reject his financiers, saying that his hands were full at the moment. Such hard-to-get tactics, which is generally used by immature youngsters to lead on the opposite sex, made everyone yearn to work with him.

Another example of the workings of his cunning mind was reflected by the large pool of financiers that he had cultivated. He juggled them around and did not collaborate with anyone more than once during the year.

But I always saw through his duplicitous nature. I saw him for what he was – a greedy, scared fat man, who adorned himself with gold rings, diamond studs and gemstone bracelets, not to showcase his wealth but to please the various Gods.

Despite wearing so many stones and regularly consulting astrologists, last evening he seemed to have lost confidence and refused to launch his son.

On a side note, I knew this even before that intrusive Parsi told me about it, but earlier, I was just playing along with him. I have my own sources. However, the Parsi's narrative helped me corroborate the incident thoroughly.

Going back to the dead film producer, my sources tell me that he did not trust his son to carry the film on his young shoulders. He had pitched the idea of playing second fiddle to the hero to his son, which the young adult had angrily refused. After training for years, his son believed that he was ready for the big break. But Rajat Rai Handa was one very risk-averse personality.

Now you must be wondering if his son, Nikhil, is one of the prime suspects. Well, let me stop you right there. As far as I believe, that young man is lost in his own delusions of grandeur and is still perfecting his autographs, for a fame that may never come.

I was never invited to Rajat's parties or premieres because I work in the investigative and crime field. And although he never felt the need to acknowledge my work or register my presence in the world, I know a lot about him, his family and those who surround him.

So, who are the accused? What are their stories and motives? Let me tell you, at least that which I know, through the bribes I have given to the constables, or from what I suspect, based on what I have heard from various sources. But one thing is for sure: every suspect has a story. The only question is, which one ends in blood?

First is the posh dame, Lady Lipika Handa, wife of the now *late* Mr Handa. She is well known in Mumbai for her charitable organisation, which raises money for improving the health and education of the destitute. These are two vital sectors of the economy, which are like a bottomless pit, and no matter how many schemes the government comes out with or spends money and resources in these sectors, these wells never seem to fill up.

Anyway, ostensibly Lipika Handa appears to be as clear of heart as her husband was clear about being financially wicked. She, along with the wives of two actors, co-owns an interior design firm and two boutique restaurants. The beautiful lady is a true entrepreneur who aims to run not just profitable enterprises but also make the society around her a better place. Therefore, the restaurants never throw the food away but give the extra to the homeless and poor. The interior company mostly uses reclaimed wood to create furniture. She believes in her team and puts in extra effort for all those who work for her. She is compassionate, which makes her put the needs of others ahead of her own. She knows the vitality of sacrificing.

In her own subtle way, she always kept her flamboyant husband on a tight leash, never allowing him to go astray or convert his bark into a bite. She had wanted her son to work in any other line but films. Unfortunately, the poor lad seems to have been living on a diet of supplements and has forcefully chiselled his body so that it has lost its originality and looks like all the other actors in the film fraternity. I suspect that the boy has practised becoming famous so much that even on bank cheque books, he could write, 'with love – Nikhil.'

Although Lipika has confessed to the crime, I am not yet clear about her motives. As far as I know, Rajat was not having an affair, nor were the couple having any financial troubles that could have rocked their marriage boat. I am stymied about why she would kill him and what she would stand to gain. I will have to keep digging, for over the years I have learnt that confessions are easy, but the truth is always harder to find.

Once I go up to their apartment, maybe I can see her behaviour and hear what the cops are asking her.

As I stand in the foyer of the building, waiting for the elevator, I see a young girl who is playing around, fall down hard on the marble floor. The girl has hurt her knees and elbow, and her shrill cries are disturbing my tranquillity. Her grandma is quick to console her and has just stated that 'nothing has happened. Shh...It is all okay. You are strong.'

I am appalled by this denial. Everybody could see that the girl fell and hurt herself, but that grandma just negated the girl's feelings, reinforced her own will on the child by telling her how she should feel and went in complete denial about her injury. I want to tell the girl that she is correct and to call out the old hag on her behaviour. Today, she is denying this physical injury; tomorrow, she might inflict mental trauma on the child and be in denial about that, too. And all this talk of *'strong people don't cry,'* I just hate it. Why camouflage issues? They must be talked about as they are. Life is so much simpler that way.

Anyway, I will now tell you about the second person who, too, has confessed to the crime. This handsome gentleman, who goes by the name of Jatin Maini, has been a childhood friend of the fat swine Rajat. The two have always been close, but compared to Rajat, Jatin comes from modest means. He is a trader of commodities and minerals and makes a steady nine per cent margin for all his efforts; yet, he is not included in the top 9% of the country. All the capital in his business has been invested by his wife, Ridhi. She is a sweet, naïve, pampered lady and the only child of her parents. Her parents are successful, sought-after gynaecologists. She is a social butterfly who looks to drift through life like a wilted leaf being blown by the wind, with no effort whatsoever on the leaf's part. Other than maintaining a close watch on her two children, Ridhi takes a keen interest in fine wine and dining. She has a close group of friends who, much to her liking, always look up to her.

Jatin does not seem to mind his wife's money; he rather seems to enjoy it. He dresses well, eats in fancy restaurants and is a frequent flyer, particularly to Delhi. He diligently carries out the trading business and regularly entertains his business guests in five-star hotels with his wife's money. He sees these splurges of money as compensation for the man-hours that he puts into the business. It would not have been so much of an issue to me if he were a straight shooter. But Jatin has a dark secret. And if it were to be revealed, he would be on the roads, penniless.

Now, it is interesting to note that Ridhi and Jatin were over at Rajat's place the previous night for post-dinner coffee and drinks. No arguments or raised voices were heard by the neighbours for the duration of their stay.

As far as I know and have heard, Jatin is well settled in his life. He is comfortably enjoying his wife's wealth and putting reasonable effort into the trading business, so why would he risk his wife's wrath and confess to murder?

Jatin has always been fond of the Handas, especially Lipika, but that fondness stems from the respect that he has had for their friendship. He would not be foolish enough to have an affair or make casual romantic passes at his best friend's wife. Even Lipika does not seem to be the kind to fall for a street-smart fellow like Jatin. Her taste is more mature.

Although, it is too early to state anything, my mind deduces that Jatin does not seem to be covering for Lipika.

While we collectively ponder over these suspects, let me introduce you to the next character who believes he has done the noble job of sending Rajat's soul back to God, as if telling Him that He had failed while creating this particular human specimen.

This tall gentleman with a dusky complexion and curly hair has a gorgeous personality. His chiselled physique, coupled with the wise brain that sits in his head, makes him a charmer. I have seen him donning silk shirts, boot cut jeans and leather boots, just like the narco gangsters of South America, and carry off the ensemble with casual ease. He is almost a decade younger than the late Mr Handa. Although I had stated earlier that Rajat never repeated his financiers in a financial year, Mr Vidit Kapoor seems to be the exception. He has had a stake in almost all of Rajat's movies, and despite all of Rajat's schemes, he has never lost a dime. In fact, some in the market wonder if he was Rajat's silent partner. But there was a big distinction between their personalities. Rajat had the knack to sell his films and create hype about them by any means necessary. At times, he made public the personal affairs of the actors, directors or whoever was important enough whose story could be sensationalised and converted into sales. While nothing was beneath Rajat, Vidit was the silent worker. A true financial wiz. He knew not only how to control the finances or curb the spending on a project, but also had the knack of finding cheaper alternatives for locations, actors and musicians. He knew where to spend the money and where to tighten his hands.

Now you may be wondering why I did not divulge this information earlier. Well, for the simple reason that I am a journalist and, in our profession, we report first and check our facts later. We always have an urgency to report. I believe that corrections can always follow later and can be reported by any junior reporter with a sorry-looking face.

Anyway, Vidit is our exception and the third in line to have confessed to the murder.

This also brings me to the point that you must take everything that I say with a pinch of salt and must not follow me blindly. After all, I am a journalist, and we always highlight the meat in any story and discard the rest for the scavenging general populous.

With a soft ding, the elevator doors open, and I silently glide out on the thirteenth floor. Instantly, my brain processes the three constables standing outside the apartment. A furtive glance around and I am able to see the nosy neighbours gathered around the staircase. Their advances are being prevented by the constables who have enforced their authority with rigour. I gather that these neighbours are from the floors above or below, as the building has only one apartment on every floor.

The constables look at me with keen, inquisitive eyes, but my gaze stops at the Handas' apartment name, *Destiny*, which I find amusing. Controlling my smile, I step forward and tell the constable that I am expected at the crime scene. As I whisper into the constable's ear, I see some of the neighbours crane their necks to try and have a good look at me, the cause of the sudden activity. Some are even swaying their necks to get a glimpse. I find their mannerisms and their urge to know comical. I hear a few of the neighbours talking to the constables below. They are repeating themselves, just to be able to linger around a bit longer.

For the next few minutes, I stand quietly in the shadows and observe a junior officer who is struggling to make up his mind about whose version of the story to believe and report to the inspector.

A moment later, the soft ding of the elevator is heard again, and I see the forensic team arriving and briskly walking into the apartment. Two sub-inspectors step out of the apartment, and one of them lights a cigarette. He takes a slow drag, exhales, and mutters, “This case is becoming a roller coaster ride. Three confessions! Are we really about to watch all of them swing for it?” The smoke curls into the night, but the question lingers in the heavy, misty air and remains unsettling.

I have a long-standing relationship with the investigating officer, so I finally stepped inside the apartment. Inspector Vijay Waghmare shows obvious astonishment at my presence. He leaves the interview that he is conducting with house staff and walks up to me.

With a hint of irritation in his voice he inquires, “What are you doing here?”

“I can help,” I reply, trying to sound humble and not authoritative.

“How?” asks Vijay, feeling bewildered by the chaos surrounding him.

“I can investigate the backstories of your suspects and unearth facts for you. Not everyone wants to talk to the police, but we journalists have our sources and ways to extract information.”

“And what do you want in return?” inquires Vijay, knowing well about my opportunistic nature.

I look around and see the gargantuan body of Rajat Handa sprawled across the plush Kashmiri carpet in the living room. The forensic team are taking photographs and samples. I notice his thick legs and belly and realise the tax his knees must be paying for carrying all the extra body weight.

Swinging my head back towards Vijay, while clicking my tongue, I casually revert, “Exclusive coverage for this crime. I want to be the first to report on any new development.”

“This is not a media trial. I cannot share details of an ongoing investigation with you, especially after knowing that you would be presenting it on your news channels and papers. And I also cannot officially engage you in any investigation related to the crime. This is a high-profile case," replied Vijay. The concern and agitation in his voice were apparent. It was too soon for the media to hound him.

But I have to squirm my way in, and so I use his phrase against him and instantly revert, "This is already a media trial, and as you rightly said, the victim is a high-profile individual. But you won't be able to keep this quiet. Why don't we work together? You don't have to engage me officially. Let me work from the shadows. I assure you; I will not publish anything you don't want me to or that the public won't find out about through other media outlets."

"Okay, but you will report everything directly to me. I don't want any surprises," says Vijay with slight hesitation. He does not seem convinced about the plan.

"Understood. What have you uncovered so far? Whose story would you like me to dig into?"

"Well, three people have confessed to the crime, but I suspect you already know that. Given that you bribed your way here, you must have bought that little piece of information too, didn't you?" He watches me closely, waiting for a reaction, but I just smirk. It's a fair accusation. I've never been the one to sit back and wait for the truth to come knocking.

"Yes, I have. You cannot blame a man for trying to earn his living," I reply, trying not to sound opportunistic and thinking that I did what I did to move up the ladder.

The society around us is so facetious; they first push you to work hard like a hamster and move up the ladder, and when you finally start moving, they are quick to judge your every move and try to pull you down, due to their narcissistic crab mentality.

Rolling his eyes, Vijay says, "Unlike your expectations, I want you to first figure out Mr Rajat's son, Nikhil's alibi from the previous evening, from 7 p.m., till 5 a.m. this morning."

"What is he saying about his whereabouts? And why him, he has not even confessed?" I questioned the inspector with the intent of extracting some more information out of him and prying into his mind.

"He may not have confessed, but he is still a suspect. And he hasn't said anything for he is missing. No one seems to know where he is."

"That's interesting."

"Find out and meet me at my station in Juhu. Till then, I will conduct a preliminary round of interviews with the three who have confessed. By evening, the forensics too would be able to reveal details about the crime, like time of death, the calibre of bullet, the victim's last meal, et cetera. So, we should be able to draw a better picture of the victim's last few hours."

"Hasn't a gun already been retrieved?"

Irritated, Vijay looked at me. Clearly, he was not happy about my knowing the real-time developments of the crime scene. Shaking his head, he replied, "Yes, a Smith and Wesson revolver was retrieved. *Prima facie*, it looks like it is the murder weapon. The gun was discharged twice, and both shots hit the victim square in the chest. The weapon is registered in the name of the deceased."

"There are no signs of forced entry, nor are there any scuffle marks or abrasions on the body. But items around the living room are scattered, and a few pieces are broken. This will have to be investigated further," replied Vijay before hurrying back inside.

It is now 10:00 a.m. and I have to go around town on a wild goose chase. Two possibilities that come to my mind. The first is that Nikhil has deliberately cut contact with his friends and family following the argument with his father the previous evening. This means that he would likely be sitting and brooding in some place where network connectivity is low, and so he is unaware of his father's death. The second possibility is that he is aware of his father's death. The former scenario hints towards him being innocent, whereas the latter scenario would point towards him being guilty. He may be guilty of something related to the murder, if not the murder itself.

But for now, I need to brush aside these thoughts and deal with cold, hard facts.

And for those amateur sleuths who think that the poor lad has been kidnapped, they need to read better thrillers. No seasoned criminal would be foolish enough to kill the father and keep the son as ransom. It is illogical. Practically anything is possible, but on a technical level, it does not make any sense. And if there's one thing I know about criminals, it's that they rarely make a move without purpose.

I believe that if I break down the characteristics of Nikhil, we can find the answers to his whereabouts. He is a young boy who, for the better part of the past four years, has been going to acting schools and dance classes to prepare himself as an actor. He has grown up on movie sets around movie stars and has seen them perform first-hand. But he has not been broken yet. Observing something can only take you so far. You have to practically do the work and get your hands dirty. To carry a film on his shoulders, he should know the nitty-gritties of filmmaking. But he never worked on the sets, not even as an assistant director. He has always been the prince who has had the privilege to take the easier path. Other than spending his father's money or his time at the gym, he has done little to hone the skills that would be paramount in his profession. Acting classes are just basic, but he should have done some theatre, participated in practical workshops or read some literature in an attempt to better understand and imbibe his field. Instead, all he worked on were his muscles and star-like attitude, which he insisted were necessary. It does not come as a surprise to me that his father felt insecure about launching him. The hot-headed, hollow personality that he is makes me deduce that Nikhil must have retreated into a shell, away from the prying eyes of the public. It would not be beyond him to go to some underground hole in a wall pub and drink away till the wee hours of the morning.

About the Author

Siddharth Maheshwari is a dynamic entrepreneur and bestselling author of three novels. An alumnus of the University of Warwick, UK, he seamlessly weaves his diverse interests in history, philosophy, science, geography, and art into his writing. His global travels enrich his stories with rich cultural insights. A lover of plays, musicals, and exotic food, Maheshwari indulges in dark chocolates and red wine, all while continuing to captivate readers with his thrilling narrativesHe resides in Delhi with his parents, his wife Sakshi —who has designed all the illustrations and sketches for his books—and their two children.

His Other Books

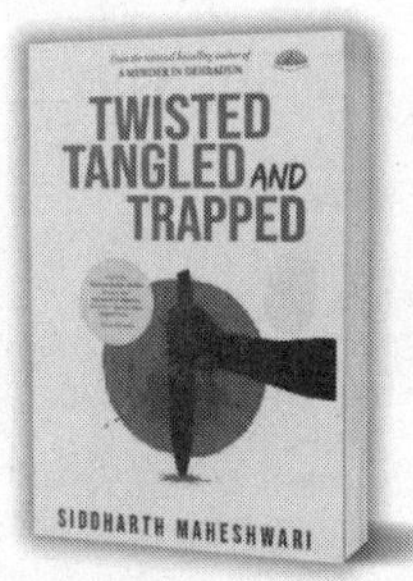